MW00574762

AMIDST THE RISING SHADOWS

Ken Lozito

AMIDST THE RISING SHADOWS

ISBN: 978-0-9899319-5-3

This is a work of fiction. Names, characters, places, and incidents either are a product of the author's imagination or are used fictitiously. Copyright © 2014 by Acoustical Books, LLC. All rights reserved. This book or any portion thereof may not be reproduced or used in any manner whatsoever without the express written permission of the publisher except for the use of brief quotations in a book review.
The author greatly appreciates you taking the time to read his work.

Please consider leaving a review wherever you bought the book, or telling your friends about it, to help us spread the word. Thank you.

Published by Acoustical Books, LLC

KenLozito.com

Edited by: Jason Whited jason-whited.com

Cover Design: Alexandre Rito

Discover other books by Ken Lozito

TABLE OF CONTENTS

CHAPTER 1
SEARCHING

Sarah's first few weeks at Hathenwood, the only Hythariam city on Safanar, had been spent in a bed, asleep. She slept as if she hadn't slept in months. She probably hadn't in retrospect. The first time she woke, a female Hythariam was standing over her, peering at her with those golden irises that marked most of their race. The eyes—so different and so familiar...*The Drake!* Sarah lashed out, screaming and gasping for breath. Verona pinned her arms down, telling her she was safe.

Sarah glared at him and drew in the energy, strengthening her muscles. Her eyes widened as she sensed Verona do the same.

Was this real? The Drake had tormented her thoughts, bending her mind to its will...but then the memories came rushing back. A portal between worlds. Aaron hunching before it as he took down the barrier. Then he was gone. She could no longer feel the effects of the Drake, but she still remembered. The muscles in her legs and back twitched, expecting the lancing pain to blaze through her following her thoughts of Aaron. She clenched her teeth and her lips drew up into a half sneer on her reddening face. The Drake could never be dead enough for the poisoning that spewed forth from its purpose. She let go of the energy and tried to stop the lump forming in her throat.

"My Lady, Aaron could think of nothing else while you were under the Drake's influence. His first and last thoughts were always of you," Verona said softly, and then he let her go.

She turned to the side and curled into a ball. Her face was hidden by the golden curtain of her hair, her eyes brimming at the ache seizing her chest. *Oh, Aaron, why couldn't you have let me go?* The very same reason she will never let go of him. *This world needs you... I need you.* In the silence that surrounded her, she yearned for his touch, desperate to feel his presence. She closed her eyes, imagining the feel of his strong arms wrapped around her, and having the remnants of his scent in her hair. To feel the press of his lips upon hers.

"He's not gone, Verona."

"I know he's not, my Lady."

Sarah sat up in her bed and swung her feet to the floor, which warmed to her touch. She flexed her toes for a moment and then stood up. Her body was fine, if a little bruised. Aaron was quite thorough when he rid her body of the Nanites. She took a few steps toward the window, and Verona opened it. The crisp mountain air seeped through her clothes to her skin. She was high up in a sea of white square-shaped buildings with the occasional dome-shaped ones poking above the trees. The sunlight caressed her face, and the energy was there, just waiting for her to reach out and use it. Each movement she made, and thought she had, no longer contained the taint of the Nanites. She was free, but at what cost? Sarah turned to Verona. His long black hair was tied back, and his handsome smile was genuine, but she could see the pain in his eyes. The absence of Aaron weighed heavily upon them both.

Verona placed a cloth-wrapped bundle upon the bed and slowly unwrapped it, revealing Aaron's swords and medallion. The crystal inlay on the pommel shone dully inside the room.

"I kept them safe, my Lady, but I think he would want you to look after them."

Sarah came before Verona and put her hand upon his shoulder; an unspoken promise went between them. They would get Aaron back.

"Thank you," Sarah said.

"I will wait for you outside, my Lady," Verona said and quietly withdrew from the room.

Sarah reached out and ran her fingers upon the medallion

adorned with the Alenzar'seth family symbol of a Dragon cradling a single rose. The sunlight reflected off the crystal in the center of the medallion, casting small rainbows upon the pristine walls of the room. Her fingers traced the Dragon, much like the tattoo upon Aaron's chest. She hung the medallion under her shirt and proceeded to get dressed. The Hythariam clothing and boots were quite comfortable, and had she bothered to notice, the boots fit the contours of her feet perfectly. Her movements were methodical and numb. She reached toward the Falcons. Aaron's swords. Part of his birthright. Sarah removed the Falcons from their sheaths, feeling them for the first time in her hands. The etchings and holes near the base of the blades would have weakened any normal swords made of steel, but these were different. They created the bladesong come to life. Each blade was about the length of her arm and remarkably light. She had seen Aaron do amazing things with these blades, and while she would safeguard them for his return, they were not hers. She preferred the single edge of a slightly curved blade native to her homeland of Khamearra.

Sarah strapped the Falcons to the belt upon her hips and left the room. Outside, she was greeted by Sarik with a quick smile, and by Braden, who with a grim face brought his fist across his heart. Garret and Vaughn came up to her and gave her a brief hug. Verona stood next to a female Hythariam, whose golden eyes she recognized as belonging to the one she lashed out at.

"Please forgive me," Sarah said.

"No forgiveness necessary. My name is Roselyn."

Sarah took Roselyn's proffered hands and gave her a gentle squeeze.

"Your recovery has been remarkable, but I would still like to make sure everything is okay," Roselyn said.

Sarah caught herself clenching her teeth. She'd had enough experience with Hythariam technology to last a lifetime.

Roselyn's eyes widened. "No, no, just a few scans to make sure the Nanites are completely gone."

Sarah glanced at Verona, who nodded encouragingly, and then back at Roselyn. It was quite obvious that they were together.

"You understand my reluctance, and I appreciate that. I would be happy with whatever aid you have to offer, my Lady," Sarah said.

Roselyn looked relieved and absently reached out to Verona.

"We are so happy to see you recovered," Vaughn said. "Please excuse myself and Garret. We're sure we will see you later this morning."

Sarah nodded to each in turn and followed Verona and Roselyn, with Braden and Sarik coming behind.

Braden came up to her side, and she could feel his connection to the energy around them. "Aaron and I always believed that you and Eric would be able to open yourself up to the energy, given some time. Where is Eric?"

"Thank you, my Lady," Braden said and then glanced at the floor for a second. "My brother was killed in Khamearra."

Sarah felt her stomach clench and reached out to him. "Oh, Braden, I'm so sorry."

"He died a warrior's death, and I avenged him," Braden replied.

Sarah nodded, having no wish to poke such a tender wound. How many had died in Aaron's quest to save her? Her chest tightened, and she felt something heavy drag her down in the pit of her stomach. And now they were without their friend...their leader...their king. *You should have let me go, Aaron. This world needs you.*

They walked in silence until coming to a door. Roselyn raised her palm to a pad of silver outside the door, which flashed as if scanning her hand. She motioned for the others to wait outside, including Verona, and gestured for Sarah to step into the room.

There were a few tables along the side. Verona had come to her room the day before and explained what little he could about the Hythariam technology. The panels on the far walls were screens that showed information. Roselyn walked over and placed her hand upon a pad like the one she saw upon entering this room. A circular section of the white floor darkened and rose a foot into the air, along with a railing.

"Sarah, if you could step up onto the platform, I will get the examination started."

Sarah did as Roselyn asked, and the overhead lights dimmed around her.

"Not to worry; a machine is going to descend from the ceiling above you. The lights coming from them will be able to scan through your clothes and put the information on the screen over here," Roselyn said, gesturing to the nearest monitor.

Sarah glanced up at the ceiling and then back to Roselyn. The Hythariam was beautiful with her exotic facial features and the feminine curve of her body. She could see why Verona was attracted to her but could hardly believe that Roselyn had made the journey with the group that went to Khamearra.

"I'm ready," Sarah said and took a deep breath.

A panel opened up on the ceiling above her, and two mechanical arms descended. At the ends, each arm held glowing metallic disks. A blue line appeared at her feet and slowly expanded, running the length of her body. As the glowing line moved up, she tried to feel it as it passed up above her chest, but felt nothing. The second arm moved down to her feet and began to circle around her. The light emanating from this scanner was a thin red line. The arm slowly circled her body, and Sarah felt a little dizzy for a moment. The arm stopped as the glowing line was at her forehead. Sarah opened herself up to the energy upon reflex and stepped backward, bringing her hands up.

"It's okay," Roselyn said and typed a few keys into the panel on the wall. The arms retracted into the ceiling, and the panel closed.

Sarah stepped off the platform as it sank back down to the floor.

Roselyn motioned for her to come over, and a smaller drawing of her body was on the screen.

"Sarah, I'm happy to tell you that there are no traces of the Nanites in your system. If there were, your scan would look a bit like mine," Roselyn said. She tapped a sequence of symbols, and a similar drawing of Roselyn's body appeared next to Sarah's. Roselyn's display showed tiny pulsating lines flowing through every inch of her body.

Sarah's skin crawled at the image.

Roselyn reached out and gently placed her hand on Sarah's. "What's been done to you is a horror I can't even begin to imagine. The fact that you're standing here beside me is a miracle. We've tried and failed to aid those afflicted with the Nanites that turned them into the Drake only a few times before. At best, we hoped to drive them from you and give you enough aid to pick up the pieces that were left, but what Aaron was able to do has pushed beyond the limits of what we might have been able to accomplish on our own."

Sarah stared down at the floor, her blonde hair covering the side of her face. "I wish he hadn't," she whispered.

Roselyn wrapped an arm around her shoulder, and Sarah allowed herself to be pulled in.

"I tried to end it," Sarah continued, "to take my own life, but it wouldn't let me. It twisted my thoughts until I couldn't tell what was real. I had power over nothing. I know you're trying to help. I look at everything in this room...all this technology, and all I want to do is draw my sword and smash this place to pieces." Sarah gasped an involuntary sob, taking comfort in the embrace of a woman she hardly knew. A woman who had risked her own life to help Aaron save her.

"I hate what was done to you, Sarah. This may be hard to see, but all of this technology here was created with the best of intentions."

Sarah nodded, wiping the tears from her eyes. She needed to be strong. She looked back at Roselyn's sympathetic eyes and allowed herself to believe that this stranger...this outsider...could be a friend.

"Thank you, Roselyn," she said. "I just want him back."

"I haven't known Aaron very long, but I believe with all of my heart that he is fighting to get back to you even now," Roselyn said.

The connection she shared with Aaron that had been so prominent had faded to barely a whisper, and she questioned whether it was there anymore at all. Her heart told her that Aaron was alive, and nothing would convince her otherwise. She wouldn't allow herself to believe that Aaron had died upon the plains of a world in its final death throes.

"What else do these screens tell you about me?" Sarah asked.

"That you're in perfect health, and time will take care of the rest."

Sarah glanced at the door. "He's a good man."

"Aaron?"

"No, Verona."

Roselyn blushed, "Yes, he is, and very sure of himself now. Not long ago I thought I had done something wrong because he was so quiet around me."

Sarah laughed, and the sound of it startled her. "Quiet? Verona?"

"That's exactly what Aaron said," Roselyn snickered.

Sarah shook her head and smiled. *Yes, definitely a friend.*

"We should head to the council chambers, where my father and Colind are meeting with the other leaders to coordinate their efforts," Roselyn said.

Sarah nodded, and they both left the room, joining the others outside. They continued through the building and came to a large elevated platform. There were so many Hythariam that Sarah felt out of place. The Hythariam and the others kept glancing toward the far wall as if waiting for something to happen. A few moments later the section of the wall before them shifted quietly to the side, and a large metallic tube came through the impromptu doorway.

"They are called trams, and they will take us to another part of Hathenwood, my Lady," Verona said.

The tram floated above the glowing points on the track and came to a stop near the platform. She could see other Hythariam through the windows, and after they exited the tram, Sarah and her group got on board. The inside of the tram had benches along the walls, but Sarah preferred to stand. The tram began to move, leaving the building, and as it did so, she couldn't feel the movement beneath her feet. If not for the trees and other buildings speeding by, she would have thought they were standing still.

"I'm glad you're feeling better," Sarik said, coming to her side. "Pretty amazing, isn't it."

Sarah smiled at him and nodded, looking at the city that the Hythariam had built. Parts of it reminded her of what Shandara must have been like before it was destroyed. No, destroyed was too strong a word. There was in fact a lot of destruction, but the bones of Shandara were still there. If they could rid the place of Ryakuls, then perhaps people would journey back and rebuild it.

The Hythariam went to great lengths to include the surrounding landscape into the layout of their small city.

The walking paths between the buildings included large trees and colorful plants that should not have been in bloom because of the cooler temperatures. The flowering plants of the gardens offered a choreography of color that was pleasing to the eye and gave her a sense of peace. How long would the peace last, Sarah wondered.

The tram came to a stop inside a dome-shaped building, and they got off. They were soon greeted by an older Hythariam with green eyes that contrasted with the sea of golden eyes she had seen thus far. He had the bearing of a seasoned warrior, from the way he stood and surveyed the area, to the way he moved his arms in precise movements.

"Hello, Sarah, we didn't have a chance to meet before. I am called Gavril."

Sarah returned the greeting and knew from her conversations with Verona that Gavril had also helped Aaron in Khamearra. Roselyn whispered something in Gavril's ear, and he nodded back to her. She could never doubt the sincerity of the people around her, but she could feel a pang of guilt twisting inside her chest at Aaron's absence. She still found herself looking for him, and even here in the crowded atrium outside the Hythariam council chambers she yearned to see him. She needed to know that he was okay. Sarah's breath caught in her throat, and she felt as if something had sucked the air out of the room. The voices echoing throughout the atrium pressed in around her, melding together until they sounded like gibberish. The golden eyes of the Hythariam turned to molten yellow with a malicious glint. Sarah spun around, looking for a window. She needed to get back outside. With her breath coming in gasps, she sprinted away. The others called out to her, but their calls trailed in her wake. She burst through the doorway, elbowing her way through a throng of Hythariam. The molten-yellow eyes of the Drake glared at her from the faces of the Hythariam nearby.

No! You won't take me again!

She burst through the doors and ran out into the gardens beyond.

Faster...I must go faster.

She drew in the energy around her and put on the speed, blurring through the gardens. She could hear sounds of pursuit behind her. She needed the high ground. Sarah leaped to the tallest branch of a tree nearby and stopped. Slowing her breathing, she squatted down upon the tree branch and closed her eyes for a moment, taking in the sounds around her. After a few moments, she opened her eyes and scanned the way she had come. The white dome building peeked above the tree line. She ignored the shouts of her name that came from a short distance away. There was no sign of the Drake, but she could feel its eyes on her, watching and waiting for a moment to strike.

No, the Drake is gone. Aaron killed the Drake.

Sarah dropped down and sank to the ground, wrapping her arms around her body. She rocked back and forth at the base of the tree, telling herself over and over that the Drake was gone.

Where is Aaron? she kept asking herself, but the silence was her only answer.

"My Lady," a voice called to her softly.

Sarah looked up to see Verona squatting before her.

"Are you all right, my Lady?" he asked.

Sarah could feel her heart thundering in her chest and her arms clutching her sides. She took a deep breath and suppressed the urge to keep running until she collapsed from sheer exhaustion.

"It's okay, you're safe now, I promise, my Lady," Verona said, and sat down across from her. "Take as much time as you need. We can head back whenever you are ready, or not at all, if that is what you wish."

Sarah nodded and took another deep breath that shook in her throat. "I'm sorry. I kept seeing...*it.* Verona, I can't get those eyes out of my mind. It's as if there are thousands of Drakes pressing in all around me. Even now at this moment, I feel it will come out of nowhere and drag me back into its clutches while I claw helplessly to escape."

Verona watched her for a moment. "The Drake is gone, my Lady. Aaron saw to that before he came for you. The Nanites that made the Drake possible are inside Aaron, who is now on Hytharia."

Sarah leveled her gaze upon Verona, "And that means they will turn Aaron into the Drake. Don't you see? We have to go after him," she said, rising. "I have to find him," she said as started to head back toward the dome-shaped building.

"Sarah," Verona called, halting her in her tracks. "We will do this together, you and I, but we can't do this alone and certainly not without the help of the Hythariam."

"What if they won't help?"

"I believe that if they can help, then they will. And if not, then we'll find another way. I have the utmost faith that if anyone can find their way back to Safanar, it's Aaron, my Lady."

"You don't understand. The Nanites are too strong," Sarah said.

Verona reach out and put his hand gently upon her arm. "You haven't seen what I have seen, my Lady. Please don't lose faith. Aaron will find a way back."

Sarah searched Verona's eyes, but his faith in Aaron was absolute and would not falter. They didn't know what the Nanites could do. Aaron needed help, but like Verona, she believed in Aaron, she just didn't know how he was going to get back. She slowly nodded, and together they headed back to the Hythariam council building.

On their way back, Sarik and Braden joined them. She could sense them all drawing upon the energy, and each

KEN LOZITO | 17

gave her a knowing look. They had come so far since the decks of the Raven. As the group approached the building, they saw Roselyn and Gavril standing together.

"Are you all right?" Roselyn asked.

Sarah nodded. "I think so," she said, glancing at the Hythariam around her but failing to suppress a shudder.

Roselyn followed her line of sight. "Is it the eyes?"

"They are just so similar to the Drake."

"You just need some time," Gavril said.

Sarah nodded, forcing her angst aside; she needed to do this.

"Please, if you will follow me," Gavril said and led them inside the building.

Gavril led them through the atrium and continued down a long hallway. The echoes of voices in a heated discussion could be heard coming from the room at the end of the hallway. There were two Hythariam in brown uniforms standing guard.

"They've already been in session for a while," Verona said.

"Doesn't sound like much of a discussion if people are shouting," Roselyn said.

They entered a grand oval chamber that had thirty-foot windows stretching to the ceiling. The center was open with two platforms where a few men and a Hythariam had gathered. The smooth white benches curved with the room and were filled with occupants. Sarah recognized Colind with his long white hair and eyes of silver. His jaw was set, and he appeared to be only staring at the space in front of him.

"We have evidence of armies gathering near Khamearra," said a dark-haired Hythariam. His maroon shirt was set off by the green cord tied above his elbows.

"There is little doubt that the High King has learned of the Free Nations Army gathering near Rexel, with similar forces massing at the smaller kingdoms, but I remind you that is but one of the threats we face," another Hythariam said. His long, silky-white hair moved in a wave as he addressed the room full of people.

"The one speaking is Iranus. He is one of the leaders of the Hythariam," Verona whispered.

As they entered the room, a slow murmur gained in intensity as many turned in their direction. Colind glanced up, and as his eyes found hers, he stood.

"Ladies and gentlemen, as you've no doubt have surmised, we have been joined by Lady Sarah of the House Faergrace. Please, my Lady, would you join me up here?" Colind asked.

The invitation was clearly for her alone, but the others took the liberty of staying at her side as she walked to the head of the chamber. Braden gave a low growl as one of the Hythariam attempted to block their access to the floor after Sarah had passed. She smiled inwardly, appreciating the support.

"Your Grace, I am Iranus, one of three elected leaders of the Hythariam people, and I bid you welcome to Hathenwood," Iranus said with a slight bow.

"Thank you, but as we are not in my father's court or any other on Safanar, then as a show of respect to the Hythariam, I would propose that you address me by my name, and I shall do the same with you," Sarah said.

She glanced around and calmed herself down as so many golden-eyed Hythariam stared back at her. She had no fear of crowds; being a princess she often had to endure the scrutiny of her father's court, even when she was cast aside after her father married another. The mixed expressions around the room were as she had feared. Some blamed her for their current predicament while others appeared to have no judgment at all.

Colind approached and took her hand in his. "I am relieved to see you looking so well, my Lady."

Sarah could see the strain behind Colind's eyes. "I think we can both agree that we hoped it would be under different circumstances, my Lord."

Colind nodded and squeezed her hand gently.

The dark-haired Hythariam cleared his throat. "I am a bit concerned by the presence of one who has been infected with the foreign Nanites. Are we sure she is not still under their influence?"

Roselyn stepped up next to her and addressed the room. "I'm happy to report that there is no trace of the rogue Nanites left in Sarah's system. She is healthy and free from the influence of the Drake."

Iranus nodded. "That should allay any fears for the risk of having Sarah at this meeting. Wouldn't you agree, Zyven?"

"It does indeed," Zyven answered. "Who better to advise us as to the strategy of the High King than his daughter? If you wouldn't mind, we would like to ask you a few questions."

Sarah studied the Hythariam and knew that if she didn't put a stop to this she would be bombarded by endless questions. It's not that she didn't want to help, it's that she had questions of her own, and given the circumstances she had a right to ask first.

"I will be happy to answer your questions, but first you will need to answer some of mine."

Iranus motioned for Zyven to be seated. "Under the circumstances, it's the least that we can do."

"Has there been any attempt to reach Aaron?"

"No, there has not," Iranus said, looking as if he regretted the words he had just spoken.

"Are you able to open the portal back to your home world?" Sarah asked.

Iranus swallowed. "It's not that simple."

"Then help me understand."

"On the other side of the portal is an army that for the past eighty years has been poised to invade this world. If we were to open a portal back to Hytharia to rescue one man, then we would put thousands more at risk," Iranus said.

Sarah glanced around the room, taking its measure. With the exception of their little group, most had the look of approval to what Iranus had just said.

"This is not just one man. Aaron Jace is on the other side. The only surviving member of the House Alenzar'seth. The rulers of Shandara. The people who opened their doors to you and gave you refuge from your dying world and civil war. Are you all saying that one such as Aaron is not worthy of a rescue attempt?" Sarah asked, her gaze narrowing as it swept the room. Despite what had occurred in her life, she had the blood of kings and queens inside her, and this group was in danger of incurring her wrath.

"I don't think you are aware of what is currently happening here. These lands are upon the brink of war. It's not that we don't want to help, but it's a matter of resources of which we are running dangerously thin. Our foes are many. Even Aaron urged us to prepare for the war with the faction of our race left on Hytharia. He knew the dangers and wouldn't want us to spend countless lives and risk everything to bring him back. It pains me to say this, but he may already be dead," Iranus said.

Sarah felt her body go rigid. "He is not dead," she hissed,

glaring at Iranus.

Murmuring began to spread throughout the room, like a rising wave of doubt that she would give no quarter to.

"He is not dead!"

Those closest to her nodded in agreement and echoed their assertions of the same.

"If you're able to open the portal to Hytharia, then I will go and take anyone who volunteers to go with me," Sarah said.

Verona, Braden, and Sarik immediately came to her side, only to be closely followed by Gavril.

Iranus raised an eyebrow at Gavril and smiled sadly. "My Lady, I would join you myself to help get Aaron back, but you don't know the destruction that would be waiting for you on the other side. When a portal is opened, it can be traversed both ways. Hordes of nightmarish creatures could come pouring through and kill everyone in Hathenwood in a matter of minutes. Aaron knew the risk and was even given a way to come back if he could," Iranus said and nodded toward Roselyn.

Sarah turned toward Roselyn, who nodded slowly to her, and Sarah dreaded what she was about to hear.

"It's true, Sarah, Aaron had a Keystone Accelerator in his possession that would have been able to open a way back to Safanar," Roselyn said.

"So you see, if Aaron could have come back, he would have," Iranus said.

Sarah's eyes drew downward as her mind raced for a way to help Aaron. She looked at Colind. "Is it possible to create another barrier?"

Colind pursed his lips in thought and then slowly shook his head. "The only living person with the knowledge on creating the barrier is on the other side of the portal."

Verona frowned. "You mean Aaron? How could that be?"

"He would have had to understand how it worked to be successful in removing the barrier and going through the portal," Colind said.

"I'm still not clear on why he went through the portal to Hytharia," Verona said.

Sarah looked up at Verona. "It's because he couldn't shutdown the Nanites. The travel crystals slowed them down, but nothing could break the cycle."

"She's right," Roselyn said. "The Nanites had a core set of instructions that they based all of their actions on. Their prime directive was to return to Hytharia through the portal. Aaron's ancestor, Daverim, created the barrier, and it was linked to the living members of the Alenzar'seth."

Verona turned toward Colind. "But you were head of the Safanarion Order, how can you not know how the barrier was made? Sarik and I can create barriers, perhaps there is something that we could do."

Colind smiled sadly, and his shoulders slumped as if a great weight were dragging him down. For a moment, Sarah could see something about the old man that she didn't expect: defeat.

"A different kind of barrier, I'm afraid," Colind said. "What you were able to do was powered through your own connections and is not something that can be maintained indefinitely. The Alenzar'seth kept that knowledge close to their chests. Reymius and I were as brothers, but there are some things that must stay within families. What Daverim did was extremely dangerous. He tethered the barrier not only to the living members of the House Alenzar'seth, but to the very core of Safanar. Over time, the energy drain eroded the very fabric of our world. Shandara became a wasteland. Ask yourself, even with the destruction visited upon Shandara by the High King and the Elitesmen Order, should not the land have recovered by now? The presence of the Ryakul would not have stunted the growth of the plant life nearest the barrier. Even the weather over Shandara was out of sync with the rest of the world. So you see, the barrier that protected our world from the Hythariam horde was also sickening the land around it. People were unaware because the Ryakul presence kept everyone out. That is until Aaron and all of you journeyed to Shandara," Colind said with his gaze settling upon the small group with Sarah.

"Aaron wouldn't want us to abandon him," Sarah said.

"On the contrary, Sarah, that is exactly what he would have us do," Colind said.

Sarah closed her eyes, feeling a pang in her heart at the truth in Colind's words. Aaron wanted to protect them all, but she would protect him, even from himself if she had to.

"Then I will apologize to him when next I see him, for abandoning Aaron is something I will never do," Sarah said.

"And neither will we," Verona said, with Braden and Sarik nodding.

Iranus quietly cleared his throat and asked for their attention. "I don't want to give false hope where there very well could be none, but there might, and I stress, *might* be a way."

Colind frowned. "What do you mean?"

"The fact of the matter is that we don't have the resources to build a large Keystone Accelerator to open a portal back to Hytharia and keep it running for any length of time to launch a rescue mission. I would like to see Aaron rescued, and if it were within my power to grant this to you, I would. What I was saying before about there possibly being a way is that in the years after the barrier was first put up, we were preparing for an invasion. We fortified Shandara to specifically be able to deal with the threat from my people. We knew the barrier gave us the breathing room we needed to prepare, but were not sure how long it would last. Together with the Shandarians we created weapons and fortified safe havens for people to gather. Daverim insisted, and I agreed, that the weapons caches hidden throughout

Shandara could not be detected by any Hythariam technology. This was to prevent the enemy from using our own weapons against us. The other thing we did was prepare a chamber to open a portal back to Hytharia."

Gasps echoed through the room, and Sarah realized that this was not common knowledge, even among the Hythariam.

"We knew there were still good people left on Hytharia that should not be doomed to suffer the planet's fate. We prepared a chamber that held certain safeguards that could suppress the threat of invasion," Iranus said.

"What safeguards did you put in place?" Sarah asked.

"Ultimately, the chamber would be destroyed, along with anyone inside. However, we wanted to open up communications with the Hythariam still on the other side. Daverim believed, as did I, that a people shouldn't have to suffer such a terrible fate because its leadership had morphed into something malicious and cruel. The Keystone Accelerator we used was able to hold the portal open for an hour before we ran out of power. At first, we launched some scouting missions, and then we started bringing more people through. They were sworn to secrecy, but we began to meet resistance on Hytharia. They had developed a way to detect when a portal was opened. We kept trying for a time after that, but something changed on the other side. The people were different and started to resist us. The groups of

Hythariam being brought back started to contain infiltrators in disguise. We started sectioning the newly arrived Hythariam until we learned whether they were serving General Halcylon. There were a number of incidents, and many Hythariam and Shandarians paid the price with their lives. More of the Hythariam on the other side began to change. They began to view us as the enemy. After we lost several scouting teams, we stopped using the chamber. The risk was too great. Years went by, and we began to discuss the idea of going back to Hytharia, but the attack from the High King and the fall of Shandara changed all that. We believed the chamber was destroyed, but we were never able to confirm. The Ryakuls and...well, you've seen Shandara, so 'might be a way' is the best that I can offer."

"It's more than what we had before," Sarah said.

"We are also in need of your aid," Iranus said. "Only those with abilities like your own can help us find the stockpiles of weapons hidden at Shandara. Aaron was going to help us when he returned. Will you help us in his stead? It could very well mean, not just our, but everyone's, survival."

Sarah took a breath, her mind continuing to race as she weighed what her actions would cost. War was coming, and her people were being pulled into it. There were good people in Khamearra, just as there had been on Hytharia, and she felt herself being caught in the middle. So much bloodshed with the sultry promise of more for those craving power. She began to wonder if any of them would survive or if they would all eventually succumb to the fires of war.

Sarah glanced at the large screens on the far side of the room that showed a depiction of the night sky. A blinking dot followed by a red pathway across a field of stars. She could almost feel the fear from the others in the room crawl along her skin. Fear of her father and his Elitesmen, but also something deeper. At times it was difficult to determine the age of the Hythariam in the room, but for some of them the haunted looks of helpless resignation to a dark fate was something she had seen before in Khamearra. The group known as the Resistance had the same desperation about them, clinging to a fleeting hope, that if they could survive another day then perhaps things would change for them. What she was about to do was more than loving Aaron and standing at his side. She was picking a side, but in her heart she knew she had a responsibility to those left in Khamearra, and it was something she would not forget.

"I'll help you," Sarah answered.

She wouldn't abandon Aaron, and some chance was better than no chance at all, which is what she faced now.

Iranus nodded and thanked her. He seemed genuinely relieved to have her help. She was invited to sit, and the meeting continued on while Sarah became lost in her thoughts. It had been two weeks since Aaron had cleansed the Nanites from her system. She had remained asleep for most of that time, which was a blessing because when she did wake up it felt as if the Drake was still controlling her thoughts. Verona had been there each time she awoke and reassured her that she was safe. Although she hadn't known it at the time, she did remember seeing Roselyn there as well. Residual effects of the Nanites' failed assimilation attempt is what she had been told was happening to her. The Nanites had begun training her mind to their twisted purpose, but now her mind was free of them. Their influence would fade with the passage of time or so she hoped.

The meeting finished, and they would be leaving for Shandara soon. With the death of the Drake, the Ryakuls had scattered, no longer claiming Shandara as their own. A camp had been setup inside the city, and Sarah and the others would be heading there to begin searching for the weapons caches and the chamber of which Iranus spoke.

Colind watched Sarah as she and the others left the hall. He hadn't been to Shandara since Aaron had freed him from his prison there. His thoughts were being consumed with Mactar and the death of his son. It was a cold world indeed when a father must visit justice upon his only son. He blamed Mactar for seducing his son with dreams of power, making him a pawn to his own designs. On a much deeper level, Colind blamed himself, and his failure burned him to his core. Reymius, his old friend and Aaron's grandfather, might have told him that Tarimus's failings were his alone to bear, but Colind knew better. Perhaps in time he might see it differently, but he couldn't allow himself that luxury now. He blamed himself, and he wanted to hunt Mactar down. That slippery fallen member of the Safanarion Order had lived too long already, and this world would bear the scars of his designs for many years to come. He could pretend to himself that he would pursue Mactar as some form of justice, but what he wanted was vengeance. He wanted it so badly that he found himself imagining trading his life for it with a perverted sense of glee. His oaths to the Safanarion Order and dead friends be damned. He wanted that man dead more than anything else.

"Colind," Iranus said.

He looked up at the old Hythariam. The hall was empty now. Its occupants had long since left.

"Do you believe we can trust Sarah?" asked Iranus.

"I don't really know her. Just what the others have told me. She wants to rescue Aaron, and those especially loyal to him want to help her. For the time being that should hold this alliance together."

"What do you think she will do if the chamber is destroyed? We can't expend time and resources to go after Aaron. I want to, and don't ever believe that I don't. I hate the thought of him stranded on Hytharia if he is still alive," Iranus said.

This had been eating away at both of them since the

moment Aaron had been trapped behind the portal. "For better or worse, Aaron is on his own and beyond our aid. I've said it before—he wouldn't want us to focus on rescuing him with the threats aligned against us. He would want us to prepare. It is our charge to protect the people of Safanar. Aaron understood this. Especially toward the end, by Gavril's account. To honor him, we shall continue preparing for war, and look for a way to possibly bring Aaron back from Hytharia."

Iranus nodded, resigned to the fact that there were limits to what they could do. "There is another thing. I've heard whispers of it since people have learned of Sarah's recovery."

"Quite the romantic story isn't it," Colind said with just a hint of bitterness to his voice.

"That's not what I meant. Some are saying we should hold Sarah in our custody as leverage against the High King."

"That would be supremely stupid of them."

"I agree," Iranus said. "But still I suspect this line of thinking will grow."

Colind nodded, accepting the fact of it. "Well, we'll need to teach them the error of this line of thinking. To hold Sarah prisoner as a means of bargaining with the High King would plant a divide among our own alliance in the Free Nations Army, as well as galvanize the High King's army. We would go from a righteous cause of rebelling against a tyrannical nation to that of criminals taking hostages."

"Let's hope the others see it that way. I've asked Cyrus about her."

"And what did my friend, the ruler of Rexel, have to say?"

"She is her father's daughter in that she has a reputation for being cold and a bit ruthless at times," Iranus said.

"Vaughn told me that they were initially quite suspicious of her when she first showed up on the Raven. But having learned a little bit about the girl, there are reasons why she would cultivate a reputation such as that. You of all people know what it takes to survive in a dangerous place."

Iranus nodded. "Indeed I do, and speaking of such places, will you be going with them to Shandara?"

Colind's first instinct was to say no. There were too many ghosts for him in Shandara. He had spent the better part of his imprisonment there, as a cursed shade sentenced to roam the realm of shadow, but now he was free.

"We've been sending in teams to help clear away the rubble. People will return to Shandara," Iranus said.

Colind drew in a shallow breath and sighed. Perhaps returning to Shandara would help put some of those ghosts to rest. From there he would begin his hunt for Mactar.

"Only for a short while," Colind said. "There are things that I must do. It's time to recall the Safanarion Order, if there are any of them still out there."

"Surely some of them have heard of your return and are

making their way to Rexel by now."

"Perhaps, but there are some that live upon the fringes, preferring a more solitary existence."

Iranus nodded. "Then I wish you good luck, and you can always reach me through the comms device."

Colind followed the Hythariam out of the room, then brought out the travel crystal and studied it in the palm of his hand. There were a number left among Aaron's things, and Verona had thought that Colind could use one. He put the travel crystal back into his pocket and headed toward the trams, resigning himself to once again go back to Shandara.

CHAPTER 2
A NEW POWER

Far to the north of Khamearra there was a small town nestled in the shadows of a dark keep with a solitary tower. The locals knew better than to venture anywhere near the place. The only indication that someone lived there was the occasional town visit from the deaf mute caretaker. A hundred years ago the place was known as Baerstone Keep, where a small plantation lord resided until Mactar appropriated the keep from him, and it had been his ever since. The townsfolk understood their place, and it was not at the keep unless Mactar brought them there. The occasion that he brought someone to the keep was usually the last anyone ever saw them again. It had been two generations since Mactar had to show the townsfolk that if they left him alone, he would do the same to them.

Mactar stood atop the tower to Baerstone Keep and gazed down at the lights of the town twinkling into the night sky.

Dawn was a few hours away, but it was the quiet at this time of night that he preferred to be alone with his thoughts. He had repaired the Drake's metallic bracer that it had used to control the Ryakul. The bracer was only half of what he needed, with the specialized call being the other half to the key of controlling the Ryakuls. That was the theory. He had yet to prove it, but he was getting close. So close that he could almost feel it.

Mactar clasped his hands together and drew from memory the strange strumming sound that the Drake used to command the Ryakuls. Other than the mere memory of the sound, he hadn't been able to crack the inner workings of how the Ryakuls were commanded.

Mactar descended the stairs that led directly toward his trophy room. A collection, of sorts, of all his victories. Hanging on the far wall were the remnants of a flag bearing the Alenzar'seth coat of arms. The fires that engulfed Shandara had blackened the flag so that you could barely discern the once-proud standard. It was meaningless now. Reymius (with the help of the Hytchariam) had gotten away, and the House Alenzar'seth had been allowed to endure. Aaron, the sole remaining heir to the ancient House Alenzar'seth, had proven to be more powerful than all his forbearers. Mactar closed his eyes, remembering how Aaron had deftly danced through a sky filled with Ryakuls. Ferasdiam marked or not, the feat had been impressive. It had been weeks since those events occurred, and he hadn't heard anything more of the Heir of Shandara. A worthy adversary. He waved his hand, sending tendrils of energy to the burnt flag of Shandara, causing it to unravel into a pile of dust upon the floor. He would strike a crushing blow against those who would oppose him, and a new order would be upon Safanar.

Mactar came before a window where a dark cylinder hovered over a small pedestal. It was by far the least obtrusive of all his trophies, and it only garnered the attention of the keenest observer. Most of those who had come into this room had grown preoccupied with the objects that gleamed. Only Sarah had noticed the cylinder when she had come to summon him to the High King. How much had changed since all those months ago. High King Amorak was correct—he did have a soft spot for his beautiful and dangerous daughter.

He had been among the first to encounter the Hythariam as they came to Safanar. A shaft of moonlight streamed through the window, reflecting off the cylinder. The device itself was broken, and it was something he would never be able to fix. The only proof he had that there were Hythariam still on the other side of the barrier. A different caliber Hythariam than those fools holed up in Hathenwood. He knew it in name only and had no idea as to the actual location of where the Hythariam called home on Safanar.

Mactar turned from the window and approached his workbench, where two bracers sat. He and Darven had returned to the mountain and found the remains of the Drake's body. They were able to salvage the other bracer and use it as a blueprint to repair the one that the Drake cast aside.

Darven quietly stepped up behind him. The former Elitesman could be the very definition of silence when he chose. This was one of the rare moments where he had truly caught Mactar unaware.

"Any luck at Rexel?" asked Mactar.

"Nothing that we don't already know. They are building airships and outfitting them with things that I've never seen before. They train their troops constantly. I can't get onto the palace grounds, and each time I tried to use the travel crystal to get there the alarms are raised," Darven said, shaking his head. "They've found a way to detect when someone enters the palace grounds by travel crystal. I was able to get into other places, like the airfield and where the barracks are. Looks like you finished repairing the bracers."

"Yes, I believe I've gone as far as I can with them. The airships are different, you said?"

"Yeah, there are additional smaller engines on the wings and on either side of the cells above the ships. I didn't see any of them actually fly, but the Rexellians are working night and day on them. One thing I did learn though. They aren't calling themselves Rexellians or even Shandara's De'anjard."

"What are they calling themselves?"

"The Free Nations Army or FNA for short. They seem to be composed primarily of the Rexellian corps and the remnants of Shandara's armies that settled there, but I also saw other kingdoms represented," Darven said, his voice trailing off.

"What is it?" Mactar asked.

"You'd be surprised what you could learn near the barracks and at some of the inns the soldiers drink at."

"I'm sure it's truly enlightening," Mactar said dryly.

"Usually when kingdoms align against a common enemy, the armies are as likely to fight each other as they are to fight their intended foe, but the Free Nations Army is different," Darven said.

"Different how?"

"Well, they rank by experience. A nobleman may be an officer, but if they are inexperienced then they will be a lower ranking officer. Doesn't matter how highborn they are. And I've seen a number of Hythariam there. Threw me off seeing their darker skin with golden eyes. I've seen some near the palace grounds, but never for very long," Darven said.

"Intriguing," Mactar said. The Free Nations Army at the moment was much smaller than the armies of the High King, but what Darven had described could almost be considered radical. "We'll see how they hold up in a real battle. You can't unlearn a thousand years of practice in a few weeks."

Darven nodded. "And they don't have Ryakuls at their command."

"Technically, neither do we. I think we need to capture a Ryakul. I know you've just returned, but are you ready to leave again?"

Darven smirked. "That almost sounded sincere. I know for a fact that you care nothing for my comfort. If you're ready to go now, then so am I."

Mactar grabbed one of the bracers and tossed the other one to Darven, which he caught easily. The Elitesman's reflexes were never off.

Darven glanced at the far wall where the standard of Shandara had hung. "Wasn't there something hanging on that wall?"

Mactar headed toward the staircase that would take them to the top of the tower. "It used to be something, and now it's dust. Let's go. We've got work to do."

CHAPTER 3
PERCEPTION

Despite whatever Mactar had said that night in the arena, Rordan knew what he saw. It wasn't trickery, it was real. The Heir of Shandara had called a Dragon—an Eldarin—to the arena. The Dragon lords were supposed to be a myth. Folklore told children of those marked by fate with the ability to speak to Dragons. It couldn't have been a trick.

He stood alone in his chambers, having dismissed his servants, preferring the solitude of his thoughts. With the deaths of his brothers, Tye and Primus, he was under constant protection of a guard who always had a few Elitesmen among their ranks. Rordan could slip away if he chose and had done so many times before. The sun was up, and the birds that frequented the palace grounds chirped away in their morning routine. He closed his eyes and heard Aaron's voice in his head.

"There is a threat to this world that none can escape from. The

Alenzar'seth have sheltered this world from an invading army. Take a good look around at those in power. Take an honest look at who counsels the High King and then the king himself."

Rordan had thought long and hard about what Aaron had said when they met. In his mind, the Alenzar'seth was many things, but a liar wasn't among them. He had debated on sharing what was said with his father, but they had been either locked away meeting with the council of the Elite Masters and the War Council, or with the armies themselves. The armies hadn't been mobilized to this degree since he had been a child. Smaller kingdoms were showing signs of rebelling against his father's authority. There was resistance even here in Khamearra, and the city had been under lockdown ever since, the district captains having orders to arrest anyone out after designated hours. Examples of stragglers had been put on display at every market square in the city. But everyday there was some type of fire. Not near any district headquarters or soldiers' barracks for now, but any inn or brothel that was known to be frequented by the king's guards were targets. When he was in the city last, there were even attempts on his own life. One problem was you couldn't tell where an attack was going to come from, but one thing was certain—anyone could be involved. From the harmless old hag wandering aimlessly through the streets to the most ordinary common folk. Now the guards only traveled with a number of men sizable enough to give the opportunists pause. That's when they started attacking the guards in groups and the Elitesmen became involved. They quelled most of the outright attacks. Yesterday, there had been reports of the letter *F* written on the front of shops in all the marketplaces in the city. The shop owners themselves were ignorant as to how the letters came to be painted upon their shop doors or windows, but they worked quickly to have them removed.

The letter F was painted with a curved sword at the cross section, which was in the style of the surname, Faergrace, the ruling house of Khamearra before his father had ascended to High King. Sarah was among the last of the direct line except for some cousins. Cousins didn't count for much, and none resided in the city, especially when someone like his father had taken out all his opposition. The Faergraces were not a threat.

Ideas could be threats, but what was the real threat here in Khamearra? Was this mysterious army that Aaron spoke of the real threat? How had the Alenzar'seth sheltered this world from anything when they had been gone for longer than he had been alive?

Rordan glanced out the window. *No billowing smoke.* Perhaps this day would be free of attack. A knock at the door came as a subtle reminder that he was expected to leave for the next War Council meeting. He tied on his sword belt and fingered the pommel at his hip. He couldn't defeat Aaron in combat, but did that necessarily mean he couldn't kill the man? He and his brothers had always tried to get the better of each other to win their father's favor. So the fact that Aaron had killed them could be viewed as a favor. He had always thought, especially in Tye's case, that he would have to kill at least one of them. They were still family, and the choice of whether they should die or not should have been up to him. Primus was his twin, and, like it or not, he felt his brother's absence more than he cared to admit. Sarah, on the other hand, was altogether different. They only shared the same father. He hadn't even known he had a sister until a few years ago when she returned to their father's court. Aaron wouldn't fight him. He had said it was because Sarah wouldn't want him to, which he found hard to believe. There hadn't been any sisterly affection before, but that may have been the result of how they had treated her. He and Primus had tried many different ways to have their sister meet with a number of unfortunate accidents. From faulty saddles to an insecure bed onboard an airship where the lines had been cut, causing the ship to tilt precariously to one side. Grease on top of the grand staircase at the palace, which had taken the life of a maid who had fallen down the stone staircase and broken her neck. He smirked at the thought, remembering the popping sound her neck had made and the vacant look in the maid's eyes as she stared lifelessly up at them in a twisted heap. After months of Sarah thwarting their attempts, they had tried to attack her in one of the shadowed passageways that most people didn't frequent. They had only wanted to scare her and scar her pretty face. When she had first come to live at the palace, many had remarked on how beautiful and fair the princess had become. Living up to the Faergrace name. Their attempts to teach Sarah a lesson had failed miserably, and he still had the scar that ran along his side to prove it. At least she didn't scar his face.

Rordan left his rooms, and the guards followed him. An Elitesman walked quietly at his side, and if he was the least bit put off by having lowly guard duty there was no indication of it. The Elitesman was older and one that he had not faced during his training sessions. He wore a silver cloak, and when Rordan glanced at him out of the corner of his eyes, he could have sworn the Elitesman's eyes had a reddish glow to them. Rordan quickened his step and made his way to the council chambers. He paused outside the door and glanced back at the quiet Elitesman, but said nothing as he went through.

There was a large table with a map of the lands strewn across. The map was older and clearly showed Shandara's borders on the side of the map that had unfurled off the table's edge. The table was surrounded by six generals of Khamearra's armies, Captain Commander Joseph and Gerric the Elite Grand Master. An angry red scar split Gerric's pale face, running from his hairline down to his jaw. Rordan wondered who gave him the scar, which had not been there until two weeks ago. The very same night he had encountered Aaron. With the destruction of one of their towers, the Elitesmen had been on the alert ever since.

"My Lord Prince," Gerric nodded in greeting.

The door behind him opened up, and his father came through.

"You're all here, excellent," the High King said. "General Khoiron, I expect that you have a report for us."

Rordan looked up to see a man with more crags on his face than the side of a mountain. His weathered hands looked as if they could squeeze blood from a stone.

"I do indeed, your Grace. Mactar's report of the forces gathering at Rexel proved to be accurate. We've also started seeing reports of troops gathering at these locations," General Khoiron said, marking several places on the map. "And these other ones along our borders are gathering troops as well. There is something about it that I don't like. They are already outfitting their soldiers for war prior to the word going out from the capital, which got me thinking. Either they anticipate what is going to happen based upon all the rumors of the return of the Alenzar'seth and people flocking to the Shandara banner, or they're preparing to rebel."

The craggy general finished speaking, and Rordan noticed

some of the other generals looking nervously at the High King.

The High King smirked as he looked at the other men in the room, "Khoiron has been my spymaster for many years, and his army of spies has served us well. His blunt nature may put some off, but I trust his keen insight. Mark the kingdoms and manors that have aroused your suspicions. We'll need to make an example out of some of them if they think to move against us, but it wouldn't serve our cause to punish a loyal vassal. Rordan, I'd like to hear your thoughts."

"My thoughts?"

"Yes, you've been to enough of these council sessions to have an opinion, and I would very much like to hear your thoughts. Do you think we've missed anything?"

Rordan stood up a bit straighter while his mind raced along with his beating heart. This was his chance to impress his father with some keen observation, but his mind was blank. As the seconds dragged on, the others around the table shifted uncomfortably.

"Father, you've sent out the call for the armies to assemble, and they will come because you commanded it, but something is missing."

"Intriguing, and what would that be?" the High King asked.

"I'm not sure what the rush is for. These other armies, in

Rexel, for example, are hundreds of miles from here. If we set out tomorrow with soldiers, airships, and cavalry, we couldn't be there for at least forty days. And that is with a hard march and the weather cooperating," Rordan said, glancing at the other men around the table.

The High King nodded. "Mobility is indeed an issue. What else?"

"We know that the other kingdoms are assembling their armies, but do we know why? Has there been any attempt to talk to them?" Rordan asked. He didn't know where the questions had come from, but now that he had asked them, more questions came to mind. "On the night that the citadel tower was destroyed, I followed the Heir of Shandara from the arena to the tower grounds."

While his father's face remained impassive, the coldness in his eyes sucked the warmth out of the room.

"What happened?"

"I caught up to him with the intent of avenging Primus's death. I attacked him...tried to attack him, but he wouldn't fight me. He told me of a threat to this world that no one could escape from and that the Alenzar'seth has been sheltering us all from—an invading army."

"Ah yes, I've heard the same lies from his own lips atop the tower. An invading army from another world is to come to our world and ravage our lands with war. You would be wise to never trust the words of your enemy," the High King said.

Rordan frowned. "What if he is right, and there is a threat? Is this something we can afford to ignore?"

"There is absolutely zero evidence to support his claim."

"But why come to Khamearra at all? It doesn't make any sense for him to come here just to sow dissension with a lie about an invading army," Rordan said.

"I can shed some light on this, my son. I caught the Alenzar'seth heir stealing travel crystals from the main charging room. He said that your sister had been captured by the Drake and he needed the travel crystals to save her. I offered my aid to him, but instead he chose to attack. So, you see, I offered a hand in friendship, and they strike at my generosity."

Rordan regarded his father for a moment, trying to decide whether his father was being completely truthful with him. Aaron did say he was here for Sarah. He had spoken of the invading army with such conviction that as much as Rordan wanted to see the man dead, he didn't believe that he was lying to him.

"The fact of the matter is," his father continued, "Rexel and other kingdoms like it have resisted royal decrees and interfered with Elitesmen sent on the king's business to apprehend the Heir of Shandara. You've asked for reasons, Rordan. How about our enemies have taken Sarah hostage?"

"But she fought at Aaron's side against us in Shandara,"

Rordan said.

"They are controlling her somehow, but there is wisdom in your words. I will send word to Prince Cyrus at Rexel, inquiring as to the whereabouts of Sarah, and what his intentions are regarding the forces being assembled there. At the same time we will rally our armies and prepare ourselves," the High King said.

"Offer terms with one hand while arming the other is a sound strategy, your Grace," Khoiron said.

"I will also have word sent to those kingdoms that are already leaning toward aligning with Rexel, announcing our intentions," the High King said.

"But...if you already suspect they are moving against us, wouldn't you be giving away our intentions by contacting them?" Rordan asked.

"Therein lies the problem. Given enough time, these suspect kingdoms could fortify their positions, making the cost of taking them by force more than we could live with. You make an excellent point, and we believe that everyone else will be under the same assumptions. And let us not forget that there is still the issue with mobility. How can we move our forces to where they need to be, when we want them to be there? Grand Master Gerric, would you like to enlighten my son and the rest of the council as to how we will overcome this very important issue?" the High King asked.

The Elite Grand Master's eyes gleamed with anticipation. "My prince, I know you are aware of the focusing crystal, but for the benefit of the others in the room, I will shed some light. As many of you know, Elitesmen are able to travel throughout Safanar with the use of the travel crystals. These crystals allow the bearers to travel to a place of their choosing with a few exceptions. We cannot use them to travel to Shandara. They simply don't work there. And the bearers cannot travel to a place where they've never been. The crystals cannot be used by the common folk, only those who have the ability to manipulate the energy can use them."

The Elitesmen were ever searching throughout the lands for new initiates and quickly squashed any attempt to setup a competing order. Try as they might, Rordan mused, the Elitesmen could never be everywhere at once, and he believed that there could be many out there who could use the energy but kept their gifts hidden.

The Elite Grand Master continued, "What many do not know is there are actually two of the large focusing crystals. One that was in the tower, used to recharge the other crystals, and one hidden underneath the citadel."

"Wasn't the one in the tower destroyed when it collapsed?" Rordan asked.

Grand Master Gerric shook his head, "No. There were safeguards in place to help protect it in the event of disaster.

In terms of mobility, we can use the focusing crystals to move our forces pretty much anywhere on Safanar."

Rordan glanced at his father and saw the wolfish smile spread upon his face. "You can move an army anywhere?"

Grand Master Gerric nodded. The other generals in the room looked impressed, but not all.

"I'll believe it when I see it," Khoiron said.

"There are limits," the Grand Master said.

"Of course there are."

"We are limited by the amount of energy used by the focusing crystals themselves. To move a large force like one of your armies can be done twice a day. Any more than that would drain the crystals to the point of uselessness."

The spymaster looked unimpressed. "And you've tested this? You know this will work? You've moved an army before?"

Gerric's brow furrowed in annoyance. "The largest group has been a hundred men."

"That's nowhere near the size of an army. The idea has merit, and if its potential proves to actually bear fruit, then you'll make a believer out of me," Khoiron said and looked to the High King. "Your Grace, there could be a lot of issues with this. Even if we could move an army into enemy territory, the men need assurances that you can get them back to safety. I can see how this could leave us over extended and expose our flank."

The High King smiled. "Your counsel has always been keen. That is why I want you and the other generals to work with Grand Master Gerric and the Elitesmen. For now, experiment within our borders, but well away from the city. No need for anyone else to know we can do this until it's too late for them. Then let them quake in their boots as the armies of Khamearra strike from anywhere and at anytime. Great change is upon us, and we've got work to do."

The other men filed out of the room, but when Rordan went to follow, his father asked for him to stay behind.

"You seem troubled, Son."

"I don't believe Sarah has been brainwashed," Rordan said.

The High King shrugged his shoulders. "Does it really matter?"

Rordan thought about it for a second. "It's all about perception."

"Yes, very good Rordan. Perception is key to having the support you need to accomplish your goals. If people see our cause as just, then many more will flock to it."

"Even if it is based upon a lie?"

His father glanced at him, and for a second Rordan wondered if he had pushed too much. One doesn't simply call a man like his father a liar.

"Love can be a form of brainwashing, Son. How many men have ruined their lives because they thought what they were doing was for love? The idealists of the world will never understand. Make no mistake. This war has been years in the making. They are preparing for war. What's important now is where and how the pieces are played."

"But what about Sarah?" Rordan asked.

"Your sister still has her uses, even if she sides with the enemy. One might say especially if she sides with the enemy," the High King said.

Rordan felt his stomach give way to the ruthless undertone of the intent behind his father's eyes. They were all pawns to him in this game, and it wasn't until now that he fully understood. Should Sarah die, no one would be preoccupied with whose side she had been on. The clear message that would pervade throughout the kingdoms was that the High King's daughter had been murdered by his enemies.

"This offer of peaceful resolution is just for show. You've already decided that we are going to war. This is all to rally the other kingdoms to your cause," Rordan said.

"*Our* cause, Son. Your sister is expendable, but you are my legacy."

Rordan swallowed and suppressed a chill as the realities of his world came to him with greater clarity.

"Come. I want you to work with the generals and the Elitesmen. You are to be more active in the rulership of this kingdom, which is about to get a whole lot bigger."

The fear Rordan had felt before was forgotten. He had won a victory. Risen above the ranks of his other siblings. There was a reason why he had survived and they had perished. It wasn't an accident of fate; it was because he was destined for this moment. He followed his father from the room with dreams of glory dancing around his head.

CHAPTER 4

OPPRESSOR'S GAMBIT

Pieces of muffled conversation went on around him as he tried to push open his eyes, but there was some type of cloth covering his face. His tongue lolled around probing the inside of his dry mouth, and he forced himself to swallow. The voices around Aaron grew louder as he lifted his hand to remove the cloth. A gentle but firm hand pressed him back down. He felt the hand slowly lift the cover from his face, and Aaron opened his eyes. Staring back at him were the golden irises of a Hythariam. The Hythariam spoke a few words that he couldn't understand. Aaron shook his head, hoping that his captor would understand that he didn't speak the Hythariam language.

Aaron blinked away his blurred vision and saw two more Hythariam in the room. He was in a gray room with a golden holographic display next to the bed. He tried to sit up and realized his hands were restrained to the edges of the bed. The Hythariam noticed and moved his hands, and the holographic display changed. Aaron felt the bed raise him to a more upright position. The Hythariam tried to speak to him again.

"I can't understand you," Aaron said.

The Hythariam closest to him had on a gray uniform with black bars upon the collar. He glanced at the other Hythariam in a black uniform that stood at the foot of his bed. He had on a belt with a silver plasma pistol holstered to his side. Their eyes locked for a moment, and Aaron met the cold, calculating gaze and knew that the Hythariam in the black uniform was the one in charge.

The holographic display morphed into a miniature version of a human body. The Hythariam in the room were taller with longer limbs. While Aaron's own six-foot-four frame was broader of shoulder and more muscled than any Hythariam he had encountered thus far, he knew they were far from weak.

A panel hissed open from the wall, and the gray-uniformed Hythariam went over and retrieved a metallic halo. The Hythariam came toward Aaron and raised it as if to put on his head. His eyes darted around, and he shifted his body as much as he could to avoid the halo. The bed beneath him glowed amber, and his muscles tensed, becoming rigid, locking him into place. The Hythariam closed in on him. He clenched his teeth, struggling to raise his hand, and beads of sweat dotted his forehead. Aaron closed his eyes, reaching out with his senses, probing for a source of energy, but felt the halo clip around his head. The ends snaked around to the base of his neck. Tiny pinpricks through his skin locked it in place.

Aaron opened his eyes and looked down at his hands. Thin metallic rods extended from the restraints on his wrists into his veins. He felt something cold being pumped into his blood. He stopped struggling against his restraints and drew inward, probing. An icy chill slid down to the pit of his clenching stomach. The Nanites were reactivating in his system. He braced himself for the pain about to erupt across his body, but nothing happened. The back of his head began to throb as a faint headache gained in intensity. Aaron took a deep breath, and after a few moments the pain subsided. He opened his eyes and was able to move his head.

The Hythariam in the gray uniform came closer, his golden eyes searching his own before he spoke. "There, that's better. Can you understand me?"

Aaron's eyes widened as he realized that he understood what the Hythariam had said. His voice sounded as if he were speaking through a tunnel. The Hythariam repeated himself, and this time it was clearer.

"What did you do to me?" Aaron asked.

The Hythariam frowned. "I won't be able to understand you yet. Give the Nanites some time. Your brain will know when to engage the translator until you can learn our language."

The Hythariam glanced toward the holo display, which showed several progress bars, and then disappeared. He gave a nod toward the Hythariam in the black uniform, and they both left the room.

Aaron tried moving his legs, but everything below his neck was still locked in place. He couldn't feel the forces that held him, gritting his teeth he tried again.

The door hissed open, and in walked the two Hythariam from before, now joined by a third. The third Hythariam didn't look older than the other two except for the eyes. They held an aged alienness that reminded him of Iranus. Knowing that the Nanites could prevent aging all together, he had no idea how old the Hythariam in the room really were. They could have been alive for hundreds of years. The eyes were old. Cold and calculating. He had the black uniform matching the other Hythariam in the room, but his had golden tips on the collar. The other two Hythariam stood to the side and silently deferred to him.

"I am called Morag Halcylon."

Aaron took a long swallow. "I'm Aaron Jace."

Halcylon studied him for a moment and tilted his head inquisitively. "You've heard of me?"

Aaron's eyes never left Halcylon's as he nodded.

"You've seen my kind before?"

"Yes."

Halcylon's eyes lit up as he looked at his companions. "We are not the last."

Aaron glanced at the other two Hythariam in the room. The one in the gray uniform remained stone faced, while the other one gave a half smirk.

"You must forgive the way my men took you into custody. You were extremely disoriented and would have died had they not taken you. There is barely any atmosphere left upon Hytharia anymore," Halcylon said.

"I'd be a lot more forgiving if I was able to move."

"Ah yes, Ronan, I think we can drop the restraints now. Our guest knows we don't mean him any harm," Halcylon said, and the Hythariam in the gray uniformed tapped a few buttons upon a black device on his wrists.

The amber light beneath the bed immediately went out, and Aaron was able to move again. He raised his arms and legs freely now, but resisted the urge to spring to his feet. Here before him was the very same Hythariam his ancestor, Daverim, had met. That fateful meeting had led to the creation of the barrier, which kept the Hythariam army from invading Safanar. Aaron looked back at Halcylon and noticed an emblem that resembled a Z.

Halcylon followed Aaron's gaze. "We are the Zekara, protectors of Hytharia."

"Where am I?"

"You're sitting in the last bastion of hope for my people. The Hythariam in this facility are all that is left on Hytharia. We haven't seen one of your kind in a very long time. We've tried every means at our disposal to go through the portal to Safanar, but always the barrier held us at bay."

Aaron watched Halcylon, trying to gain some insight into why his ancestor, Daverim, believed that this Hythariam standing before him was the tyrant that Iranus had described. There was a harshness to his golden-eyed gaze, and Aaron felt as if he were being scrutinized just as closely.

"How did you manage to come through the portal to Hytharia?"

Aaron's mind flashed, remembering how he tricked the Nanites and freed Sarah from their influence. He searched within, but could only feel the faint whispers of his connection to Sarah.

"How long have I been unconscious?"

Halcylon regarded him a moment. "A few days. Your body became ill as you acclimated to this world."

Days? The others would have tried to rescue him by now if they could. Iranus wouldn't take the risk, and Aaron couldn't blame him. He was only one man, but he still wasn't sure what to make of General Halcylon. He looked over at Ronan, and a flash of uncertainty zipped across his face. Aaron began to suspect that he was being lied to.

"What did you do to me?"

"We've injected Nanites into your system. The ones that were in your system were quite different from what we have now."

Aaron glared at Halcylon, "So you know what they've done?"

Halcylon seemed to nod to himself. "When the portal became closed to us, we had to take other measures to ensure our survival. Since we could not force our way through the barrier, we had to come up with another way. We sent a ship bearing a new prototype Nanite, designed with a singular purpose of assessing the barrier and opening the way for us to escape this dying world."

Aaron felt the bile rise in his throat. "I've seen firsthand the results of that singular purpose. Do you realize how many lives were destroyed in the process?"

Halcylon fixed him with a withering gaze that could crack stone. "Do you know how many lives have been destroyed by the actions of your people? Our survival hangs by a thread, and now you are tied to Hytharia's fate, as are we."

At last Aaron saw it. The tyrant of which Iranus spoke. The ruthlessness in Halcylon bubbled to the surface. Ruthlessness bred from desperation. Didn't he go through the portal, as an act of desperation to save Sarah? Halcylon would use any means necessary to ensure the survival of his people, but when Aaron looked into Halcylon's eyes, he saw a hardened edge devoid of any compassion.

"How were you able to come through the barrier?"

Aaron slowly rose to his feet. The Hythariam in the black uniform rested his hand upon the pistol at his hip.

"I took down the barrier and came through."

"You purposefully came through to a dying world. Didn't you have any plans on getting back?" Halcylon asked.

"I had a way," Aaron said, glancing around the room. "But I lost it."

Halcylon gestured toward Ronan. Another panel hissed open, and Ronan retrieved his Keystone Accelerator.

"Is this what you lost?" Ronan asked.

"Yes," Aaron answered, his eyes lingering on the device, gauging his chances of taking the Keystone Accelerator and opening a way home. They didn't look good.

"The portal opened from such a small device would last only seconds before it shut down, if it worked at all," Ronan said.

Halcylon shrugged his shoulders. "Seconds was all he needed. What disturbs me is that you were willing to come through the portal and then head right back to Safanar, but I don't know why. What was the point of you coming here?"

Aaron remained silent.

"Gone quiet now, have we?" Halcylon asked, after a few moments. "Weren't you even curious as to what was on the other side of the portal?"

"I've already seen what was on this side," Aaron said. "An

army. An invasion force prepared to rain destruction down upon Safanar. You took action to ensure the survival of your people, and mine have taken action to protect their people."

Halcylon took a deep breath and sighed. "I had hoped to keep this civil. You have answers that I need. The very lives of the remaining Hythariam I'm sworn to protect are at stake."

The halo on Aaron's head buzzed to life, and he dropped to his knees.

Halcylon squatted down so he was eye level with him. "I have an abundance of patience. One way or another, I will get the answers I seek."

Aaron struggled to push the halo off his head. His fingers numbly grasped it, and he pushed. The halo scraped away his skin as it came off his head. He slammed it onto the ground, and the halo bounced away. A plasma blast scorched the ground next to him. Aaron looked up into the barrel of the pistol pointed directly at his face. He felt a strange tingling at the back of his head, and the golden holo display sprang back to life.

"Are we online?" Halcylon asked.

"Yes, we should be able to disseminate his thoughts now. It took a bit longer to calibrate to human physiology, but it did require that he be conscious. I would advise caution though. This one is not like the others," Ronan said.

Halcylon tilted his head inquisitively again studying

Aaron. "Still, only human."

Halcylon's cold, dead eyes slid away from him. Aaron tried to get to his feet, but found that his limbs wouldn't work right. His head swam, and the blood drained from his face as he felt something pulling along the edges of his mind. He tried to summon the bladesong, but it remained stubbornly out of reach. He needed a clear head in order to summon the energy within. Aaron blinked slowly as he glanced up at the display above him. Images passed as if from a movie. The breath caught in his throat as his mother and father figured prominently on the screen.

Protect your sister. His father's dying words echoed in the recesses of his mind.

"What is this place? This is not Safanar," Halcylon said to Ronan.

The two Hythariam were too preoccupied with the holo display to pay him any mind, but the soldier in the room watched him intently.

Aaron glanced back at the display, which now was a multitude of images from his own life. He saw Sarah's face, her golden hair shimmered along the display for a moment, and his pulse quickened.

What wouldn't you do... The last words spoken by his grandmother, who had fallen victim to the Drake, whispered in his mind. Aaron closed his eyes and breathed slowly, calming himself. True mastery came from a focused mind.

He pulled together the pieces of his consciousness unaffected by the Nanites and ignored the rest. A translucent form of the barrier coalesce in his mind.

"Why is there interference?" Halcylon asked.

"I don't know," Ronan said, his hands waving through the interface like the conductor of an artificial symphony.

Aaron fed the barrier in his mind, and he felt the skin along the tattoo of the Dragon upon his chest begin to stir.

"It's him, sir."

Halcylon's eyes flashed toward Aaron and narrowed. Then he nodded back to Ronan.

Ronan brought up a miniaturization of Aaron's head upon the display. His hand flicked through the options beneath and then turned expectantly to Aaron.

The sensation of the Nanites felt strange, like tiny beads of light invading his vision as they attempted to wrest control of his mind. The barrier held, and Aaron pushed outward. The holo display went dark.

"What happened?"

Ronan's eyes lifted in shock. "He's resisting the Nanites somehow."

Aaron struggled to his feet, glaring at Halcylon as he stood. His legs shook with effort. "I'll never submit to you."

Halcylon grabbed Aaron by his hair, pulling him upright. "I don't need your submission, human. What was that other place we saw?"

Aaron met his gaze and smirked silently.

"If you love Safanar so much, perhaps we can go to this other place instead."

Just then, the display came back online, and Aaron heard the voices of himself and Verona as he told him about where he came from.

"Earth," Halcylon smiled wolfishly. "Tell me human, where is this Earth?"

Aaron felt his strength ebbing away as he hung at Halcylon's mercy. "Like Safanar, Earth is beyond your reach, Hythariam."

Halcylon grabbed Aaron by his shirt and flung him across the room. "Safanar is not beyond my reach, human!"

Aaron crashed into the wall and lay sprawled upon the floor.

"Sir, what do you intend to do with him?" Ronan asked.

"He'll stand trial for war crimes against the Hythariam. The Zekara will have justice," answered Halcylon.

"Very good, sir."

Aaron sat up against the wall. The Hythariam soldier leveled his pistol at him, but it didn't matter. He doubted he could stand at the moment. Though the Nanites had ceased their assault, he could still feel them crawling inside him. He had to think of a way to turn them off. Aaron looked up at the holo display, and where there were foreign symbols before, now he could read them.

"The tribunal will meet within the next thirty minutes. I want the prisoner brought to central shortly after it starts," Halcylon said.

The Hythariam soldier stood over Aaron and slapped two metallic shackles to his wrists. Halcylon and the soldier exited the room.

Ronan keyed in a sequence into the display, and Aaron could feel the Nanites go dormant. With his strength returning and his head clearing, Aaron rose to his feet.

"We don't have much time," Ronan said.

"For what?" Aaron asked.

"Tell me, are there any Hythariam left alive on Safanar?"

"You think I'm going to tell you anything?"

"I was part of a special force of infiltrators, tasked by Iranus to bring others from Hytharia back to Safanar."

Aaron clenched his mouth shut and glared at the Hythariam.

"We came through a different portal from Shandara," Ronan said.

Aaron let out a mirthless chuckle. "Now I know you're lying. There was only one portal on Safanar. The one with the barrier put in place to keep the likes of you, and your psychotic leaders, from ruining our world as you've already done to yours," Aaron said nodding toward the door.

"You're wrong. We built another place capable opening a secret portal from within Shandara. Mine was part of the last mission to come here. We were part of a covert mission to bring back more of my people, but something must have happened because the portal never opened back up for us to return."

Aaron pressed his lips together in thought. "When was this covert mission?"

"Twenty-five cycles of our dying star," Ronan answered.

Could it be? Could this Hythariam be telling him the truth? Iranus or the others had never said anything about another portal being used.

"Shandara has been destroyed," Aaron said.

Ronan looked away with a pained expression. "Destroyed...but that would have been impossible."

"I assure you, I've seen it for myself."

"We knew the risks in coming here, but what happened to all of the other Hythariam that were living in Shandara?"

Aaron regarded the Hythariam. He couldn't tell him about Hathenwood, despite the sincerity of the Hythariam before him.

"Please, I need to know."

Aaron leaned back against the wall, staying silent, but part of him wanted to tell him something.

"I can help you. I have already helped you. Do you still feel the Nanites?"

He didn't feel them anymore, but that wouldn't stop someone else from turning them back on. "You could give me the Keystone Accelerator."

"It won't do you any good. The charge has been drained from it."

"Can you remove the Nanites from my system?" Aaron asked.

Ronan slowly shook his head, "This is something I cannot do."

"Then what exactly can you do?"

"You need allies here if you wish to survive," Ronan said.

"I want to live, but I won't betray my friends."

"Halcylon will use you. You have no idea what he's capable of. You don't know what he has done to our people. Everything you see--," Ronan said, but was cut off as the door hissed open and soldiers, armored head to toe, came in.

Aaron instinctively glanced at the wall, looking for a clock. Had thirty minutes passed already? The spartan gray walls had nothing even remotely close to a clock on them. Ronan returned the Keystone Accelerator to the panel in the wall and closed down the holo display.

Aaron had no illusions of a fair trial here, but he'd much rather walk than be dragged to wherever the Zekara wanted him to go.

The towering soldiers in their dark armor filed in around him, and each held some kind of rifle. The soldiers were easily seven feet tall, with their faces hidden behind a helmet. The door hissed open, and they left the room to the musky damp smell of a hallway carved from dark stone. The jagged edges of the hall had an unfinished look, and Aaron wondered how long the Zekara had been there. There was track lighting with cables running along the edges of the floor. They came to a large reinforced door where two more soldiers were posted. Small drones zoomed down the hallway, pausing briefly at small panels that opened, allowing them through.

The large door opened, and a small breeze came through. Aaron's eyes widened at the enormous cavern before them. An intricate network of catwalks sprawled throughout the place. Dark stone walls extended beyond his field of vision, becoming shadows, leaving him to wonder whether they were underground or inside a mountain. A Zekara soldier shoved the butt of his rifle into his back, moving Aaron along.

There was a buzz of activity throughout the place, and Aaron could see thousands of Hythariam going about their business. None of them appeared to look anything like the hordes he had seen when he had peered through the portal and got his first glimpse of Hytharia.

They stepped onto a floating platform. Railings rose up in front of them, and Aaron grabbed on. The floating platform whisked them away, flying overhead toward the central part of the vast cavern they were in. Aaron marveled that the Hythariam carved all of this out to escape the destruction upon the surface. He knew they were technologically advanced, but being able to dig all of this out was a monumental feat in and of itself. Over to the right was small field of green that looked to be a hydroponic garden. There were several throughout the cavern that he could see. Aaron wondered how they weren't running out of air with so many Hythariam about.

"Are there more caverns like this?" Aaron asked.

"No talking!" the solder at his back said and slammed his rifle into Aaron's back again.

Aaron winced and sagged on his feet. He turned back and glared at the soldier.

"Turn around, human," the soldier barked. "Better yet, give me a reason. I want you to. Just one reason. BANG!" he said brandishing his gun. "No tribunal...nothing. Problem solved."

Aaron turned back around, and his soldier escorts grumbled under their breath. Ronan's face was a mask of impassiveness. He couldn't trust him. He could feel it in his gut. As the platform began to descend, Aaron's mind raced, searching for a way to survive this. Even if he could get away, where would he go? The dying planet was a death sentence.

The platform landed in the middle of a small stadium. Several drones zoomed in, and large displays flicked on around the stadium. Aaron's head figured prominently on screen. The Hythariam gathered in the stadium grew quiet as the platform finished its descent. A soldier secured his shackles to a small pillar rising out of the ground and joined his other escorts to stand well off to the side. More soldiers filed into the stadium, circling around the edges.

Murmuring swept through the crowd. Aaron looked at the display of himself. His brown hair had grown past his shoulders. His clothing was almost in tatters, and he looked every inch the criminal that he assumed the Hythariam thought he was. Despite being chained to the small pillar that came up to his hip, Aaron stood taller, with his shoulders back, and faced toward the dais where five Hythariam sat. They must be the judges serving in this tribunal.

The Hythariam in the stadium began to cheer as one of their own stepped down from their ranks and walked midway between the tribunal and Aaron. Halcylon's golden collar sparkled atop his pristine black uniform. He held up his hands, and the Hythariam in the stadium went silent in a hush.

Aaron was a bit surprised that someone of Halcylon's position didn't preside over the tribunal himself, but came to the realization that he didn't need to.

"You know me as your leader, a general of the Zekara, and savior of the Hythariam. Normally, I would sit at the head of the tribunal, but not this time. This time, I want the decision from this tribunal to be yours, and yours alone. We have here before us a human. One from Safanar. One of the gatekeepers that have kept us from our salvation, along with the traitors of our own kind. The hour is late, but as I have always said, the way to Safanar will be open for us through the portal. We will not perish with our beloved Hytharia. You have put your faith in me. Even when others of our kind took their chances among the stars, leaving us to our fate, trusting their cryostasis tubes to keep them safe while they traveled to the nearest inhabitable planet. A journey that would take them the better part of fifty of our cycles with no guarantee of success once they get there. They could only take a fraction of us, and I was one they had wanted to lead them. Yet I stayed here with you. I did not do this because it was the easy choice; I stayed because it was the right choice, but this is not why I've called this tribunal. I've called this tribunal because of this man...this human that came through the portal, proving that the barrier that has been in place is no longer a factor."

Murmurs spread through the crowd like waves, and Halcylon waited for it to die down before he continued.

"It saddens me to say this, but it was not peaceful intent that brought this human to our dying world. I've spoken with the human, and he cares nothing for you or for the struggles we've had to endure since the portal to Safanar became closed to us. The civil wars we've fought while our enemies have sewn discord among our very brothers and sisters. The Hythariam will endure as we always have. Look at the human."

Almost as one, the shift of thousands of heads turned in his direction, and the glare of golden-eyed Hythariam bored into Aaron. A soldier approached him and cut Aaron's shirt from his body, exposing his muscled chest. The Dragon tattoo of the Alenzar'seth, with its hints of gold and silver, glistened on the large screens throughout the stadium.

The Hythariam screamed their rage and denial, shaking their fists into the air. Aaron's heart thundered in his chest, but he wouldn't allow himself to cower, even in the face of this madness. Halcylon was making him the embodiment of all the wrongs endured by the Hythariam, and the crowd believed him. He wasn't sure how the truth of matters would stand in the face of so much fear and desperation. He looked around the stadium at all the Hythariam. There were men and women, but there were also children. Not many, but enough for him to notice. Aaron couldn't have imagined what it must have been like to have your whole world crumble around you.

"The mark on his chest," Halcylon said, approaching Aaron, "is the mark of the Alenzar'seth, the rulers of Shandara. The very same people who turned their backs on us. I've spoken to the human before calling this tribunal. After speaking with him, I learned that there wasn't a morsel of remorse for what they condemned upon our race. But don't take my word for it. You can hear it from his own lips."

The screens flickered to Aaron in the room from earlier that day, *"You took action to ensure the survival of your people, and mine have taken action to protect their people."*

Halcylon glared at him. "Protect your people! What gives your people the right to visit genocide on the Hythariam?"

The crowd erupted in fury, and Aaron's head whipped around expecting them to charge out from their seats and tear him apart. He focused himself and began probing for a source of energy around him.

"Through the use of the Nanites we have gleaned information of another world entirely that is also thriving with life. Information that our guest would have kept to himself. Earth, another world, a place we could share with the humans and not only survive, but thrive. But no, the Alenzar'seth will never allow that. He would have the gates of Earth and Safanar be forever closed to the Hythariam. Condemn us all to death. What are we to do?" Halcylon asked, spreading his arms wide, inviting the crowd to respond. "Should we hear what the human has to say? I bet he will tell us of a tale of suffering and trials enough to endear himself into our own hearts. Do you want to hear from him? Hear him tell us why we have to die?"

The crowd was united in their screams, lusting for his

blood, as if that would give them any semblance of justice. Hytharia was a place of death, and madness was its warden.

Halcylon waved for him to speak. "Speak to us, human. This is your chance to sway the tribunal before they render judgment. The Hythariam are not an uncivilized race."

The way Halcylon almost spat the word, human, left little to the imagination of how his race was viewed by the general. Aaron took a moment gathering his thoughts. He glanced at the shackles on his wrists and felt the stirrings of the bladesong within. He cast his gaze upward to the jagged ceiling of the cavern above, and then at the angry faces of the crowd all around him. There were no arguments he could make that would spare his life. The Hythariam needed someone to bear the blame for their suffering. He could fight and most certainly die here at this moment, upon this world, away from the people that mattered most to him. He glanced at Halcylon, who stood waiting for him to speak with a menacing glint in his eyes. There was only one thing he could think to do and that was to honor the most basic teachings. When his grandfather had died, thrusting him headlong into this mess, his father had told him there were no perfect solutions. Never were truer words spoken. When faced with uncertainty and having to take responsibility for offenses arrayed against you, the truth cannot only be your shield, but the beacon that shines even in the hour of your death.

Aaron looked up to speak to the crowd. "Your general is right. I didn't come here for the benefit of the Hythariam. Nor did I come here to wage a war that began ages ago before I was even born. I came here to save the woman I loved. She was pulled into this conflict, saving my life, but in turn it would have cost her more than I was willing to allow. The actions I took to save her brought me here, and are something I will never apologize for, to anyone. It is true there are Hythariam alive and well on Safanar, and they all grieve for those left behind. I've seen the sorrow that haunts their footsteps and the pain behind their eyes. They grieve for you and given the choice would choose peace over war. It wasn't me that put the barrier in place, barring your people from Safanar. But given the choice, I never would have come here. It is true I took the barrier down, but not for you. They were for my own selfish reasons. The Hythariam on the other side of the portal fear the war you will bring them. They fear your leaders and the measures that will be taken if you were to ever make it to Safanar."

"Measures indeed, tell me, Aaron, what wouldn't you do to protect your people?" Halcylon asked.

"My ancestor, Daverim Alenzar'seth, created the barrier to protect his people and his world. I cannot know what was in his mind when he committed the act. I'm already betting my life that he wouldn't have taken such an action if he hadn't believed it was necessary. You found Safanar through an accident of fate; who says you should live at all? What desperate measures have you taken to survive? The Hythariam on Safanar paint a bleak picture of what life was like on Hytharia and the measures the Zekara had taken to achieve its goals."

"Doing what is necessary is never wrong," Halcylon countered.

"Was it necessary to murder your own people? Sacrifice entire cities so that you should live?" Aaron asked.

Halcylon studied him for a moment. "We've had to make tough choices in order to survive."

"That's exactly the point. My people also made a tough choice in the name of survival, and yet here I stand, waiting to be judged by your tribunal. Who will judge the actions you have taken?" Aaron asked.

"Indeed you are here to answer for the genocide that your people have committed against mine. Can you justify that?"

In that moment, Aaron knew it was hopeless. "It's not genocide if the Hythariam are alive on Safanar. You've had almost eighty years, and are you telling me that in all that time the Hythariam didn't come up with a contingency plan? That it was either make it to Safanar or die?"

Halcylon regarded him with an icy glint in his eyes. "Make no mistake, human. We will be going to Safanar, and when we do, the Safanarions will have much to answer for, as will the Hythariam there."

The roar of the crowd shattered the silence, and Aaron could hear the echoes of the other Hythariam throughout the great cavern outside the stadium they were in. The roars outside were deep and bestial, beyond that of any normal Hythariam. Aaron felt the stirrings of the bladesong within, and the muscles in his arms grew rigid, straining against the shackles on his wrists. He looked at Halcylon, understanding once again why Iranus was so fearful of his coming to Safanar. If he were to die here, then perhaps he could make his death count for something. He pulled the energy in hardening his muscles and skin. He kept his gaze upon the ground and took a breath. In the last second before he would jump, he looked at Halcylon.

The Hythariam watched him, waiting for Aaron to reach out toward him. "Do it, human," Halcylon hissed.

The moments ebbed away, and the only reason Aaron didn't move was because it was exactly what Halcylon wanted. Instead, Aaron turned to the tribunal and waited.

The crowd came to a muttered silence as the five members of the tribunal rose from their seats.

"We of the Hythariam find the human guilty of the war crime genocide against the Hythariam race. His sentence is death to be carried out immediately," a member of the tribunal said.

Halcylon stepped up. "I have a better idea that I would like to present to the tribunal and one that would serve the justice we of the Zekara would seek."

"The judgment has been rendered and cannot be changed."

"Yes, it has. What I propose is that we condemn the human to the same fate that he and the other Safanarions have doomed the rest of us to. When the portal is once again opened upon Safanar, the human will watch and remain alive long enough to bear witness that the way back to his home is right in front of him, but forever beyond his reach. He can die with our beloved Hytharia."

The crowd roared their approval. The cheers of righteous fury changed to fear as the ground shook violently beneath Aaron's feet. Pieces of rock detached from the roof of the cavern and slammed into the ground around them. The Hythariam in the stadium were thrown to the ground. The tremor finally passed, and Aaron noted that Halcylon was completely unfazed by what had happened.

Halcylon turned and waited for the tribunal to respond.

The members of the tribunal regained their feet, and a member spoke. "We find that your suggestion is in keeping with the good faith of our judgment and will be carried out upon the human."

Aaron glared at Halcylon, but he wouldn't move. He wouldn't strike out against the general even though he was such a short distance away from him. They had a way to get to Safanar. A glimmer of hope ignited deep inside Aaron that he may yet be able to return to Sarah. It was that hope that would keep him from casting his life away, and the look on Halcylon's eyes confirmed that this is what the general had planned the entire time. Halcylon had used Aaron as the rallying cry for the Hythariam. As he looked around the stadium at the hateful leers of the Hythariam, Aaron almost doubted that he would live long enough to even see the portal open to Safanar.

"Have no fear, human," Halcylon said, so only Aaron could hear. "The last thing you will see is your home through the pale light of the portal. Mark my words, Safanar will be forever beyond your reach."

Halcylon stepped away, and four soldiers took up guard around him. The Hythariam in the stadium came onto the field, hungry to see their human prisoner who they had condemned to death. All the while Aaron kept thinking that Iranus was not mistaken in his judgment of his own people. The slippery slope stemming from desperate measures in the name of survival had sapped the soul of the Hythariam race, leaving a yearning hatred to the purveyors of their own destruction. War and a struggle to survive had become a way of life for the Hythariam, and the only thing keeping them together was the promise of retribution for all the wrongs that had been visited upon them. It was madness, and Aaron was caught firmly in its web.

CHAPTER 5
FALLEN CITY STIRS

Colind looked at the rubble-strewn ground that stretched away from him. Shandara had been his home and his prison. Now it appeared that the fallen city was waking from a fitful slumber. The imbalance of energy and constant twilight were gone. The barrier that held the Hythariam at bay no longer drained the land. Sunlight bathed the city in a warm glow, and the city seemed to breathe a great sigh as if it had cast off a terrible burden. The cries of the dead still echoed in Colind's mind, causing him to wince at times. Nothing remained of the people who couldn't escape, and what fire hadn't consumed the passage of time claimed for its own.

The Hythariam had been slowly clearing the streets and restoring the buildings. At least they had shelter, and the underground springs that fed the city still worked.

"I keep expecting to see a Ryakul lurking around every corner," Garret said.

"They've scattered, but there could still be some here," Colind answered.

"Without the Drake to control them, I'm afraid it's only a matter of time before they terrorize the smaller cities and towns that have little or no defenses," Vaughn said.

Garret frowned, taking stock of the area, "What I don't understand is how the Ryakuls even survived here for so long. What did they eat? It's not as if there was a ready food supply anywhere near here."

Colind's stomach sank, and he closed his eyes, wincing, "They ate the most readily available food supply: other Ryakuls."

They glanced at each other, their mouths drawing downward, disgusted at the thought of this new revelation.

"I've seen it," Colind answered. "My body was trapped and my soul doomed to dwell in the twilight of this place. The past, whatever else it is, is gone."

The silence gave them men a brief respite from bitter thoughts. They turned down a street that had been cleared. The rubble had been moved to a place away from the city. Roselyn, Iranus's daughter and a brilliant scientist, had been able to create smaller Keystone Accelerators for them to use to open portals. They were less powerful than the prototype that Aaron had used, but they did work just fine. They were limited to a few uses in a given cycle and currently had to brought back to Hathenwood to be recharged. Iranus had assured them that new versions of the accelerators would be able to recharge on their own.

"Even though the barrier has been down a month there have been reports of animals returning to the surrounding forests," Vaughn said.

Colind nodded, "That's good. I know Cyrus has been getting a lot of requests from people wishing to return here. Resources at Rexel are being spread thin, but it will do them no good to get here and not be able to feed themselves."

"There is a long road ahead if Shandara is to be rebuilt," Garret said.

Colind nodded, "Yes, but if Shandara is going to protect anybody we need to repair the walls."

"They are using the rubble from throughout the city, reshaping it into pieces to fix the damaged sections, but simply put, it's a big wall," Vaughn said.

"We still have some time," Garret said. "Precious little though there is. Have the others had any luck finding the chamber or the weapons caches?"

Colind shook his head, "The place that the chamber is believed to be is in one of the most damaged parts of the city. They are still working their way toward it, but they need to be cautious lest they destroy the very place they are most eager to get to. As far as the weapons caches go, they think they might have found one. Sarah and the others are heading there now."

Vaughn frowned, glancing where Colind had nodded his head.

"What is it?" Colind asked.

"I'm worried about Sarah. Her patience is growing thin with finding the chamber. Each day that passes, her will erodes away that much more," Vaughn said.

"I want Aaron back too," Colind said.

"Do you think he is alive?" Vaughn asked, and Garret glanced back at them.

"Yes," Colind said without hesitation.

"How can you be so sure? Verona and the others say the same thing. It's as if they won't believe for a second that Aaron may, in fact, be dead."

"It's not blind faith, my friend, I can assure you. Think about it," Colind said. "We know the Hythariam are on the other side. Aaron saw them. So they must be monitoring the portal and would know if someone came through. I believe Aaron is being held captive by the Hythariam on the other side."

Garret swallowed, "Being held captive could be worse than death. This is the same race that created the Drake. I can only imagine what they could do to Aaron, especially if they knew who he really was."

"They know who he is," Colind sighed.

"How?" Garret asked.

Vaughn's eyes grew wide. "He bears the mark of the

Alenzar'seth upon his chest."

"Yes, and Halcylon would never forget who is responsible for putting the barrier in place. Given the amount of destruction where the chamber used to be, I have little hope that we will be able to mount any rescue attempt for Aaron. He is on his own."

The uneasy silence dragged on.

"I'm beginning to understand Sarah's attitude," Vaughn said quietly.

"If they know who Aaron is then they will recognize his value. Wouldn't they keep him alive then?" Garret asked.

"That's what I'm hoping for," Colind said.

"There has been some good news. Zsensibar's armies are gathering in the south. King Nasim has been in contact with Cyrus this morning," Vaughn said.

"That is good news. At least now we are only slightly outnumbered by the High King's armies instead of overwhelmingly so," Garret answered.

"Have they moved?" Colind asked.

The Hythariam had set up what they called a command center at their camp in Shandara. Vaughn had spent most of his time in there, meeting with the rest of the Free Nations Army leaders and using the tracking devices of the Hythariam to keep an eye upon the High King's army.

"No, they are merely gathering, but it can't be much longer before they move out. It's just a matter of figuring out where they will go first," Vaughn said. "Also, this morning there have been reports of Ryakul sightings. They are sweeping west of here. Some of the new airships...the FNA Air Corps is what they are calling themselves, have been dispatched to hunt them down. There has also been a shortage of airship captains. They are going to need to start promoting some of the newer recruits up through the ranks sooner than expected."

"Would one of those new captains happen to be a Zsensibarian prince?" Garret asked.

Vaughn smiled, "Indeed, he would. Although it took some convincing. Jopher had been adamant about staying on board the Raven to serve under Morgan, saying he needed more experience."

"Normally I would say that was very wise, but we're going to need for everyone to move a bit faster than they would like," Colind said.

"Admiral Morgan agreed with needing more experience, so he assigned some of the more senior officers to serve under the prince and packed him off onto one the newer airships," Vaughn said.

Colind found himself laughing with the rest of them.

"Anything more on helping the nations that have allied with us in defending their own cities?" asked Colind.

"The Hythariam have some type of canon. We've seen them in action on the airships, but again there is an issue of powering anything to do with Hythariam technology. I don't think they were prepared for the scope of what's involved. They are preparing weapons and generators to power them, but it's slow going," Vaughn said.

"Perhaps finding some of the weapons caches here will help with that," Colind said.

They headed back toward where the digging was commencing for the chamber. He would be leaving them soon. He needed to find more members of the Safanarion Order. They were needed. Colind glanced at Garret and knew he would be hard pressed to leave the other man behind. Perhaps he shouldn't leave him behind then. Knowing the armies were gathering and war with the High King was imminent, Colind wondered what would be left of them to stand against the Hythariam if they survived. The object in the heavens, a space ship, Iranus had called it, was still heading in their direction. Colind couldn't help but feel as if they were missing something. A looming threat that lurked among the shadows just beyond his reach, but would strike out and catch them all off guard. He had to begin his hunt for Mactar, who was even now roaming free virtually unchecked. His time here in Shandara was at an end, he decided. He would be leaving by nightfall.

CHAPTER 6
A CALL FOR AID

It was their third day in Shandara, and Sarah glared at the mountain of rubble before her. This was supposed to be an entranceway that led to the chamber where they might be able to open a portal to Hytharia. Sarah would be surprised if there was a place in this cursed city that had suffered more destruction than where she was right now. She all but scowled at the Hythariam working to remove the remnants of the buildings that used to be here. No one was moving fast enough. One quiet Hythariam, Tanneth, had urged her to be patient and had warned her that they could cause further damage if they weren't careful. Sarah glanced over to her left where the quiet Hythariam stood with Braden. The Hythariam made sense. She just didn't like it. They were about to trek out among the ruins again, looking for the weapons caches that were supposedly hidden throughout the city. *They are there*, she corrected in her mind. It was just her frustration getting the best of her. The more time passed, the more her emotions spun wildly inside her. She even found herself getting angry at Aaron for leaving her. The nights were the worst, when tears came when she least expected. *He's not dead. I will get him back,* Sarah told herself over and over again.

Her fingers caressed Aaron's swords. He had been able to use them to lift a house-sized boulder, allowing them to free Colind from his prison. She had tried the same, but though she could wield Aaron's blades, she couldn't evoke the bladesong with them like he had. Gritting her teeth, she turned away and walked in the opposite direction.

Braden and Tanneth came to her side and silently followed. She remembered how dark Shandara had felt upon their first trek into the city, as if they were all about to be swallowed into the ground. Sarah hadn't realized how profound the feeling was until she came back here. The barrier had been sucking the life out the land surrounding Shandara, and if left in place, would have plunged more of Safanar into darkness. They all believed that Aaron wasn't dead. Not that she needed their faith in that, but it did make her feel a little bit better. She said a silent prayer to the Goddess that he would survive to return to her. They thought Aaron had been captured by the Hythariam military and the dominant faction known as the Zekara. Sarah didn't care what they called themselves, but the fact that they had Aaron and she couldn't get to him burned her up inside. She drew in a shaky breath and tried to keep her anger in check.

"My Lady," Braden said. "We're heading up to the northern part of the city. Nearest the palace. Tanneth scouted it a bit last night, and he thinks he has found something, but will need you to confirm."

Sarah nodded. Next to her only Sarik, Verona, and Braden could tap into the energy enough to determine whether the caches were near. The others had all newly come into their powers, but she pushed them on without mercy. They trained together whenever they made time for it and never complained, urging her to drive them harder. They all knew what was at stake, but deep in her heart Sarah knew it would take more than the four of them to balance an engagement with the Elitesmen.

They were all good men, even the Hythariam Tanneth, and she was grateful for their support. None of them bore her any ill will, but she could sense the uncertainty from some of the other Hythariam, particularly Iranus. His word carried much weight, and while he hadn't said anything directly, there were others on their council that viewed her as the daughter of the High King. Perhaps even some believed they could use her to barter against her father. She was no stranger to this game and wouldn't have survived in her father's court this long without having learned how it was played. She wondered how the Resistance in Khamearra had faired since Aaron's visit. So far they had no news and no contact. Verona had given her one of the leftover travel crystals, and she was tempted to return to Khamearra to see how things were in the city. She entertained the thought of offering to do some poking around on behalf of the FNA, but couldn't do it. They were still her people, even if she didn't stand with her father. Maybe Aaron was right in his belief that there could be no end to this conflict without bloodshed. But then again, Aaron had the chance to face her brother Rordan and chose not to fight him. Verona's account had left her momentarily speechless, and she felt a warmth blossom inside her chest at the thought even now. Despite what had happened to him, Aaron was a good man, which he had proven time and time again. But deep down Sarah knew there was only so much a Dragon would take before it would unleash its fury. She almost found it hard to believe that he had reached out to not only her brother, but her father as well. A fool's plea some would say, but he was *her* fool. Aaron believed wholeheartedly that the people of Safanar needed to unite if they were to have any chance at all to stand against the might of the Hythariam military. She shared his belief that the people of Safanar should unite, but it would be difficult, if not impossible, for them to unite against a foe that for all intents and purposes was a myth. The Zekara were not here. Right now the only armies gathering upon the field were native to Safanar. The perfect time for a strong enemy to sneak in and position itself for a devastating strike was now. In Khamearra there were Elitesmen who followed the old code; perhaps now they would stand with the Resistance and overthrow the current regime.

They walked deeper into the city, and the blackened skin of the buildings had begun to show flecks of white as the years of weathering stripped away the past. The first time they had seen Shandara, the destruction had a deep effect on all of them. It was one thing to learn about something as part of history, it was quite another to actually see where the event happened. To smell the stale air. To see all the lives that had been twisted and snuffed out by the fires that had consumed the city. Devastation brought about by her father and his victory was celebrated in Khamearra to this day. She felt her stomach rise up and settle back down, as if she were on an airship.

"Tanneth, what did you find last night?" Sarah asked.

"A part of the city that has been virtually untouched."

Sarah nodded and quickened her step.

Birds flew amid the buildings, and fresh nests could be seen, but Sarah was at a loss for where the birds collected the bits required for building them. The forests were quite a bit away from where they were now, but the birds were determined to make a home.

They turned a corner, coming to a wide-open street lined

with some of the biggest statues she had ever seen. The statues were of men and women appearing in succession, depicting a person standing at first, then progressed with each showing the movements of the slow forms that Aaron had first taught them onboard the Raven. Sarah allowed her eyes to glide over them down the long thoroughfare, fooling her eyes into seeing the motions of the very still statues.

"This place is amazing," Verona said.

Braden bowed his head, brought his fist across his heart, and whispered the Warden's Oath of the De'anjard. The rest of them bowed their heads in respect, including the Hythariam. As they progressed down the wide street, Sarah's eyes took in the stunning details of the statues. The folds of the clothing draped over lean muscles in each depiction of the slow forms were shown to perfection. The faces carved into the statues were generic ideals, and she drank in the sight of them as did the others. The tension drained away from her shoulders, and she found herself standing straighter, becoming infused with the majestic energy exuding from this place. The succession of statues spoke to the potential in each of them, and Sarah was grateful that amid all the destruction throughout Shandara this place had been spared.

Tanneth stopped in front of a statue about halfway down the street and nodded to Sarah.

"You think there could be something here?" she asked.

The others spread out examining the area, but Tanneth and Braden stayed at her side. The pedestal upon which the statue stood was adorned with an intricate design of laurel work, drawing the eyes toward the center. Sarah traced her fingers, following the path of the design, and closed her eyes. Her fingers glided along, and she could feel Aaron's medallion grow slightly warmer where it rested upon her chest. She drew in the energy around them and focused on the base of the statue. She sent tendrils of energy to follow the laurel vines away from the center to their point of origins that had become distinct. She fed the tiniest morsel of energy into each origin point and retrieved the warm medallion from under her shirt. The origin points glowed, and she heard Braden call the others over. Sarah brought the medallion to the center of the pedestal and pressed it firmly into place. There was a faint but audible click, and the white pearl in the medallion's center flashed momentarily. They heard the grating sound of a stone doorway reveal itself around the corner of the pedestal away from the street.

Sarah hung the medallion back around her neck and followed the others. Faint glowing orbs pulsated to life inside, growing brighter and revealing a stone staircase. Just past the entranceway, the air tasted stale and old, leaving Sarah to guess when the last time someone had ever been down there. Having drawn in the energy, her eyes immediately adjusted to the dark. They came to the bottom of the stairs, and more orbs began to glow, stretching out along the walls away from them.

The orbs nearest grew brighter as did the others, revealing a long room that housed racks of weapons. The racks closest to them held bows and swords covered with a layer of dust, but the farther they ventured, the types of weapons began to change. One rack held golden rods with handles that slipped over your forearm and a grip for your hand.

"Shields, like the one Braden carries," Verona said.

"They're good at deflecting the Elitesmen's attack orbs," Braden said, then looked at Tanneth. "Now you and Gavril can test your pistols against one of these shields and stop asking me for mine."

Tanneth smirked, taking one of the rods off the rack. He attached it to his arm and engaged the trigger in the handle. Within a second, a golden oblong shield fanned out.

"I never get tired of seeing that," Verona said.

"Braden, do you think it can do what you've done with your hammer and shield?" Tanneth asked.

Braden's brow furrowed in thought for a minute. "Too risky to try in here. Would cause too much damage, but we can try later."

"I don't see any more war hammers like yours here," Verona said, gesturing toward the black-and-gold-etched hammer that Braden carried.

"What can you do with the shield?" Sarah asked.

"I found this hammer beneath the Citadel of the Elite. I had assumed it was taken from Shandara at the fall. When I strike the shield with it I'm able to use the energy to focus the vibrations and push things away," Braden said.

"Things?" Sarah asked with a raised brow.

A hungry look broke through Braden's facade. "Elitesmen, my Lady."

"Indeed," Verona said, "and he's been reluctant to give a demonstration ever since."

"Do you think you can teach the others to do it?" Sarah asked.

"Perhaps now that we have more shields, but it's not for the weak. It requires a strong hand to guide the waves coming off it. This may sound strange, but I felt the shield's potential when I focused with the energy drawn within. While my hammer seems to be well suited to the task, it might work with something else," Braden said.

"I think the hammer suits you, my friend," Verona said.

"So you focused these waves, and it pushed the Elitesmen out of the way?" Sarik asked.

"Violently."

"Couldn't they just move out of the way? I mean they can move pretty fast," Sarik said.

"Not fast enough," Braden said.

"I think I'm fast enough," Sarik answered.

Braden laughed. "All the young ones think they are fast

enough."

"I don't know, Braden," Verona said. "Sarik is pretty fast nowadays. Like you, my friend, he's picked up a few new tricks."

"As entertaining as this is, I think we should keep moving. Look, Tanneth is leaving us behind," Sarah said.

She always liked their camaraderie. The bond between them was strong, and she felt fortunate to be a part of it. At first to them she had been Sarah, daughter of the High King, but now she was one of their own. She glanced at Braden, who tended to look out for her as an older brother or uncle she never had. Their protectiveness for her stemmed from their loyalty to Aaron, but she appreciated it nonetheless. After all, they accepted her into their group through her own loyalty to Aaron.

"The weapons here are all finely made, but if they were preparing for a war with the Hythariam military, wouldn't they have different sorts of weapons and armor here?" Verona asked.

"These aren't ordinary. The alloys used show signs of the combined efforts between our peoples. But wait," Tanneth said, stepping up to a smooth metallic wall.

He stood there for a moment and brought up his wrist, tapping commands into the comms device. Two panels hissed open simultaneously, and a screen flickered to life. Tanneth stepped up to one of the open panels and began moving his hands in a sequence that Sarah couldn't begin to guess at. The screen in front of them changed.

"This is a map of the city," Tanneth said, his voice growing excited. "And these are where the other weapons and supply caches are hidden."

The map was invaded by blue dots throughout the city with the exception of a flashing yellow one. Sarah recognized the street above them on the map, which had a flashing yellow dot. Tanneth keyed in another sequence, and a section of the far wall pulled back revealing a smaller room.

"Gavril told me that the creation of these rooms was a joint effort with the Shandarians. It required a Shandarian to open the way into these vaults, but it required a Hythariam to access the more specialized weapons and devices," Tanneth explained.

"Why couldn't you bring up a map like this at Hathenwood?" Sarah asked.

"These vaults were here before Hathenwood was built, and for more protection the records of these locations could only be accessed from one of the vaults. It's what we call a closed system," Tanneth explained.

Sarah nodded. "What's so special about the weapons down here?"

Tanneth smiled. "They are a blend of the finest Shandarian craftsmanship mixed with Hythariam technology. Some are powered and are able to shoot bolts of energy, others help with defense, and there are more things like the comms devices."

Sarah studied the map. "Is that the palace?"

Tanneth nodded.

"What's there? That dot looks different from all the rest."

"It was where the city's defenses could be managed. We've been trying to reach it, but it's off the main palace, which is largely intact. When the invasion does happen, Shandara will become the last and best hope for us," Tanneth said.

Sarah glanced between Tanneth and the screen. "What about the other cities?"

"We're doing the best we can, and we will help them as much as we can, but we had years to prepare Shandara for invasion. The expectation was that the frontline battles would be fought here," Tanneth said.

They were interrupted as his comms device lit up.

"Yes, Colonel," Tanneth said as Gavril's face appeared on the screen.

"You've done it, Tanneth. Good work," Gavril said.

"Yes, sir. I uploaded the other locations to Hathenwood. This will allow us to narrow our search. Sarah was able to open the door for us."

"This is great news," Gavril said, sounding relieved, then he looked at Sarah, and his gaze softened. "My Lady, I need for you to return to our base. We've had word from the

Resistance."

An icy grip spread throughout Sarah's chest. "We're coming."

Without so much as a backward glance, Sarah headed for the exit. Each step she took, she drew in more energy, lengthening her strides. She emerged into the sunlight with the others quickly following. Tanneth and Braden quickly activated their gliders and stepped on. After a quick look at the others, Verona followed suit. None of them could jump like she could. Sarik gave a half smile and dashed off down the street, blurring away from them. Sarah nodded to the others and launched into the air. The wind brushed past her face, and she felt her long braid trailing behind her. She landed and immediately took off again, closing the distance to their camp. Braden and Tanneth followed her using the Hythariam gliders. The dust clouds rising from the city streets were the only indication of where Sarik was. He could move so fast now, possibly faster than she could. She kept seeing the look in Gavril's eyes in the back of her mind. Her people were in trouble. She was torn between her need to rescue Aaron and her duty to those she swore to stand with.

"Oh, Aaron...I'm sorry," she whispered as she made the final jump that landed her in the middle of their base camp, startling a throng of Hythariam and people working nearby. The others weren't far behind, arriving in their own fashion.

Verona and Sarik had come a long way since the decks of the Raven. It would only be a matter of time before they could jump as she and Aaron could. Braden, she suspected, wouldn't be able to jump like that. His abilities with the energy came in a different form than the others. Braden's abilities centered around his use of strength, which suited the De'anjard perfectly.

Gavril was one of the few Hythariam whose golden irises had a greenish tint, and they flashed in surprise as they came into the tent. The old soldier recovered quickly and nodded toward the display.

An older man's face appeared on screen. The bleeding wound upon his head stained his gray hair, but it didn't look bad.

"I am Nicholas, one of the Resistance leaders here in Khamearra. We need help. We're being slaughtered by the High King's guards and the Elitesmen. They are sweeping the city. There is no place left to hide. A number of our people have escaped and are making their way to Lorric. There are armies massing outside the city walls. They are planning something big. Please help us," Nicholas pleaded before the message went blank.

Sarah swallowed the lump in her throat and closed her eyes. "I need to go to them."

"What about Aaron?" Sarik asked.

Sarah cast her eyes downward as Sarik's question echoed

in her mind. "Is the chamber intact?"

Gavril shook his head grimly. "We haven't been able to reach it yet. I'm sorry, but it doesn't look good."

Sarah felt her knees turn to water before every muscle in her body went rigid as she turned away from Gavril. Her eyes welled up with tears threatening to spill over. "I can't help Aaron here," she said in a harsh whisper. "But I can help my people. I'm going to Khamearra," she said, retrieving the travel crystal.

"Not alone you're not, my Lady," Verona said quickly.

The others all nodded with the clear intention of coming with her. She felt her lips lift into the slightest smile, and her eyes softened. "Thank you, but I can't take you all with me. They need you here. I need to be able to move quickly, and I can't do that if all of you come with me."

They all protested at once, saying how they couldn't let her go alone. Only that alone is how she had made her way through the world, that is, until she had met Aaron. She could tell they weren't going to let up, and she had too much respect for them to just up and disappear.

"I can only take one of you with me when I use the travel crystal because it's getting weaker," she lied.

Verona stepped toward her first, but she shook her head. "You're needed here. The Hythariam need you to open the other vaults throughout the city, and Sarik can help you."

"What about the medallion?" Verona asked.

Sarah withdrew it from under her shirt and reluctantly passed it to him. "Take it."

"One second please," Tanneth said. He went over to one of the metallic cases stacked upon the floor and rummaged inside for a minute. He withdrew a round plate about an inch thick and set it atop of the case. The plate came to life as he tapped in commands to his comms device.

"Put the medallion on top," he said.

Verona did as he was bidden. After a moment, the medallion rose a few inches into the air and was bathed in a red glow. An exact duplicate of the medallion came up on the screen. Verona retrieved the medallion and handed it back to Sarah.

"We'll be able to make a copy of the medallion, which should allow us to open the vaults throughout the city," Tanneth said.

Sarah frowned. "Are you sure? This medallion has been infused with the energy of Aaron's ancestors. That cannot be copied with that device."

Tanneth nodded. "You are correct, but I think the medallion's use at the vault was more as a key. The energy to open the vault came from you."

Sarah nodded slowly and hung the medallion back around her neck, relieved that she could at least hold onto this small piece of Aaron. *Foolish girl,* she chided herself. She glanced at Braden and was about to speak when he cut her off.

"Do not think you're leaving me behind, my Lady. Since my Lord is not here to protect, I will protect what matters most to him," Braden said and gently placed his hand upon her arm.

Physical contact was all that was needed to accompany someone using the travel crystal.

Verona stood, struggling with the fact that he wasn't going, but like Braden wanted to look after her. He shared a hard look with Braden and said, "Safe journey to both of you."

"I will send word when I can," Sarah said.

"Please do so," Gavril said. "We can be of aid and make the journey to you using the accelerators, but it will take a few hours. If you can coordinate with us we can help them escape."

Sarah nodded and looked at Braden. "Are you ready?"

Braden nodded, hefted his war hammer from his belt, and gave her a gentle squeeze. Sarah drew in the energy and focused it on the crystal, picturing a place in Khamearra, her home. After days of their frustratingly fruitless search for a way to rescue Aaron, she was eager to be of use, but at the same time she feared what she would find when they got there. With a silent prayer for the Goddess to guide her path, she activated the travel crystal.

Verona stood helplessly as Sarah and Braden disappeared. He silently cursed his duty for a moment, but knew that he was exactly where he needed to be.

"Let's go find the other weapons caches," Verona said.

Gavril reached out to him. "We'll start making plans for the evacuation now and have a team of FNA soldiers standing by."

Verona nodded and left the tent with the others.

CHAPTER 7
A WANING HOPE

Aaron had been left in the stadium, chained to the stone pillar. Halcylon had invited all the Hythariam to look upon the human. The soldiers posted would prevent anyone from killing him, but his body ached everywhere. The first stones thrown hurt the worst. The Hythariam here looked at him as if he were some type of animal.

Sometime later, the soldiers had chained his legs to the pillar, making it so that he could hardly move. He occasionally slipped into a restless sleep until the pain in his aching arms from which he hung woke him up. What passed for food was brought sparingly, but the tasteless, slimy white goop was the only thing they served. He had to endure. It was the only way to get back to Sarah. The faces of his friends faded in his mind as more time slipped past. His arms and legs failed to obey him, and his mind felt as if there were a great weight pulling down his thoughts.

The ground beneath him shook, rattling the chains that bound him, and snapped him awake from a dreamless sleep. He was strewn upon the ground but couldn't remember how he had ended up there. He slowly turned his head to the sound of footsteps approaching upon the hard rocky surface. He opened his eyes, and the smoky gray fur of a wolf padded up to him.

"Zeus!" Aaron gasped and started coughing. His grandfather's wolf half-breed that had died at Shandara watched him with his large slate eyes.

Am I dying?

He could hear Zeus's panting, but as Aaron raised his head, the wolf vanished.

"Get him up," Halcylon ordered.

Rough hands grabbed Aaron and brought him to his feet.

"Look at the screen, human," Halcylon said.

Aaron raised his head to watch as the large screen in front of them flickered to life. Elitesmen crowded his field of vision, which then melted away to a sky filled with Ryakuls. The scenes were all disjointed, but all of them had been of events in his life.

"Explain this. How are you able to do these things?" Halcylon asked.

Aaron sucked in a slow breath. "All Safanarions can do this. They've been preparing for you for the last eighty years. When you bring your army to Safanar, you will be hopelessly outmatched. If you come peacefully, they may allow you to live."

Halcylon's golden eyes narrowed. "You lie, human. We can see your memories. We know what's waiting for us on Safanar. You spread ideas like wildfire."

One the Zekara soldiers jammed the end of his rifle into Aaron's stomach.

Aaron collapsed to the ground, his limbs failing to work properly. He struggled to his hands and knees.

Halcylon squatted down to Aaron's eye level. "This shall be the pose of all the Safanarions."

The bladesong flickered inside him, coming from deep within. Aaron could hear the deep growl of the Eldarin. His mind cleared, and he looked into Halcylon's baleful gaze. He struck out with his hand, grabbing the Hythariam by the throat and surged to his feet.

"We will never kneel before you," Aaron growled.

Halcylon's eyes widened in shock as he gasped for breath. The soldiers rained down blows upon his back, and Aaron collapsed to the ground. The bladesong went silent inside him, and he writhed on the floor in pain. When the soldiers stopped beating him, he found himself staring at his feet. The breath caught in his throat. His feet looked deformed, sticking out at odd angles. He blinked his eyes, and they returned to normal. Aaron shook his head, trying to clear it.

"Will it be ready, Ronan?" Halcylon asked, his voice

sounding gravelly.

Aaron couldn't even raise his head to see the Hythariam.

"Oh yes, sir. The Akasul won't last long. Maybe a month at the most. We've rushed its development," Ronan answered.

"Will the memories stick?" asked Halcylon.

"We're pushing the boundaries of even the Nanites, but yes, it will work."

"Excellent, the best weapon is the one they'll never see coming," Halcylon said.

The Hythariam walked away, their voices fading. Even the soldiers left him. Chained and weakened as he was, he wasn't going anywhere.

Aaron lay upon the ground, staring up at the column above him, his eyes tracing the lines of it. Something appeared out of place. He closed his eyes, trying to draw in the energy around him, but it was getting harder to do. What once had been so easy was being stripped away. Two green eyes opened and stared at him. The rest of the creature's body blended in with the column.

"Someone is always watching, human," the creature hissed at him.

Aaron tried to speak, but he couldn't form any words.

"Don't try to speak, human. You and I have the same goal," the creature said, and for a moment its body quivered. It crept down lower along the column. Its body was small, only about four feet in length, but its claws were able to penetrate the rocky column with ease. The creature's face was dark, but Aaron could see the points of its teeth when it spoke.

"We both wish to kill Halcylon," it whispered.

Aaron struggled to open his mouth, but couldn't.

"Don't consume what they bring you. It is bad," the creature said.

"Name?" Aaron asked in a voice barely above a whisper.

The creature cocked its head to the side, listening. The creature turned its gaze upon him and moved its head as a hunter studying its prey. "I have no name, only what my captors used to call me...Thraw."

Thraw came inches from Aaron's face, sniffing.

"You smell bad. I'm not sure you will be much use," Thraw said.

"...Fight..." Aaron croaked.

The door of the stadium opened, and the soldiers were heading back his way. Aaron glanced up at the column, but the creature was gone.

CHAPTER 8
RETURN HOME

Sarah and Braden stood on a hill just outside the city of Khamearra. They wore ordinary brown cloaks, which for the most part concealed their weapons. Sarah scanned the skyline of the city and noticed the missing tower at the Citadel of the Elite. One still remained, but the blow to the Elitesmen and the lack of one of their towers was a constant reminder that their power was not absolute. Airships dotted the skyline over the city, their hulking masses moving lazily. She had gotten used to the FNA airships that were quicker and more agile.

Her gaze drifted over to the palace, which towered above the city, casting long shadows around it.

"Braden, at some point I will need to go to the palace," Sarah said.

Braden nodded. "Okay."

"Alone."

Braden reared up. "My Lady, I cannot protect you if I'm not there with you."

"I've been looking after myself since I was a child. I know the palace and how to get in and out unseen," Sarah said.

"Then you can get us both in unseen, my Lady."

Sarah sighed. "Very well," she said, deciding not to push the issue, at least not yet.

Braden brought out the comms device and read the small screen. "Tanneth says they are putting together a plan to rescue any of the Resistance we can get out of the city."

"Where will they take them?" Sarah asked.

"Shandara," Braden said, frowning as he read the message again. "Rexel is bursting at the seams, and Shandara is the one place they are least likely to be found."

Sarah nodded. "I see. When can they be ready?"

"In about six hours, but I'm not sure if it's enough time for us. We need to find out what's been done to the Resistance and where they are being held," Braden said.

"First things first then. Why don't we have a look around and then try and make contact?" Sarah said.

"We should find Captain Nolan. He runs one of the interior districts. He gave us aid when we were in the city last. They were starting to lock down the place when we left a few weeks ago."

Sarah nodded and tried to ignore the pang of guilt she felt whenever she was reminded of what Aaron had done for her. If only she hadn't allowed the Drake to capture her...

"My Lady, are you not well?" Braden asked.

"I'll be fine. Let's have a look around."

Sarah drew up her cloak, and the cloudy skies began to drizzle. At least they would have a reason to keep their hoods up. She kept her head down, thinking about the last time she had been home. The Elitesmen Council had sent men to capture Aaron in Rexel. It seemed so long ago, and so much had changed since then.

Braden gasped, snatching her attention. Lining the main streets leading into the city were crudely constructed frameworks where men and women hung suspended by glowing shackles. The dead people were being collected and thrown into a large wagon that took them away from the city. The rank smell mixed with that of a cheap perfume almost caused her to gag as the cart passed by them.

Sarah and Braden looked back up at the people still hanging helplessly, secured by the glowing shackles used by Elitesmen.

"Pay them no mind. They're traitors," a gruff voice barked.

Sarah glared at the guard from under her hood.

"You there, you've the look of a warrior. Volunteers for the High King's army report in at the west gate," the guard said, eyeing Braden.

Braden nodded. "Thank you. I'm certainly here to fight, but can you tell me what these people have done to deserve..."

Braden said, gesturing up.

If the guard caught on to Braden's double edged comment, he didn't let on. He narrowed his gaze and said, "They were part of some sort of rebellion in the city. Mind you, there is a curfew in effect. If you're out after dark, up you go," the guard grinned.

Braden nodded, and Sarah didn't trust herself to speak, because if she did they would be fighting for their lives.

They entered the city proper and left the smell of rotting corpses behind. She couldn't believe the barbarism she had just seen, no doubt ordered by her father. She had heard someone remark how there were similar setups for suspected Resistance members at all twelve gates into the city. Her hands balled into fists; these were her people. She clutched her sword and glanced at the passing guards. She couldn't understand how Braden, who wasn't known for keeping a cool head, had been able to remain focused throughout the exchange with the guard. One telling look from him was all she needed. He was just as furious as she, but a smart warrior will fight upon a battlefield of his choosing.

There was the appearance of things settling down the farther they ventured into the city, but the people were on edge and hurriedly retreated into their houses.

"Do you recognize that?" Braden asked.

Sarah looked where he pointed, and her eyes widened in

shock. Painted upon the side of a building was a curved sword at the cross section of the letter F.

"It's the sigil for the House Faergrace, my mother's family. They were the rulers of Khamearra before she married my father," Sarah said.

Braden frowned. "I've seen it on a few places throughout the city. Why would they be painted on the sides of buildings?"

"I think they are a reminder of a time before the rise of the High King," Sarah said.

"My Lady, this place is poised to collapse into a war. What would they do if they learned of your presence here?"

They continued walking while Sarah mulled over the question. "More people will die, but they are my people. I can't let this go on."

Braden nodded, pressing his lips together. "What do you intend to do?"

A child's face appeared behind the window above a shop and watched them. After a few moments, the child was ushered away by their mother.

"I'm not sure," she said.

They continued on, coming to the district headquarters, and Braden led them inside. The clerk at the front desk looked up as they entered the room, his eyes registering Braden's towering form filling the doorway.

Braden leaned in. "Is Captain Nolan here?"

The clerk frowned and told them to wait over at the benches off to the side. Ten minutes went by, and Sarah was losing her patience. The answers she sought were at the palace and not in some district headquarters.

A black uniformed guard came up and told them to follow him. The guard led them through the building toward the offices in the back. Sarah glanced at Braden. His face was a mask of impassiveness, but his hand strayed to the war hammer on his belt.

The guard brought them just outside a room and knocked on the door. The door opened, and the guard gestured for them to go inside. Sitting behind a desk was an older man, fit and trim, with his blondish hair tied back into a pony tail.

Captain Nolan dismissed the clerk that was in the room and instructed the guard to wait outside. He pressed his finger to his lips as they left and motioned for Braden and Sarah to come closer.

"I hadn't expected to see you so soon, but I'm glad you're here," Captain Nolan said, clasping hands with Braden.

"Neither did I," Braden said.

The captain tried to glance at Sarah's face under her hood. When she removed her hood, the captain's eyes widened and darted to Braden who nodded.

Captain Nolan immediately bowed his head. "Your Grace," he whispered.

"Quietly, Captain," Sarah said.

"We received Nicholas's message, and the Hythariam are preparing a way to get your people out," Braden said.

Captain Nolan sighed deeply. "It's been bad since you were here last. We were able to get some out of the city, but that stopped last week. They've captured and executed two of the leaders of the Resistance, and each day there are less and less of us around."

"What about help from the Elitesmen of the old code?" Sarah asked.

"They help, but their numbers are few. They work mostly in secret," Nolan answered.

"Your family?" Braden asked.

"They are safely away from the city, on an extended holiday with my wife's family in the country," Nolan answered. "I keep waiting for them to check on that story and come barging through that door to take me away when they find that they're not there. My Lady, I'm glad you are safe. Aaron was quite worried about you but wouldn't go into any details. I wish we had his help now."

A sharp pang of guilt seized Sarah's chest. "As do we all. Please believe me when I tell you that if he could be here, he would."

Nolan glanced between them, noting their troubled looks. "Is he okay?"

Sarah felt her bottom lip quiver for a moment before she clamped down on her emotions, focusing herself upon the task at hand. She calmly met the captain's gaze and shook her head, but before he could speak she said, "I need for you to make contact with the other members of the Resistance. We need to pass the word that we're working on a way to get them out of the city as soon as possible. Are you still able to gather in any of the meeting places?"

"Of course, my Lady. I will send word at once. There are still some places that we can meet, but you must understand most will only come if it means leaving the city. I don't have much to offer in way of hospitality, but I do have a place where you can wait."

"I appreciate that, Captain, but I'm not staying. I'm going to the palace," Sarah replied.

Braden pulled a comms device out from his cloak and handed it to Nolan.

"I know you've seen this before, so we'll be in contact," Braden said.

Sarah leveled her eyes at the captain. "Do you intend to leave with the rest of the Resistance?"

Nolan looked back at her for a few moments. "To be honest, I'm not sure, my Lady. The people in my district need protection, what little that I can afford to give, but my family..."

Sarah laid her hand upon his arm. "I understand, Captain."

"Not that way," Nolan said as they went to open the door to leave his office. "There is another way out of the building," he said and rose from his seat.

Nolan opened the only other door in the room that Sarah had assumed was a closet.

"It might be a tight fit for you, Braden, but it will take you out through the back," Nolan said and stepped inside. The side wall opened up to a small passageway.

Braden leaned into the closet and glanced doubtfully at the passageway. The man was huge and his 'muscles had muscles' as Verona would say.

"He'll be fine," Sarah said with a smile. *He did insist on coming.*

Braden groaned and ducked his head, going into the passage first. The passage wasn't all that long, and Sarah could appreciate its uses for a district captain. They emerged outside near the rear of the building, and Sarah drew up her hood. The rain had stopped, but the cadence of dripping water sounded off throughout the area. There wasn't enough rain to wash the filth that was her father's rule out of the city. She was a princess, but without any real power here. True, she had the Resistance, but her father commanded the armies and the Elitesmen. But the Elitesmen were beginning to fracture, and she wondered if that was a weakness she could exploit.

Sarah drew in the energy around them and leaped to the top of the building next to them. She heard Braden grumble from below as he began to climb up. She looked toward the palace, with its many gray towers and walls that separated it from the city proper. Khamearra was old, and each ruling family had added to the palace, contributing to the grandness that it was today. Normally she looked at the walls and towers with a sense of pride, but now they were washed in blood. The people were crying out for the return of the Faergrace. She needed to find a way to protect her people, but with all the looming threats upon the horizon, it seemed more like an impossible task. If not from her father, then it was the threat of the invading army from Hytharia.

Braden crested the top of the building, slightly out of breath, but he didn't complain.

Sarah held out her hand. "I've got an idea," she said, bringing out the travel crystal.

Braden took her hand, and she used the crystal to take them into a private chamber near her rooms in the palace. Sarah led the way, taking the least used pathways through the palace. More than once they had seen Elitesmen walking the grounds. No doubt Aaron's last visit to Khamearra had set the security of the palace to an all-time high. Something tugged along the edge of her senses. They were passing one of the training areas that her brothers had often used. She wasn't sure who was in the room, but they were certainly channeling a lot of the energy. She cracked the door and peeked inside. Rordan was there, shirtless with his body dripping with sweat. Sarah threw open the door the rest of the way and walked inside.

Rordan turned at her entry, his mouth falling open for a moment, and then he chuckled. "You've returned," he said.

Braden closed the door behind them.

Sarah studied her half-brother for a moment. Last she saw him had been at Shandara, when they had tried to capture them. The spoiled innocence of privileged youth was no longer on his face. He looked older and more dangerous.

"Now this won't do for Father's plans at all," Rordan said. "How is the man you've betrayed us for?"

Sarah ignored the question. "How could you let the city come to this state, Rordan? They are killing people in droves. Not even I thought you were this cruel."

Rordan swallowed. "That is not my doing. That was Father's solution to those foolish enough to openly rebel against him. This all started because Aaron was here."

"I know," Sarah said.

"And now he is gone, but you return...*alone*. What a fortuitous turn of events. I'll have Father disband the armies since you're now here safe and sound," Rordan said with a smile that left his face appearing unhinged.

"What do you mean disband the armies because I'm here? Who would believe that?" Sarah asked.

Rordan turned away from her. "Truths created to fill a need, but it's not all you. The actions of the Alenzar'seth here in the city help put this into motion. Have you seen the

Citadel?"

"We can't afford to go to war with each other now. There is another threat to this world; you must help me make Father see reason. The killings must stop," Sarah said.

Rordan looked back at her, narrowing his gaze. "He and I spoke, you know. This Aaron Jace. He told me that we didn't have to be enemies. That I could be better than Father." He looked away from her, his eyes growing distant.

Sarah's heart beamed in her chest. Aaron had reached out to his enemies to unite them all toward a common goal. He had done it for her, and it sent her heart both bursting and tearing at the thought.

"He also spoke of a greater threat to this world, as if war with Father was some inconsequential thing," Rordan continued.

"And what will you do?" Sarah asked.

"Do? What could I do? No one can defy Father. At least not for very long. The Alenzar'seth will learn this soon enough," Rordan said.

"How long will you hide in Father's shadow?" she sneered.

"For as long as he is in power, which will be for some time. No kingdom is safe. There are none beyond our reach now," Rordan said.

Sarah studied him for a moment. He looked as if he almost meant the words, but something in his eyes gave her pause.

"You sound as if you believe that, more or less," Sarah said.

"And how long do you intend to skulk about the palace before going to see Father?"

"How long will you go about pretending that you don't live in fear every moment of every day of your life?"

Rordan stepped toward her, his hands clenched, and Sarah had her sword out and at his throat before he could blink an eye. She could have taken his life then and there, but she wouldn't. Rordan simply stood there with her blade resting upon the side of his neck.

"The next time you raise your hands against me, my blade will cut you, brother or not."

Rordan took a step back with his hands slightly raised from his sides. "I'll send Father your regards, Sister."

"No need. I'm heading there now," Sarah said and left the room.

Braden quietly followed. "There is something wrong with him," he said after a few moments.

"I agree, but what do you mean?" Sarah asked.

"Couldn't you sense it? I've been around all manner of men from murderers to those believing themselves to be heroes, but there is definitely something off about your brother."

"Half-brother," Sarah said quickly and cursed her vanity in trying to separate herself from the likes of Rordan.

"Perhaps it's the voices or the whisperings. You know when you tap into the energy and you hear the whispers of the souls from ages past?"

Sarah's brows furrowed in thought. "You do have a point. I just couldn't see it."

"Not surprising, my Lady. Most have a blind spot when they have family in their sights."

"Thank you, Braden."

"For what?"

"For coming with me."

"It's what Aaron would have wanted."

"I know, but still I appreciate it," Sarah said.

Braden's lips lifted in a half smile. "And you're one of us now. We have to look out for one another. Are we really going to see the High King? I'm here to help protect you, but I have no wish to be captured by the Elitesmen."

Sarah looked away, staring at nothing, but her eyes taking in everything. "I have to."

They walked along in silence down the deserted hallway.

"Eric saved my life by throwing me out a window. In a split second, when the Elitesmen had attacked the inn, his first thought was to get me to safety. He rightly assumed that I wouldn't leave his side and would have fought and died there along with him. He took the decision from me, and I can't forgive him for that. Not now at least, and maybe not ever. So I'm not going to stand in your way and keep you from making a last stand against the High King. However, I think you should consider whether your actions honor the sacrifice that brought you here," Braden said.

Honor...Sacrifice...Duty, Sarah whispered in the depths of her mind.

"I have no intentions of throwing my life away or yours for that matter. If I don't do something to help these people then I wouldn't be honoring anyone's sacrifice," Sarah said, looking out of the windows to the grand expanse of Khamearra. "We need to get them out. All of them."

"Who?"

"The Resistance, they need to quit the city if they wish to live," Sarah said.

A door swung open from down the hallway, and an older man with long gray hair that spilled onto his leather duster beckoned to them.

"Elitesman," Braden said, "we thought you were--"

"Dead?" Isaac asked. "Not yet. Come inside."

Sarah had a throwing knife in her hand and quickly sheathed the blade and followed Braden through the door. The dark and dusty room was little more than an attic, filled with mismatched furniture.

"What happened to you?" Braden asked.

The old Elitesman took in the sight of Sarah as if making sure she was real. Sarah met his gaze. This was the Elitesman that had helped rescue Verona and the others when they were captured by the Elitesmen. He was like Beck, the old Elitesman who came to the manor where she grew up and trained her.

Isaac went down to one knee. "Your Grace, I'm glad the Alenzar'seth was successful. He wouldn't say exactly what had happened to you, just that he needed travel crystals."

Sarah's mind snapped into the hazy memories of using the crystals to help reset the Nanites. It was Aaron's last-ditch effort to save her.

"It's time for you and your brethren to come out of the shadows. The Resistance needs you, and so do I," Sarah said.

Isaac returned to his feet. "Beck always spoke highly of you, your Grace. We've been helping the Resistance where we can. Gerric has the Elitesmen everywhere. They are wise to our presence here in the city."

"We need to get the Resistance out of the city, and rescue as many as we can," Sarah said.

Isaac divided his bushy-browed gaze between her and Braden. "Where can they go?"

"Shandara," Sarah answered.

"No one can get to Shandara. The place is in ruins, and if that weren't enough, the Ryakuls would feast upon any who would go there," Isaac said.

"No more. The Ryakuls are gone. The darkness that sickened the land is gone," Sarah said.

"And the Heir of Shandara?"

Sarah unclenched her jaw. "He's...gone."

"He's dead?"

"No," Sarah and Braden said at the same instant.

"Then where is he?" Isaac asked.

"He's trapped in another realm, and we're trying to get him back," Braden said.

"We got word from Nicholas that the Resistance was in trouble, which is why we're here," Sarah said.

Isaac frowned. "I sense that you're not telling me everything, which is fine. Nicholas's message was putting it mildly. The High King and Elitesmen are culling the inhabitants of Khamearra, murdering anyone who has ties or shows any signs of defiance. So much so that the cracks are beginning to show in the foundation of the Order of the Elite."

Sarah's eyes widened at the implication. "Do you think some would break away?"

Isaac nodded slowly. "We were trying to get the younger initiates out, before they could be corrupted any further, but they are as likely to turn you in as want to escape. The older ones... some may, but fear keeps them inline. It's hard to tell who to trust."

"Where are they holding prisoners?" Sarah asked.

"They don't hold prisoners very long. They are either executed or volunteered into the army," Isaac replied.

"Conscripts," Braden said grimly, "usually don't make good soldiers."

Sarah's mind raced, a plan already formulating in her

mind. "We can't help the ones in the army, at least not now, but we can help the people in the city. We should focus there."

"I'm open to suggestions, your Grace," Isaac said.

"The Hythariam are in preparations to send aid. We go tonight," Sarah said, looking around. "We need a map."

Braden brought out his comms device. "I have one, my Lady."

Sarah smiled. "I thought you didn't like to use those things?"

"I don't," Braden grunted, "but they are damn useful, and Tanneth has been teaching me and Verona about them. Sarik is already well versed in how they work. What do you wish to see?"

"A layout of the city," Sarah said.

Braden's beefy fingers tapped in the sequence, and after a few grumbles and suppressed curses, a small map lit up the room in a yellowish hue.

Sarah frowned. "This might be useful if Tanneth or Gavril could follow along, which would help coordinate the efforts from their side."

Braden's brow furrowed in thought, and a smile split his square jaw when Tanneth's voice answered the call.

"Okay, Braden and Sarah," Tanneth said, "I've added Gavril and Verona so they can hear us and see the map."

"Braden, I'm impressed you managed not only to call, but

put up a map of the city," Verona's voice chimed in.

Braden glared at the comms device. "That shield of yours won't protect you from me, Verona."

"We'll see, my friend. How are things in Khamearra?" Verona asked, his tone taking a more serious note.

"It's bad—public executions and people being rounded up. We need to get them out," Sarah said.

"How many are left?" Gavril asked.

Sarah glanced at Isaac, who answered. "Thousands of them."

The silence dragged on until Sarah spoke up. "Are you still there?"

"Yes, my Lady," Verona answered. "We're trying to come to grips with this. Who is there with you?"

"The old Elitesman, Isaac," Braden said.

"Not as old as all that," Isaac said quickly.

"Where can they go?" Gavril asked.

"The only place available to them. Shandara," Sarah said. "No buts; they are dying, and they have nowhere else to go."

"We can't use the flyers to get out that many. How many could you get out with the travel crystal?" asked Gavril.

"Not nearly enough. The travel crystal can only do maybe ten people at a time if it's fully charged," Sarah replied.

"Okay, let's take this one step at a time. Are you able to get the remaining members to converge upon a few key locations in the city? Preferably some of the gates, which would be the weak points along their perimeter?" Gavril asked.

Sarah glanced at Isaac, who shrugged his shoulders.

"Tanneth, can you add Captain Nolan? He was our contact when we first entered the city and may be better able to advise us as to what the Resistance can or can't do." Sarah said. "But be discrete; we don't know who will be around him, and he's understandably on edge as it is."

After a few moments they heard Nolan's voice whispering into his comms device. They brought him up to speed and posed the question of organizing the Resistance to converge upon key locations in the city.

"Which locations?" Nolan asked.

Sarah glanced at the city map. "I'm thinking the gates along the east and southeast part of the city. They are farthest away from the palace and the Citadel, and it would take the armies camped outside the city the most time to muster any type of support."

"Sir," Tanneth said, "I think it's time we try them out. It's their only shot at getting out of there."

"I know, I just don't like it. They need more field testing," Gavril replied and sighed. "What Tanneth is suggesting is an all-or-nothing plan. If anyone gets left behind, they will be on their own because we will only get this chance once. Then the High King will fortify against such a strategy again."

"Let's hear it then," Sarah said.

"We bring a small force and hold the three gates that you've suggested. We open a portal at the gates that will take the Resistance directly to Shandara," Gavril said.

Sarah frowned. "I sense a 'but' there. What is it?"

"We've been able to create smaller portals that have two uses before they need to be recharged. The thing is we've only tested them with small groups, and the portal was never open for very long. So to move the amount of people you are suggesting, there is a risk that many could be left behind if the portals fail to remain open."

Sarah took in Braden and Isaac's grim expressions. This was too risky. If they failed, they would effectively be handing the remaining members of the Resistance over to the High King.

"A slim chance is better than no chance at all, but I think the decision on whether they will take that chance should be up to the people we're trying to help. How soon could you be ready to come?" asked Sarah.

"About four hours' time," Gavril answered.

"Nolan, is that enough time to spread the word and get the people to the gates?" Sarah asked.

"Four hours? Barely enough time. They will be able to bring only what they can carry. I will spread the word, but there is another thing to consider. The High King, the guards, and the Elitesmen aren't going to sit idly by while thousands of people race toward the city gates," Nolan said.

"You're right. They won't, but I think I can keep the High King's attention for a little while at least," Sarah said. "Gavril, I'm not an army general, but I've listened in on enough of my father's War Councils to know that if you do this, they will treat it as an act of war. That the Free Nations Army struck first."

"We are already at war, my Lady," Verona said. "Armies are assembling throughout the lands. I'd say that the risk is worth it if we can help the remnants of the Resistance get to safety."

"Verona is right," Gavril said. "We made a promise of support to any who would stand with us. They've done more than their share to aid us, and this will be our chance to return the favor. Also, we can add our own bit of distraction that will draw attention away from where we don't want their eyes to see."

They spent the next few minutes outlining the plan. It was rough and quickly thrown together, but they were desperate. If Sarah hadn't seen the flyer-class SPTs for herself, she wouldn't have believed they would make the trip. Tanneth and Sarik would pilot the Hythariam ships and give support from the air. Given that the airships in Khamearra could do little more than provide target practice, she was confident they would be relatively safe. It was the portals that worried her. Too many things could go wrong.

There were so many things that could fail to come together, but people were being killed in droves. Sarah believed that the people who made up the heart of the Resistance would jump at the chance to get to safety; she just hoped that they wouldn't be meeting their own demise.

Braden put the comms device away, and Isaac eyed him.

"Are you able to jump great distances?" Isaac asked.

Braden shook his head.

Isaac frowned. "But you can draw in the energy and enhance your strength?"

Braden nodded.

"Well then, you can land at least if you drop in from a high place, like some alcove somewhere. Just something to keep in mind," Isaac said.

"Perhaps," Braden said, his brow furrowed in thought.

Isaac turned to Sarah. "You've been teaching them?"

"I have, but Aaron was the one who was able to show them their connection for the first time," Sarah answered.

Isaac nodded. "Your Grace, I will spread word to those of us that are left of the Old Order of the Elite. Something for you to consider is that there are some, many, that would see the return of the Faergrace rulership as good for Khamearra."

Sarah met the old Elitesman's gaze. "Would they follow a queen?"

"No, not just any queen, but they might follow you," Isaac

said, and then he took his leave of them.

After a few moments Braden broke the silence. "I find that Elitesman infuriating, but he might have a point."

Sarah had hoped to bring her father around, but there seemed to be little chance of that happening. Her mind wandered to her mother's family sigil they had found painted throughout the city. Perhaps that was the people's way of reaching out to her. A war of succession was a bloody thing, and that didn't tempt her at all. What drew her in to even consider the thought was to help the people of Khamearra get out from under the power of the Elitesmen and her father.

Sarah and Braden stayed in the attic, laying out some plans and mostly waiting to hear back from Nolan or Nicholas about the status of the Resistance. They moved unseen through the palace, collecting little bits of information about the readiness of the High King's army, but what troubled Sarah was all the talk of secrecy. Something big was being planned. Something that would change how wars were fought on Safanar, and she needed to find out what that was.

Try as she might, Sarah couldn't get it out of her head that her actions were providing the spark that would take all of Safanar into war. The histories in all the great libraries glossed over these points. The dates and battles were cold and factual, but provided little insight into the worries and fears of the people who fought them. Were they doing the right thing? Beck had often told her that doing what is necessary is never a bad thing. Perhaps Verona was right and they were already at war, and the good people of Safanar were caught in the middle. Would future generations look upon her actions as the catalyst that changed their world, leading it into one of the darkest times of their history? Is that how they would view Aaron?

"My Lady," Braden whispered. "Nolan sent word. Whoever would leave Khamearra will be at the designated gates. They are going to start assembling now in the surrounding buildings and wait for the signal. They will be ready to go at the beginning of the nighttime meal. That is a few hours after Gavril said they could be ready, but I think that will be fine."

Sarah nodded.

"What is it?"

"When I first became involved with the Resistance, we would achieve specific goals. We worked against corrupt district captains or shipments bound for the Citadel. I never knew they were part of the De'anjard, but now it makes sense. Then they banded together in force, to aid Aaron, and now they are fighting for their lives."

Braden nodded in understanding. "They've always been fighting for their lives. A wise man told me that the tyrants of this world will use the blood of innocents to sap the will of any who would oppose them. Fear and brutality are their primary weapons. There is a time to survive and endure, and then there is a time to fight. This is a time to fight, my Lady."

Sarah smiled sadly. "A truly wise leader would have found a way not to fight at all."

Braden shrugged his shoulders. "We didn't make this world."

They rested for a time, both of them silent in their thoughts.

"I think we should be going now," Sarah said.

Braden frowned. "This is my least favorite part of the plan. I can't protect you if you go in alone."

"We've been over this, Braden. They will kill you on sight. I have the travel crystal if I get into trouble, and failing that, you will be there to rescue me," Sarah said.

"This is no joking matter. Verona told me what the Elitesmen did to them when they were captured."

"I know," Sarah said grimly. "They won't harm me, and if it looks like you won't be able to get to me, then get yourself out of the palace the way we discussed earlier."

Braden shook his head. "I'll be able to get to you, my Lady."

"Yes, but just in case."

"I will get to you, my Lady," Braden said, and the determined look in his eyes left little room to argue.

They left the recesses of the palace and headed toward the Great Hall, where her father would be hosting the evening meal. There was no way to know who would be in attendance, but Sarah knew the Elitesmen would be present. She could feel their presence throughout the palace. She left Braden in an alcove with access to a catwalk that the servants would use to polish the chandeliers that hung above the Great Hall. This would give him the best vantage point.

Sarah made her way down to another level, where she used to observe her father's court. It was in this room where she had last seen her brother, Primus, before he stabbed her in the back at Shandara. She remembered slipping into unconsciousness and then Aaron calling out to her from the dark recesses.

Sarah shook off the bittersweet memories and focused on the Great Hall. Her father's hulking presence resided at the head table with Rordan at his side. Rordan didn't touch his food but kept scanning the room. She wondered whether Rordan had told their father of their little meeting, but in the end she decided it didn't matter.

The noise in the Great Hall grew as the evening meal started in earnest. Sarah said a silent prayer to the Goddess Ferasdiam to guide her way and to watch over her people. She closed her eyes and made a small circle with her thumb upon her forehead. Her hand drifted down to Aaron's medallion that lay nestled against her chest beneath her shirt. Gritting her teeth, she left the room.

Sarah came to the servant's staircase where two guards waited, eyeing her approach. She pulled back her hood, revealing her golden braid. The guards gasped in surprise, and Sarah drew herself up with all the dignity of a princess of Khamearra.

"I will see my father now," Sarah said. One of her hands hidden in the folds of her cloak grasped the hilt of a throwing knife, ready to use it if necessary, but the guards nodded and brought their fists across their heart, bowing their heads in unison.

She moved past the guards and then heard the heavy footsteps as one ran off. She emerged midway into the Great Hall to a sea of nobles and decorated officers of the Khamearrian army. Her hard gaze slid past her nose as she took in the scene before her. Here these people ate and drank their fill, while the dead piled up at the gates. Her hand clutched the hilt to her sword while servants and nobleman alike scurried out of her way.

Some guards with the silver Dragon emblem gleaming upon their pristine black uniforms moved to intercept her. One of the guards held up his hand to block her path. Sarah drew in the energy, enhancing her strength. She reached out and bent the outstretched hand back on itself, and the guard cried out in pain.

"Get out of my way," Sarah said, keeping her eyes upon the other guardsmen.

She proceeded past them without a backward glance. If they were fool enough to get in her way again, she would draw her sword. Sarah's gaze was fixed at the head of the Great Hall, drawing her father's eyes to her. She strode forward, and the High King narrowed his gaze.

"My daughter has returned to us!" the High King's voice boomed across the Great Hall, silencing its occupants.

Sarah came before the head table and glanced at Rordan, who coolly met her gaze. To the side she could sense Elitesmen closing in around her.

"I have returned, Father," Sarah said.

"What a joyous event this is to have you here now, but I'm a bit out of sorts. Where have you been?"

"Why are you having so many of our people executed, Father?"

Sarah's question echoed through the Great Hall, and her father's playful gaze withered.

"I didn't realize I was answerable to you, my daughter. Regardless, these citizens are a sickness that has plagued our beautiful city. I'm afraid that there is only one way to root out such a vile infection."

"Entire families! Why not let them leave?"

"The infection runs deep. Examples must be made, that any who align with the Resistance are to be punished by death," the High King answered coldly.

"You go too far," Sarah shouted. "I stand with the

Resistance; will you have me executed?"

Gasps erupted throughout the Great Hall.

The High King leaned forward. "And your Alenzar'seth suitor. Do you now stand with him?"

The Elitesmen inched closer to her. "Come at me if you will, Elitesmen; I never grow tired of dispatching any of you."

The High King's pained expression almost seemed genuine, but she knew better.

"I see you've been infected by the Alenzar'seth. He will be brought to justice, like all the other kingdoms that would foolishly clamor to Shandara's banner."

"He will never bow to you," Sarah hissed. "And neither will I."

The room darkened as the High King stretched out his hand toward her. The medallion became as ice against her skin. Sarah shut her eyes, wincing against the sudden cold. For a second she saw a dark figure chained to a column. The vision appeared as if she were looking through a window with water streaming down, giving occasional glimpses of golden clarity.

Aaron! She saw him.

"She is shielded. Take her!" the High King shouted.

Sarah shook off the vision and leaped to the side, circling around one of the Elitesmen who tried to grab her. She sprang to the top of the nearest table, whose occupants scrambled out of the way. Two Elitesmen chased her, and she kicked out, knocking them off the table.

Sarah jumped to the next table over, bringing her closer to her father, and saw guardsmen pouring into the Great Hall. An Elitesman leaped to the table in front of her, landing hard, sending plates of food crashing to the floor. He drew his sword with practiced efficiency of one at home with a blade in his hands.

Sarah took a step back, drawing her own blade, its single curved edge catching the light around them. The Elitesmen charged, and their blades clanged out. She dashed forward, inside his attack, and pulled him off balance. Sarah spun, deflecting another attack and kicked the Elitesman in the back, sending him face-first off the table. She drew in the energy and jumped to the far side of the Great Hall. She glanced at her father and could have sworn a prideful smile tugged at his lips.

The Elitesmen blurred toward her, passing the guardsmen as if they were standing still. She reached inside her cloak and grasped the travel crystal, but an attack orb glanced off her sword and knocked her off the table and onto her back.

The loud war cry of the De'anjard sounded from above as Braden landed atop of the guardsmen, sending them sprawling. Braden unfurled his Shandarian shield and lashed out with his war hammer. Attack orbs from the Elitesmen blazed into the shield and ricocheted away into the fleeing nobles. Braden let out another war cry and slammed his hammer on his shield. He planted his foot behind him, bracing himself, his face a mask of grim concentration.

Sarah felt the pressure of the sonic waves as they barreled off Braden's shield. Braden focused the blast, sending guardsmen and Elitesmen alike flying through the air. The pressure built up in her ears, blurring her vision. Sarah grabbed the travel crystal and at the same time grabbed Braden's outstretched arm. They were pulled into a purple abyss, bringing them safely away from the palace.

Sarah and Braden gasped, catching their breath. She took them to the first place she could think of, which was near one of the designated gates that the Resistance would use to escape.

"What happened to you back there?" Braden asked.

She got up off the ground. "I had a vision of Aaron."

"Where?"

"I don't know. It was so dark. He was chained to a stone column," said Sarah.

"How were you able to see him? Can you do it again?"

"I...I don't know. They tried to capture me, and the medallion became as ice on my chest."

"What medallion?"

"Aaron's," she said, taking it out for Braden to see.

He studied it for a moment, then they both looked up as

two golden Hythariam flyers streaked across the sky. Alarm bells began to ring throughout the city. People were filling the streets, and she heard the guards manning the gates behind them call for archers. Sarah grabbed Braden's arm and used the travel crystal to bring them to the streets below.

She marched up to the guard commander of the gate. "These people are leaving the city."

The commander's eyes widened. "Your Grace, I have orders not to allow anyone to leave."

"I'm giving you a command; you and your men are to quit the gate," Sarah said.

The commander's eyes darted to the approaching crowd and back at Sarah.

Sarah leaned in with a whispered threat. "You can't stop a mob. Save your men."

"Archers, ready bows!" the commander cried.

The guardsmen at the top of the gate towers drew their bows and nocked their arrows.

"Your Grace, if they come to the gate, I will order my men to fire," the commander said.

Sarah drew her sword and in a flash had the end of her blade at the commander's throat. "Call them off," she hissed.

"Stand down," Braden bellowed.

The guardsmen at the tower aimed their arrows down at them.

"I don't want to kill you, Commander, but if you give that order, you will be the first to die," Sarah said.

"With all due respect, your Grace, if I don't give the order, the king will see to it that I die anyway," the commander replied.

Sarah lowered her sword. "You shouldn't have to serve under such conditions. I cannot sit by while my father murders the good citizens of Khamearra. Would you join a cause worthy of laying down your life for?"

The commander met Sarah's eyes, and something gave way inside. He held up his hand, and the archers stood down.

"They will have us executed for this," the commander said and glanced up at the people tied to the poles beyond the gate. "Cut them down," he ordered his men.

Some of the guards looked as if they would protest the commander's orders, but decided against it.

"Thank you, Commander," Sarah said.

"Your Grace, if you're taking these people away would you consider taking a few guardsmen along?" the commander asked.

Sarah studied the commander for a moment and nodded.

Hythariam soldiers, riding upon gliders, swooped over the walls wearing dark armor. The leader removed his helmet, revealing Gavril's face.

Gavril glanced up at the guards and looked at Sarah

questioningly. "I'm glad things are so calm here. There was some fighting at the other gates."

"We don't have long," Sarah said.

Gavril nodded and gestured to his soldiers who immediately put the equipment they were carrying on the ground. They opened a tripod of legs and rested a large cylinder atop. The cylinder began to glow, and a beam of light spread out from it, forming a large oval that bent the very fabric of the world around it. A great hum pulsated from the portal as it stabilized into a glittering doorway of light.

A Hythariam soldier tossed a small metallic ball into the air, which zoomed through the portal. The Hythariam soldier studied the readout upon his comms device and nodded toward Gavril.

Gavril waved over toward the crowd, urging them through the portal. At first they approached warily.

"It's all right; you will find safety on the other side," Sarah said. "Please, you must hurry."

Flashes of light erupted around them, and two Elitesmen appeared. Sarah dashed forward, lashing out with her sword. The Elitesmen met her attacks, but she pressed on, hoping to distract them. One Elitesman disappeared in a flash of light. Sarah pressed her attack, keeping the Elitesman on the defensive. She felt the energy flow through her, guiding her blade as she unraveled the Elitesman's defenses. In moments, the Elitesman collapsed to the ground after her blade stabbed him in the heart.

The crowd pushed forward as more and more people disappeared through the portal to Shandara. Sarah jumped to the top of the nearest building, catching a glimpse of the Hythariam flyers as they laid waste to the airships on the far side of the city. A figure leaped up next to her, and Sarah turned, seeing Verona.

"Apologies, my Lady, but I couldn't stay away," Verona said and waved to Braden down below.

Braden nodded up to them and continued to wave people through the portal.

"The Elitesmen will be back anytime now," Sarah said.

Verona nodded grimly, his face darkening at the thought. "The others are all through. This is the last portal."

The gate beneath them came crashing down, trapping the fleeing people on the other side. Sarah and Verona leaped to the ground. The trapped people began to panic. Braden muscled his way through, shouting for them to stand clear, and grasped the gate.

"You can't lift it. We need to hook up a team of horses to get it up," Verona said.

Braden ignored them, the corded muscles in his back straining. He roared with colossal effort, and the heavy gate slowly lifted off the ground. Sarah and Verona quickly pushed a nearby wagon under the gate, and Braden eased the gate down.

As the last of the Resistance raced through the portal, the Hythariam soldiers converged around them. Bright flashes of light lit up the street, and Elitesmen had them surrounded. Attack orbs were flung in their direction. The Hythariam soldiers fired their plasma pistols, catching the Elitesmen off guard. Gavril waved them through the portal, and they retreated from the bloody streets of Khamearra.

They emerged into the quiet twilight sky above Shandara with the great white walls before them. The heart of the Resistance that was the De'anjard rejoiced to return to their homeland after being away for so long.

Sarah looked around her at all the people they had gotten to safety, and her heart ached for all those they had left behind. Verona and Braden stood next to her.

"And this is only the beginning," Verona said.

Sarah walked among her people, and many bowed in her direction. Verona was right, this was only the beginning, and it left her wondering what the price of this war would cost them in the end. Would they look back and deem the price worthy of the cost, or would they dread the silence of thousands of dead souls as their only answer?

CHAPTER 9
A DEMONSTRATION

"Dek, I tell you they are out there just beyond the tree line. The whole town is in danger," Resel said.

"Ryakuls, you say?" Dek asked.

"That's what I'm trying to tell you. I was a few miles out, checking my traps, and I heard them out there," Resel said, clenching his dirty hands. "You're on the town council, shouldn't you raise the alarm or something? Send out a search party?"

They were less than a mile outside of town when Dek had been told that Resel was screaming like a madman running from the forest. His eyes narrowed at the otherwise normal tree line. The air was crisp, and the skies were clear. Nothing out of the ordinary for their remote northern town.

"You should send word to Rexel and this Free Nations Army they have there. They could come up here and slay the beasts," Resel said, pacing.

Dek frowned. "It's two days hard riding to Rexel. Plus, they would need time to send someone up here. If the beasts are even out there."

"Oh, they're out there. I heard them," Resel said.

"You heard something, I'll grant you that. But did you see them?"

"I didn't stick around. As soon as I heard those deep growls, loud enough to rattle my teeth, I hightailed it out of there."

"It could have been a bear."

"It wasn't a bear, I tell you. The trees all started swaying violently, though there was no wind. Bears don't do that. I tell you there are Ryakul up near the peak, just like the reports warned there would be."

Dek frowned. Ever since news came in from the other towns that Ryakuls had been attacking some outlying farms, he was getting scared trappers like Resel coming to him with an alleged Ryakul encounter every other day. "All right, calm down, Resel. We'll head back into town, get a few of the hunters together, and go out and see what's got you so spooked," Dek said, putting his hand on Resel's shoulder. He didn't need the old trapper starting a panic.

"Gentleman, pardon me, but did you just say there are Ryakuls around here?"

Dek and Resel turned around, and behind them were two men in black cloaks. The one who spoke was the shorter of the two. He had greasy dark hair and eyes that seemingly took in everything around them.

"We mean you no harm," the taller man said.

Even beneath the cloak, Dek could tell he had the bearing of a warrior. How had they gotten so close to them?

"Yes," Resel said. "Just north of here, about five miles away."

The two regarded each other for a moment and started to head north without another word.

"I'm not sure if there are any Ryakuls up there, but it may not be safe for you," Dek called to them.

"Safer for me and my companion than most. Thank you for the information," the shorter one said, and they continued on.

Dek wasn't sure why, but he felt a cold shiver run down his spine. He motioned for Resel to follow, and together they headed back to town. Both men set a brisk pace, eager to be back among people and away from mysterious strangers who appeared out of nowhere and went looking for Ryakuls.

***

"Maybe luck will be with us here," Darven said.

"It certainly wasn't with us before. Not that I believe in luck," Mactar replied. They had been hunting for Ryakuls, but without the Drake to control them, the beasts had scattered. Remote towns like these were often reporting

Ryakuls seen in the area.

"Just in case there are actually Ryakuls here, let's go over it again so we don't have a repeat like the last time," Darven said.

Mactar resisted the urge to glare at the former Elitesman, who seemed to adopt a particular fondness of pointing out their recent failure. They had a chance encounter with a Ryakul a few nights ago, and when Mactar had tried one of the calls that the Drake had used, the Ryakul launched into the air and flew away. At least it hadn't attacked. Dead Ryakuls were no use to him.

"That wasn't my fault. The bracer failed. Regardless, it's fixed now," Mactar said.

"I hope so. It wasn't you who was out there as bait the last time," Darven said dryly.

Mactar chuckled. "You're not losing a step or two in your old age, are you, Darven?"

"Not in the slightest," Darven replied softly.

Darven had always been gifted, even for an Elitesman, but his ambitions ran beyond those of the Elite Order. Without another word, they both drew in the energy and sped ahead. Anyone watching would have seen them disappear, which wasn't accurate at all. They were still there, but moving at speeds beyond the capabilities of normal eyes to track. It was an advantage that the Elitesmen had perfected, and the knowledge had been given to them by Mactar himself.

Miles went by in mere minutes, and they came to a halt. Mactar extended his senses out away from them and could detect two hidden Ryakuls. He pressed the button on his bracer, and it came to life in a soft glow. Mactar strode into the clearing, and after a few moments Darven followed.

Mactar recalled the memory of the call the Drake had used to control the Ryakuls. He crossed the clearing and could hear the loud snorts of the beasts as they lay in wait. Crossing into the tree line the sunlight above all but vanished, sending them into perpetual twilight. Directly in their path was a Ryakul; its bat-like wings were folded in on themselves, and a low growl came from its saber-tusked maw. Foamy white liquid pooled below the beast's mouth, and its eyes bored into him hungrily.

Mactar locked his eyes on the beast, all the while wondering where the other one was. A piercing scream came from above, and Mactar felt a hand roughly pull him back into the clearing. Sounds of snapping tree limbs filled the air as the Ryakul on the ground followed. A dark shadow crossed the ground, and Mactar saw the second Ryakul swooping down at them.

Got you.

Mactar used the energy, sending out the strumming sound in a freakish rhythm, and the effect on the Ryakul was almost instantaneous. The Ryakul on the ground, the one that had been closing in on them, stopped in its tracks and kept shaking his head. He was so surprised that he almost lost his hold upon the energy. The Ryakul reared back, roaring, and lunged forward, snapping its jaws at him.

Mactar held out his hand and blared the Drake's call. The Ryakul stopped less than a foot away. The beast's wretched hot breath washed over him. The Ryakul closed its mouth and regarded Mactar warily. He sensed the life energy around the Ryakul, but its inner emotions were closed off to him.

"You're mine," Mactar said, and though the beast couldn't understand his words, it understood the meaning behind them.

The second Ryakul landed near them, its massive head sitting atop an elongated neck coiled up like a viper about to strike. Using the Drake's call, Mactar brought his will to bear, and the Ryakul's head lowered in submission. The wild eyes of a predator glared back at him in a mask of pure hatred. Mactar reached out and ran his fingers along the pebbled skin of its neck. He could see the shafts of energy imbued around each of the beasts, being both vibrant and dark. Without controlling them, the Ryakuls were almost mindless, moving on instinct alone.

"I can feel them," Darven said. His own bracer glowed, and the Ryakul allowed him to approach. "How do we tell them what to do?"

Mactar moved away and motioned for Darven to follow.

He scanned the clearing for a suitable target. A gnarled old tree with a massive trunk caught his eye. In his mind he pictured the Ryakuls shredding the old tree with their massive claws. As soon as the thought formed in his mind, the Ryakuls snapped their heads in the direction of the tree, but they didn't move. They were waiting for something. Mactar sounded the Drake's call, and the Ryakuls bounded off, decimating the old tree. After the tree was destroyed, the Ryakuls turned on each other, taking grand swipes with their talons and spiked tail. Mactar pressed the button on the bracer, which sent out a barely audible sound, but it snatched the Ryakuls' attention instantly.

"That's interesting," Darven said. "They attacked each other. We'll have to keep that in mind or this could get out of control really quick."

"They seem to react to my thoughts, but I can't gain any insight into theirs. It's as if the beasts are giant living shells. Not fully alive, but not fully dead either. But you're right, we need to practice," Mactar said, then he glanced to the south.

"The town?" Darven asked.

"I could think of worse targets, but we only have two Ryakuls at the moment. Come on; I've got an idea."

***

Dek called for the hunters to gather in the town square so that Resel could relay what he had heard in the forest. The old fool was sincere if nothing else. He was surprised to see how the hunters listened to the old trapper, confirming some whispered fear lying along the edges of their thoughts. Their grim expressions spoke volumes, and some watched the sky warily.

"We'll need to assemble more men and sweep out to the north," a hunter named Carl said.

"How many men?" Dek asked.

"I'd say at least a twenty. Tell them all to bring their bows," Carl answered.

"Are you sure we're not overreacting? What if we don't find anything?"

"Then we'll be safer for it," Carl said.

"Fine," Dek said. The townsfolk had gathered in the square, waiting for them to convene. Dek stepped away from the others and addressed the crowd. "Then it's decided. We need twenty volunteers to head north of the town to investigate whether there are any Ryakuls in the area."

Hands slowly rose, and before long, they had their twenty volunteers. Dek was about to speak when two brief flashes of light shone along the tree line beyond the village. It happened so quickly that he almost questioned whether he saw anything at all. A loud screech made them all jump, and a blurry, dark form swooped out of the sky. The tips of the wings slashed through the people in the square, washing the paving stones in red.

Dek stood frozen as the dark beast spun about with its spiked tail demolishing the buildings, sending splinters of wood into the scattering people. Some people fell in a mad dash to get away. Hunters fired their bows in a futile attempt to slay the Ryakuls, but their arrows bounced harmlessly off their armored hides.

A second Ryakul landed, tearing at both buildings and people alike. In moments, the town was in ruins, and all Dek could do was watch, unable to move. The Ryakuls caught sight of him and bounded forth. The last thing Dek saw was the cavernous black maw ringed with bloody teeth the size of swords rushing toward him.

***

"There, you see? An effective test," Mactar said, looking down at the ruins of the town. "Now think of what ten Ryakuls could do to a castle, or fifty to an army on the field."

Darven nodded. "They are impressive. There is no doubt about that. Once we assemble the numbers you have mind, what's our next move?"

The Ryakuls had moved to the outskirts of the town, chasing down anyone who couldn't find cover. As the Ryakuls moved farther away, Mactar heard a few survivors that must have huddled in the basements of the buildings. A few mangled bodies littered the streets with some twitching in their final death throes.

"We'll rejoin the High King's army and prove why we're more effective than any army mustered by man. Even those with Elitesmen among their ranks," Mactar answered.

"You mean to challenge Amorak?"

Mactar chuckled. "Goodness, no, then who would I put in his place? Rordan is too young, and I have no wish to rule in his place. Do *you* want to be king?"

"No, like you, I'm interested in the real power behind the throne and not the illusion of sitting on it," Darven said.

"Hence I keep you around. Now we need to find more Ryakuls," Mactar said.

Darven called to the Ryakuls, and they immediately took flight, heading in a northeasterly direction.

Mactar's eyes narrowed. "Where did you send them?"

"To seek out their own kind. We can follow along and bring them under our power," Darven replied.

"Our power?"

Darven bared his teeth in a wolfish smile. "You need me, and we cannot both search for more Ryakuls and attack the enemies of the High King at the same time. So yes, *our* power."

"Very well," Mactar said, allowing Darven his own illusion.

***

Rordan stood in the Great Hall of the High King's palace. He would be joining his father in the encampment on the outskirts of the city. Since his sister's appearance, measures had been taken to fortify all the city gates. Reports had steadily come in from three of the gates where an open portal was used by thousands of people fleeing through them. The strangest of these reports were those of black-armored men flying through the air with some type of machines on their feet. Normally such reports would have been dismissed outright, but these came from Elitesmen who had witnessed the events with their own eyes. The Elitesmen, while many things, had never been keen to exaggerate, especially about such a large breach in their defenses. Thousands of people fled the city, people who were no doubt aligned with the Resistance. But the symbol for the Faergraces still showed up. His father's mood had settled into that of a cold fury, and the king had added that those who escaped his grasp would only escape for so long before they were punished.

Rordan activated the travel crystal and emerged on the field outside the High King's tent.

"We will find them. I think we can guess where they went," the High King said.

Rordan stepped inside. They were still talking about the attack last week. The attack that suspiciously occurred when Sarah had paid them a visit.

"What concerns me are these portals," General Khoiron said, his craggy face frowning deeply. "Your Grace, if the enemy has the means to use these portals, then I think we need to move up our timetable."

"In this we are agreed, my old friend. Our reports say they used some type of machine to create the portals. We will circulate the description of it and have it be a target in future engagements," the High King said.

Rordan made his way through the crowded tent. "Mactar sends word that he has been successful, but he needs more time to gather more of them to make a difference in battle."

"Excellent news."

"What has he been successful in doing?" Khoiron asked.

"This, I'm afraid, I will not be sharing with the War Council. Not just yet," the High King said. "Elite Grand Master Gerric, the time for testing with the crystal is over. The attack will be at dawn."

"As you wish, your Grace. What are the targets?"

"These four kingdoms, bordering our lands," said the High King, drawing their attention to the map. "They won't know what hit them. There will be four more kingdoms the day after. Each group will take a contingent of Elitesmen. I expect the cities to fall by the end of the day. Inform the men that they will get their share of the plunder from these cities. That should rally them."

Rordan's heart pounded with excitement. War on this scale had never been possible before. He would be going with Khoiron tomorrow and was eager to test his mettle in battle.

A small voice lingered in the back of his mind about the threat to them that Sarah had spoken about, but he banished it as soon as it came. Stepping out of the command tent and seeing the thousands of men assembled that were all part of the High King's army made him more than confident. Knowing full well that there were eight more encampments with as many men in them gave the High King the most powerful army Safanar had ever seen. Safanar would be reforged and would someday be his to rule. Despite himself, his mind drifted to the Heir of Shandara.

He will never bow to you, Sarah had said in the Great Hall, and she had meant it. Even knowing what their father was capable of, she sided with the Alenzar'seth. Sometimes in the quiet moments he thought of his own encounter with him. Could they ever be anything other than enemies?

Rordan followed his father and the other members of the War Council. Anyone who stood against them was an enemy. The sooner the kingdoms learned that lesson, the better they would be. Even if this threat that his sister believed to be lurking over them proved true, it could never stand against the might of the Khamearrian army.

CHAPTER 10
LEFT BEHIND

"We've lost it, sir," the Hythariam's gaze bored into his screen, and his fingers danced across the controls with practiced precision. "I'm sorry, one moment it was there, and next it was gone."

Gavril shared a glance with Iranus. "Acknowledged," Gavril said. "Flight team, do you have a visual on the target?"

Eight of their flyers were in the upper atmosphere, waiting to intercept the vessel sent from Hytharia. Iranus still gave himself a mental kick for missing the danger brought to their attention by Aaron. He brushed away the mournful feelings for the young man and focused himself on the screen in front of him. The moments dripped by as they waited in the command center at Hathenwood. The Hythariam and the few Safanarions in the room held a collective breath.

"Negative, we don't have a visual. Permission to sweep the area of the ship's last known trajectory," Tanneth said.

Iranus didn't have high hopes that the search would be successful, but they couldn't afford not to search.

"Granted," Gavril said. "It was a long shot at best. Our satellites aren't military grade."

"I want all the satellites tracking the continent. We can rely on our own search algorithms to alert on anything of Hythariam design," Iranus ordered.

The techs at the consoles began tapping away, carrying out his orders.

Vaughn, one of the few native Safanarions in the room, came quietly to his side. "Do you think they will find anything?"

"The ship must be equipped with military-grade technology, which means it can evade our means to track it. Tanneth will lead the search, and we'll have to wait and find out," Iranus answered.

Gavril came over. The old soldier still had his sleek, black armor on that molded itself to the wearer, almost like a second skin, and was very light in weight. The Hythariam who remembered what life had been like during their last dreadful days on Hytharia all had a deeper set to their jaws and a quieter manner than the others. They hardened themselves for the battles yet to come.

***

The Hythariam vessel had traversed the vastness of space, and the onboard ship's artificial intelligence engaged the protocols for the last leg of its journey. The dataset it had for the planet was eighty years old, but the intelligence it yielded was acceptable. Its target was located in a remote central-northern area of the land mass below that had little inhabitants. The AI detected passive scanners and engaged stealth protocols to evade detection. The ship's designers had equipped the vessel with state-of-the-art cloaking technology, so that even if one were standing just outside it, they wouldn't be able to see the ship. The precious cargo entrusted to the AI would be delivered, and the prime directive assigned to it more than thirty years before would be fulfilled.

The ship breached the atmosphere over the planet's vast oceans, away from the marks detected by it sensors. The cloaked ship zoomed across the sky in a staggered approach with its mass displacing the clouds in its wake, but nothing else marked its passing. High above the land the ship flew, rapidly approaching its target. The ship came to a halt and hovered in the air, running a threat assessment of the valley it had chosen for its primary target. The criteria set for the AI was met, and it was green for the final stages of its long journey. In seconds, the onboard computers mapped every inch of the valley below. The ship began its descent using its lasers to cut away a landing area with enough room to carry out its tasks. The countdown timer was engaged. The next actions were essential if it were to achieve its prime directive. Two smaller craft detached themselves from the hull and raced ahead, each two hundred feet in length. They slammed into the ground, anchoring themselves in place. Panels opened up, and the batteries of the trans-dimensional Keystone Accelerators ignited to life, charging up as they waited for the final calculations from the ship.

The main spacecraft landed with the ground giving way to the reinforced landing gear. A small army of machines exited to perform their assigned tasks, reading the area for the host that would come through the portal. The subroutine finished, and the AI ran another check against the star maps of Hytharia's last known position. The AI calculated Hytharia's current position, taking into account the singularity that had been steadily feeding away at the system of planets for which it had been apart. While the data was being fed to the Keystone Accelerator pylons, the AI engaged the passive drones and sent them out, and another subroutine was dedicated to track the positions of all the satellites surrounding the planet.

The small panels opened upon the roof of the ship, and cyber defense drones zoomed into the air, rapidly accelerating away.

Data transfer complete...

The AI waited for the timer to reach zero, giving the drones enough time to take their positions.

The pylons ignited with bolts of energy running the length

of each shaft before reaching across to join the other pylon. The energy aligned into a matrix that spread between the pylons, and a portal sheared to life, opening a doorway to a dying world.

***

Alarms blared to life throughout the command center deep in the heart of Hathenwood.

"Sit rep," Gavril said, standing at the central pavilion.

"Energy spikes being reported, sir," the tech said frowning at his screen.

Gavril punched in the command to bring it on the main screen for all to see, but it was completely washed out.

"That can't be right. Run a diagnostic," Iranus said, coming to Gavril's side.

The seconds dripped past while the techs clattered away at their work. "The system is clean, sir; the report is accurate. The energy spikes are everywhere according to our sensors."

Gavril felt as if the floor was suddenly pulled away from his feet. "They've blinded us. The Zekara are coming," he said, giving word to Halcylon's military faction.

"Are you sure?" Vaughn asked.

Gavril's grim face didn't move from the main screen. "I'm sure. This is an act of war. They blinded us to their doings by flooding our systems with false energy spikes reporting from all over the continent. They knew we would be looking for them. Halcylon wasn't taking any chances. With the failure of the Drake, that ship was their last effort and must have an AI with a full-complement cyber warfare suite."

The occupants of the room remained still in a stunned silence.

Gavril turned to Iranus. "We have to find the command center in Shandara; that's where this war was meant to be fought."

"I know," Iranus said, "but we need Aaron to bring the defense online there."

"What do you mean?" Vaughn asked, dividing his gaze between the two of them.

"Hathenwood has been our home since the fall of Shandara, but it wasn't meant to be. Shandara was to be our safe haven in the event of invasion. We poured all our resources there. However, access to the system is genetically encoded to only be brought online by a member of the Alenzar'seth," Gavril said.

"Aaron," Vaughn whispered.

"Yes, Aaron," Iranus said. "Since his return we've been searching for it. Daverim wouldn't safeguard his city to anyone other than his line."

"Surely Reymius would have done things differently," Vaughn said.

"Yes, he would have, but the fall happened so fast. The High King caught everyone by surprise. We couldn't put contingencies in place should all of the Alenzar'seth perish.

Plus, Shandara was cut off from everyone by the Drake and the Ryakuls there," said Iranus.

"In addition to the weapons caches, we've been trying to dig our way to the command center amid the ruins," Gavril said.

Vaughn frowned. "Wouldn't it have been destroyed with the city along with any of the defenses you had in place?"

Gavril shook his head. "No, the system never came online, and many of the city's defenses were protected underground. We've been clearing the ruins away, but they can only be brought online by the command center in Shandara."

"What if..." Vaughn began and stopped, "...what if Aaron is dead?"

"Then we'll make every effort to bypass our own security measures in place to bring the system online, but first we need to get access to it. It's buried in a part of the city that is almost completely destroyed," Gavril said and frowned at the main screen. "After all these years we still got caught by surprise."

"We couldn't have known," Iranus answered.

"*I* should have known," Gavril said, then he addressed the room. "Stop tracking energy spikes, it's useless. We need to focus our efforts and narrow potential targets for us to investigate. Let's make a grid and check these areas. The ship will likely choose a place remote from any city."

"How do you know that?" Vaughn asked.

"It's what I would do," Gavril answered.

"They wouldn't have come here?"

Gavril shook his head. "The ship could land anywhere. Halcylon will not charge out and blindly attack. He will evaluate and prepare before he makes his move. He will try to remain hidden while he grows in strength."

"You sound as if you know him," Vaughn said.

"I did know him. I served under him in the military. I'm not sure whether he is alive, but these events with the ship are reminiscent of the tactics used by the general. He was nothing if not effective."

"You almost sound as if you admire him."

"He's crazy. Brilliant, but the good man he may have been is gone. I aim to stop him and take him out if I can," Gavril said.

They resumed their work, and Gavril set himself to the task of facing the embodiment of an old nightmare that hadn't plagued his dreams for eighty years and prayed he was up to the task. He was most senior of the Hythariam military that came to Shandara and knew that if he failed, they all would perish.

***

The ground rumbled, and pieces of the hollowed out mountain came crashing down. Aaron stirred awake. He didn't know how long he had been unconscious. Across the stadium an entire section had been pulled away, and a gleaming portal lit up the last bastion that housed the Hythariam, while their planet slowly died.

He was a huddled mass upon the ground with a column digging into his back. Only his eyes moved; the rest of his body felt off, as if his parts were in the wrong place. The Hythariam were flocking to the portal, and Aaron's pulse raced, trying to catch a glimpse of Safanar. Flashes of light washed through the hollowed out mountain as the Hythariam poured through. A long line of equipment trekked across the way and disappeared in a flash, journeying to the place he longed to return. Aaron tried to move his arms, but they wouldn't respond. He forced his lungs to expand, taking in as much of the thin air as he could. He focused his mind, looking inward, trying to make sense of the wrongness he felt to his core. Nothing worked. Part of his mind scattered at the thought before focusing upon the portal. He remembered gaining consciousness in a blurred dream, and when he wouldn't eat, the Hythariam forced the food down his throat. The beast called Thraw he hadn't seen again, and Aaron wondered if he had imagined it all. His eyes shut as if great weights forced them. When he opened them again, the long line of Hythariam heading toward the portal was gone.

"Beautiful is it not, human?" Halcylon asked. "No, don't get up. I doubt you could even if you wanted to."

Aaron lifted his head, which took every ounce of will he had. "Home," he whispered.

Halcylon squatted down, his cold eyes peering at him. "You really are a mess, but *this* is your home now, *human*. You've been sentenced to the same fate that your kind would have visited upon my people. Hytharia has scant time left, and you will be the only one to witness her passing. Initially, I thought to just kill you outright, but I find that this is a fitting end for you."

Halcylon rose to his feet and had to balance himself as the ground shook violently. More of the mountain caved in on itself, and the night sky was exposed on the far side of the cavern. The air began to rush away.

"My time here is up. But know that your beloved Safanar will be in good hands." Halcylon began to walk away, but then turned around. "So much for the strength of men."

Halcylon and his soldiers disappeared through the portal, and after a few moments it vanished, plunging everything into darkness.

Aaron's heart sank as he lifted up his hand in a vain attempt to keep the portal open by sheer will alone, but he had nothing left to give. The air was thinning, and the ground shuddered underneath him. Giant fissures tore the ground open, forming deep chasms.

This is it. I'm going to die. The thought was strangely comforting, but for the deep rumbling of the Eldarin from the recesses of his mind. Aaron tried to focus so he could draw the energy into himself, but failed.

As rocky pieces of the mountain continued to fall, something glittered in front of him that wasn't there before. It took a few moments for the glittering object to register in Aaron's failing mind. He glanced up, and standing before him was a dark figure with green eyes. Hints of the creature's pointed teeth lay inside its mouth, but its body remained blended to its surroundings.

"Thraw," Aaron whispered.

"This is the device you need, human; get us out of here," Thraw said.

Aaron looked at Thraw's form for the first time. The creature had the brown complexion of the Hythariam and a shaggy black mane. Each foot ended in a metallic claw protruding from hairless skin. The green eyes were reminiscent of the Hythariam, both in size and shape, and most importantly intelligence.

"You're part Hythariam," Aaron said and felt his body jerk against the column.

Thraw picked up the small Keystone Accelerator at its feet and shoved it in into Aaron's lap. With a swipe of its claws, the chains fell away from Aaron's arms.

"There is no time, human. You must use the device, or we'll both die," Thraw said.

Aaron's hands clumsily snatched at the Keystone

Accelerator in his lap. He swiped at the top, and the cylinder flared to life, casting a bluish light around them. Aaron stared dumbly at the portal to Safanar before him. If his mind had been working right, he would have known that the portal would only last seconds.

Thraw grabbed the human by the arm and leaped through the portal as Hytharia gave a final shudder and the ground beneath them gave way to darkness and flame. The portal closed immediately behind them. Thraw's eyes almost squinted shut in the sunlight. The human lay unconscious in a huddled mass of misshapen arms and legs, which left him to wonder if it would be a mercy to simply kill the human to put it out of its misery.

Hunter senses kicked in, and Thraw leaped into the nearby tree line as more of the humans came running. The beast climbed the tree and watched as the humans gathered around. The sunlight here was almost blinding, as he had never seen the outside, but for images that would play for the Hythariam. The fresh air burned the inside of his lungs, but he bore it all in silence. He had heard the others talk of climate acclimation and had assumed he would need time to get used to his new world. Then it would be time to hunt. His gaze returned to the humans as they carried off one of their own and Thraw set off, eager to be away and do the one thing he had been bred to do: hunt and kill. Only the Hythariam were his prey, and Halcylon was his target.

CHAPTER 11
REUNION

Along the outskirts of Shandara the sun was hours away from setting. The rune-carved staff rested with part of its heft sticking up from the earth. Grass had returned in patches, transforming the barren area into the potential for green fields. The staff hadn't been moved or touched since it had been stuck it into the ground. Sarah closed her eyes. She could still see Aaron stumbling toward the portal, the Nanites coursing through his system. Her hands clenched at her helplessness as she kneeled there upon the ground, hardly able to move. The Nanites that Aaron tricked into leaving her body had left her weak and disoriented. She opened her eyes, letting the memory fade. The runes along the staff glowed dully. She knew that the staff was connected to Aaron somehow, and after seeing that her people were provided for, she came here to feel closer to him. Braden was with her of course, and he spoke quietly with the De'anjard that guarded the staff. Her eyes glided over the runes being drawn into the pulsating rhythm. A soft breeze pulled at the wisps of hair that had escaped her braid. No one had wanted to touch the staff for fear of cutting Aaron off from Safanar. Barely two months had passed, and she was no closer to Aaron than she was when she first woke. The rune-carved staff was a mystery, and she had to know its secret. Could it help her find Aaron? More importantly, could it bring him home? She brought her hand up to the staff and could feel the hum of energy along its carved surface. Her fingers grazed overtop, and the quickening of energy from the staff seeped into her fingertips. Sarah quieted her mind and focused on Aaron. She could almost smell his earthy presence in a mixture of fire among the fringes of her senses. The runes on the staff flared brightly for a moment before the staff went dark.

Braden and the De'anjard guard came running over. "What happened?"

"I don't know. I barely touched it, and suddenly it went dark," Sarah said.

They stood there for a moment, not saying anything. All of them staring at the staff.

"Does that mean he's..." the guard asked.

The fear in her eyes was mirrored in Braden's for a moment. "No, he's not gone."

The comms device chimed up, and Braden withdrew it

from his pocket.

"Braden. Is Sarah with you?" Verona's voice asked through the device.

"I'm right here, Verona."

"Good. We need for you to return to Rexel. There have been reports of the High King's army attacking," Verona said.

"We'll be right there," Sarah said.

Braden closed the comms device. "You didn't tell him about the staff?"

"I will when we get there," Sarah said, bringing out the travel crystal.

Braden nodded and instructed to the guard to stay with the staff. He took Sarah's hand, and she engaged the travel crystal. Within a moment they emerged at the Free Nation's Army encampment outside Rexel. Verona greeted them. He wore the forest green clothing that the Hythariam wore. Roselyn stood at his side with her hand upon his arm. It was clear that the two were in love. She was happy for them both, but at the same time she felt a tinge of jealousy at their happiness. Sarah clamped down on those thoughts immediately. If it weren't for the efforts of Verona and Roselyn, she might not be standing here at all. Roselyn watched her with the keen golden Hythariam eyes that were almost feline but not quite human.

They exchanged greetings, and Verona led them through

the camp.

"I'm glad we were able to help members of the Resistance escape the city, my Lady," Verona said.

"We were able to get a lot of them out, but there are still people there who need our help," Sarah said.

"The Khamearrian army has been attacking our allied nations. Reports are still coming in, except we don't know how they are able to attack so many places at once," Verona said.

"They could be using the travel crystals," Braden offered.

"We thought of that, but the reports speak of a large attack force, laying siege to castles and small cities. Seems like a tall order for a travel crystal, even with the Elitesmen," Verona said and then went into the numbers of the attacking forces being reported.

"You're right. It's too many for the travel crystals traditionally used by Elitesmen, but they certainly aren't marching there, otherwise they would have been seen. They must have found a way to augment the travel crystals to move larger attack forces," Sarah said.

"That's what we're afraid of. We've been advising the nations allied with us to stay on alert, but we're having trouble coming to any of their aid. So far they've hit places close to the Khamearrian border, and not everyone that was hit was allied with the FNA."

"My father is sending a message to the other kingdoms.

That no one is beyond his reach. They could attack here at any moment," Sarah said, noting the heightened activity around them.

"What's happening?" Roselyn asked.

A crowd was gathering a short distance from them, so they decided to head over. The crowd was gathered around one person, who stood taller than most of the men gathered around him.

Verona frowned, peering into the crowd. Then his mouth fell open, and he turned to Sarah, "My Lady...The Goddess has blessed us this day. Our wayward friend is back."

The breath caught in Sarah's throat, and she began running. Aaron stumbled along, looking as if he had walked a great distance. Some people came to his aid, but he waved them off. His clothes were in tatters, and he was covered from head to toe in bruises and dried blood, but she didn't care. She ran to him and took him in a fierce embrace, and the crowd around them melted away. Sarah gazed into his honey-brown eyes with hints of gold on the edges, expecting to see the man she loved; instead she found a stranger looking back at her through Aaron's eyes. A sudden coldness sucked the breath from her. The crowd around them cheered. Verona and the others came up behind them smiling.

Aaron leaned in to press his lips to hers, and she flinched back instinctively. A gnawing doubt rapidly spread through her core. *This is not my Aaron.* The people closest around looked at her in shock. Her breath quickened in her chest, and she studied Aaron uncertainly. The crowd around them knew what Aaron had sacrificed to save her, and here she was spurning the miracle of his return, but she couldn't help it. This was not Aaron, and the certainty of it crawled along her skin.

Aaron didn't seemed fazed that she had pulled away. He looked around at the others tiredly and fell to the ground, going unconscious. Verona and Braden carried him away. They pointedly didn't look at her, and some others scowled in her direction before moving on.

Sarah stood rooted in place, unable to move or shake off the feeling that something was terribly wrong. A gentle hand touched her arm, and Roselyn's eyes drew up in concern.

"What is it, Sarah?"

Sarah's eyes darted around, and her breath came in short gasps. "It's not him, Roselyn. I know this must sound crazy, but when I looked into his eyes I swear the man we knew wasn't there."

Roselyn narrowed her gaze inquisitively. "Are you sure? Look at him. He's been through quite an ordeal."

Sarah grasped Roselyn's arms. "It's not him. You have to believe me. He saved me in Shandara using his own life force to keep me from dying. Since then we've shared a connection, and now it's gone."

"It's all right," Roselyn said soothingly. "I will examine him, and we'll be able to see if he is, in fact, Aaron Jace."

"Do whatever you like, but I would know my love if I saw him."

Some of the men passing by glanced in their direction, and Roselyn stepped closer to her. "I have a sample of his blood at Hathenwood. I will get another one from him and compare, but you need to calm down. If you start flinging accusations you may find that there are some here who would harm you."

Sarah clenched her teeth, the muscles in her body becoming rigid. "You know something." It wasn't a question, and the look in Roselyn's golden eyes confirmed it.

"Nothing you don't already know. You're the daughter of the High King. There are some who think you are just a spy. Others believe you to be a perfect bargaining piece to negotiate terms with him. And still others say that you manipulated Aaron into sacrificing himself for you."

Sarah had to fight to keep her mouth from gaping open, but deep down she knew what Roselyn said was true. She had been too preoccupied with trying to find a way to rescue Aaron and help the Resistance to pay the naysayers much mind. If she openly voiced her doubts about Aaron, then they would use it against her.

"I've been blind," Sarah said.

"No you've been working to find a way to help Aaron. We all have. People will talk and have opinions regardless. I want to help you. If that man isn't Aaron then he is not here for our own good, and we need to remove that threat, but what if it is Aaron?" Roselyn asked.

"It's not."

"What if something was done to him that changed him to his very core? Like what was done to you?"

Sarah opened her mouth to reply, but nothing came out. Roselyn had a point.

"He's been gone for months. Who knows what's been done to him in that time," Roselyn said.

Sarah glanced at the backs of the receding crowd. "I have to trust my heart."

Roselyn nodded. "There is just one more thing. If what you suspect is true, then where is the real Aaron?"

Sarah shook her head and scanned the people around them as if Aaron would suddenly emerge.

"Let's go," Sarah said.

They headed in the same direction that Verona and Braden had taken Aaron in. Off to the side of the road, a group of men were stacking sacks of grain into a wagon when a crippled-looking man muttering to himself lurched by, knocking into one of them. The men on the ground shouted and kicked the crippled man who flailed his arms clumsily and his shouts grew louder, sounding like gibberish. The workers screamed at him, and each began laughing and taking a shot. The cripple swung his gnarled hands and tried to wheel around, but stumbled and fell. The workers closed in on him hungrily.

"You men, stop that at once!" Sarah shouted at them.

The men turned around and took note of her golden hair, giving her a slight bow before going back to work. Sarah kneeled down. The crippled man kept his deformed hands covering his face. His clothes were caked with mud, and it was matted through his greasy hair. He drew ragged breaths. Sarah reached out and gently pulled his arms down. Dull-brown eyes darted around before coming to focus on her. He pulled back and squeezed his eyes shut. His mouth opened and closed rapidly. He was hideously deformed as if every bone in his body had been broken. He lurched to his feet and took a few steps away.

"Len," a short man called, coming down the road. He had a homely face and was dressed in simple clothes, but he had a gentle manner to him. He called out again, and the crippled man swung around repeating the name.

"Thank you for looking after him, my Lady. He wandered off the moment my back was turned," the man said.

"It was no problem. Those other men were beating him," Sarah said, glaring at the group of men who had finished loading the wagon and were moving away from them. "I'm sorry, but I didn't get your name."

"Apologies, my Lady, my mum exhausted herself with instilling manners into me, but I'm afraid it was all for not today. My name is Wes, and this is Len," Wes said with a smile and nod to both Sarah and Roselyn.

"Len," Sarah said, but the crippled man was looking away from them. "That's a strange name."

"Hardly a name at all, my Lady. They found him in the woods yesterday and that was the only word he has said since," Wes said.

"It's very kind of you to look after him," Sarah said.

"Well he's quite strong, and I'm short, so I look after him, and he helps me lift stuff when I need it."

"Len," Len said, his eyes growing distant for a moment, but then darted around following things that only he could see.

They bid the men farewell and headed back into the camp. Sarah caressed Aaron's medallion under her shirt, lost in thought, and before long they came to a heavily guarded tent.

Roselyn started to head inside, but Sarah reached out to her. "I can't go in there."

Roselyn considered her words for a moment and nodded. "We'll meet up later then."

Sarah stood alone outside the tent, and her insides squirmed. She found herself wanting to plunge headlong into the tent and give into the fantasy that Aaron was inside waiting for her, but she couldn't. She heard many voices coming from inside, from Verona's boisterous laughter to Braden's grumbling.

Backing away from the tent, she engaged the travel crystal and left. She emerged under a star-filled sky. The trickling water of a fountain of the Goddess Ferasdiam stood amid a remnant castle long since gone to ruin. At first she didn't recognize where she was until a vision of Aaron burned through her mind. This was a place he had taken her when he had tried to rid her of the Nanites. Verona later told her that the fountain was where a Dragon had spoken to them. She gazed at the stone carving of a woman standing resolute above the pool of water that served as the fountain's basin. Sarah collapsed to her knees, her eyes brimming with tears, and wept. All the while cursing herself for doing so. She twisted around and sat with her back against the fountain walls. She withdrew the medallion from her shirt, tracing the carving of a Dragon cradling a single rose with a crystal in the center. She moaned Aaron's name and sank to the ground, passing out of thought and mind, but for the soft trickle of the water and the resolute stare of the stone carving of the Goddess above her.

CHAPTER 12
SHADOWS DESCENT

"I'm here, my Lady," Verona said.

Roselyn looked up from what she had been working on and smiled at him.

"My Lady?" Roselyn asked.

"In this case I mean it quite literally," Verona quipped.

Roselyn laughed and kissed him. "Fool."

"Always for you, my Lady," Verona said, feeling her silky raven hair glide across his hands as she stepped back.

"You should have seen the looks I would get when I asked why you were so quiet."

"I see my reputation precedes me," Verona grinned.

The smiled melted away from her face, and the muscles above her cheekbones rolled as she chewed her bottom lip. He was still learning all her quirks, but this was one he knew well. There was something she wanted to talk to him about.

"How is Aaron?"

Verona noted the slight frown on her face when she asked. "He rests. Braden is with him."

"Did he say anything about how he escaped?"

Verona shook his head. "Not since you examined him yesterday. He more or less passed out."

Roselyn nodded and addressed the flashing light on the screen she was working from. She had setup a small lab with some of her Hythariam equipment that he couldn't even begin to guess how they worked. "What are you working on?"

"I'm running some tests on Aaron's blood."

"What are you looking for?" Verona asked.

"Anomalies. I'm comparing this sample from what we had at Hathenwood," Roselyn said.

Verona frowned. "You kept his blood?"

"It's not as ghastly as you make it sound," Roselyn grinned. "But yes, we did. If you recall, he was infected with the Ryakul poison, and we were trying to help him. Our blood, yours and mine, hold detailed information about us."

Verona nodded. "And why are you comparing his blood samples?"

"He's been gone for months on Hytharia. Captured by my people there. These tests might give us some insight into what has been done to him, if anything. I know on the surface he appears normal, but in the time you were with him has he acted any different?" Roselyn asked.

"He was captured. I don't mean to bring this up, but we both know what that was like," Verona said. The images of the Elitesman Sevan torturing people while he and Sarik kept up a shield still came to him in his dreams.

"I realize that, but Sarah believes that the man that came yesterday isn't Aaron," Roselyn said.

Verona blew out a breath. "Do you realize how crazy that sounds? If I hadn't known about the Nanites and that they were capable of changing the very foundations of our minds, I would think she lost her senses."

"And now?"

"I see Aaron before me. What do you see?"

"I'm not sure what to think. So far the blood tests match, but I have more tests to run," said Roselyn.

Verona came to her side and reached out to her. "What do you see, my Lady?"

"I see Aaron, but Sarah is my friend. She and Aaron are connected in ways we're only beginning to comprehend. If she has doubts, then we should listen to her."

Verona was silent for a moment, considering his words carefully. "Could she still be suffering from some remnant of the Nanites? The way I understand it is that they retrain the mind."

"I've considered that, but don't you find it suspicious that Aaron just showed up here out of nowhere?"

"I thought of it more as a blessing, but I see your point. If he has returned does it also mean the rest of the Hythariam have arrived?"

The comms device chimed from both of their wrists, and Roselyn brought hers up.

"It's a message from Gavril. They want to see us at the command tent," Roselyn said and started packing up her things.

"Roselyn, I think we need to give Aaron some time," Verona said.

"Something we're lacking at the moment. There are too many people who seek to use Sarah as some type of pawn with the High King or believe that she is here spying for him," Roselyn said.

They headed toward the command tent.

"Rumors," Verona said. "She's the daughter of the High King; of course there are rumors. I have no doubts where Sarah's loyalties lie."

"Even if she refuses to believe that Aaron has returned?"

Verona felt his teeth clamp down. "You paint a dark picture, my Lady." His thoughts drifted to Aaron's return and the look on Sarah's face as she pulled away from him. How could she have known anything so quickly? And now Roselyn was running blood tests looking for Goddess knew what. They had enough enemies to face without being suspicious of one another.

Outside of Rexel was a city of tents and makeshift shelters.

More permanent structures were being built, but not fast enough to accommodate the Free Nations Army. They came to a behemoth-sized tent, and he nodded to the guards posted outside and entered. There were various groups gathered inside the tent. Some groups were being led by Hythariam there to teach others the basics of how their technology worked. Others were gathered with leaders of the various factions that made up the FNA, poring over maps and discussing tactics. Verona had sat in enough of those to know how useful they were. The maps of Safanar since the dawn of the airships were more accurate than anything they had before, and the Hythariam satellites up in the heavens augmented those as well. He had yet to see so many of the things that Roselyn spoke of, but he had come to trust and rely on the Hythariam technological wonders.

A small crowd gathered at the meeting area, and standing along the outskirts was a familiar face although not as young as he was a few months ago. Jopher had turned into a fine officer.

"Got your feet back on solid ground?" Verona asked.

"For the moment. The admiral put me in command of a ship of my own," Jopher said.

"I don't know how you did it, but you've wormed your way into Nathaniel Morgan's good graces," Verona said.

"I'll tell you how he did it," came Admiral Morgan's voice from behind him. "With honest to goodness hard work. You princely types are all the same. You come to me all high and mighty, thinking that what comes out of your ass doesn't stink like the rest of us. A few weeks or months getting your hands dirty tends to change all that."

"I'm sure you expected it to take months in my case," Verona grinned.

"You both did well. I couldn't be prouder if you were my own sons. The truth of the matter is we need ship captains, and that means some of you will need to grow a bit faster," Admiral Morgan said.

"Did you happen to see my request?" asked Jopher.

"Aye, I did, lad," Morgan said, "You want Hatly, the Raven's engineer. I bet you'd take the Raven too if I was of mind to let you, but I'm not. You're going to one of the newer ships."

"Come now, Nathaniel," Verona said. "You get what you want, which is for Jopher to captain a ship for you, and he gets what he needs, which is an exemplary engineer to keep her flying. You taught him well."

"Too well apparently. Yes, I will approve the transfer," Morgan said after a moment.

"Thank you, sir."

Verona grinned at them both, and the admiral took his leave of them.

"Is it true about Aaron being back?" Jopher asked.

Verona nodded. "Causing quite a stir. He more or less

passed out shortly after arriving. Braden is with him. I have a question for you, but not as an officer in the Free Nations Army, but for the heir apparent of Zsensibar's throne."

"That's making waves among my many brothers and sisters still in Zsensibar," Jopher said.

"I can imagine, but they will learn. With Khamearra's armies attacking, we need a commitment from your father. Do you know if he's willing to grant that now?" asked Verona.

"You would think that the sheer fact that I am here would be a measure of his commitment, but I understand what has leaders of the War Council concerned. He will be coming here soon enough," Jopher said.

"Hopefully he doesn't intend to bring his whole army. Resources are spread thin enough as it is, or so my uncle keeps saying."

"Troop movement is going to be one of the topics of discussion. He has used the comms device, but he doesn't like them," Jopher said.

"I actually agree with him in that regard. The comms device has some limitation, and some things are best discussed in person," Verona said.

"Are you getting set in your ways, Verona?" Roselyn asked.

Verona gave her a sly grin. "Not at all, my Lady. There are some I'd rather see in person as opposed to a voice through one of your machines. Your voice, while music to my ears, doesn't hold a candle to actually standing at your side, which is music to my soul."

Roselyn giggled and leaned into him. He brought his arm around her shoulder, and for a brief instant their worries were far away from them. At that moment the thing sitting in the middle of the floor lit up around them. He couldn't remember what it was called. Roselyn would know, but he wasn't of a mind to ask her about that. He was more of a mind of stealing away with her so they could be alone, but there was little chance of that happening. A large display of light showed the people in Hathenwood.

Roselyn eyed him. "Do you remember its name?"

It was almost like she could read his thoughts. "A holographic display," he said.

"What about the device on the floor?"

Roselyn was nothing if not determined to teach him about the Hythariam and their infernal devices that he couldn't remember the names of. It was almost like when he was younger with Vaughn and his history lessons.

"I haven't got a clue, my Lady."

Roselyn stared at him with those golden eyes of hers that would have chased away any of the words that came to mind, except that he knew this was important to her. Jopher stood on the other side of Roselyn and mouthed some words. The answer lit up in his mind like a beacon in the sky. "A holo projector."

"Very good," Roselyn said. "Perhaps you should keep Jopher with you to feed you the answers."

Dammit, she caught us, he thought to himself. "My Lady, you scold me. I am deeply sorry. But I could bring up the finer points of archery."

Roselyn leveled her gaze at him coolly. "You could."

Verona often found it interesting that some rules between men and women, including Hythariam, didn't necessarily apply both ways. Perhaps he was being too hard on her. Roselyn did try shooting an arrow from a bow, but it didn't go well. She had been as bad as Aaron was when they first met.

"Thank you, everyone, for joining us on such short notice," Iranus said. "We have a great many things to discuss."

Sarah came to his side so quietly that he didn't know she was there until she placed her hand upon his arm. Her cheeks were red as if she had been out in the wind, and her eyes held the remnant swollenness of someone who had been crying. Verona went to put his hand upon her back and felt the crisscross of sheathed blades there.

She still carries Aaron's blades.

Roselyn came to Sarah's other side, and they turned their attention back to Iranus.

Iranus began speaking again. "We've have reports of the High King's armies attacking neighboring kingdoms near

Khamearra. Not all of them have openly allied with the Free Nations Army, but we believe the High King is sending a clear message to anyone who may have been on the fence about joining us. We must find a way to respond to these attacks. We've put protocols in place so warning can be sent as soon as possible, and a ready force will be on standby all day and night from now on."

A quiet murmuring began at that. Verona had known about the ready forces being assigned as the strategy had been discussed previously, and his uncle, the prince, had informed him that they wanted him to lead one of those forces. Verona almost missed the quiet days when they were just trekking to Shandara, and prior to that, finding trouble in whatever city they had been to in the Waylands. Verona had made his own proposal to the War Council for a more proactive fighting force with aims of striking back at the High King. He was still waiting for the final approval of it, but he had already been trolling through the various FNA camps, looking for a specific type of fighting man. Men who weren't afraid to take risks and were able to improvise. Braden had aims of resurrecting the De'anjard and with his Warden's Hammer he made a formidable addition to any group of men that Verona would put together. Now that Aaron was back, Braden would probably be going back to guarding him. The only thing he could do was to convince Aaron to join him, which begged the question as to whether

Aaron was fit to rejoin the fight now that he was back. *If he is back*, said a quiet voice in the back of his mind. He glanced at Sarah through the corner of his eye. Her intentions where Aaron was concerned had always been good, and he wasn't sure why she would believe that the man who came back to the camp yesterday was anyone other than Aaron. Part of him believed it was still some remnant effect of the Nanites, but what if she was right and they were all being fooled? The implications could be disastrous for all of them. It made him uncomfortable to even consider the notion.

"Lady Sarah," the holographic image of Iranus addressed her formally, "do you have any opinion about these attacks?"

"I think you are correct. My father is sending a message that he can strike whomever and wherever he wishes at any time. But as you said, with our allies increasing their readiness they will be better prepared to defend against an attack," Sarah said.

"Thank you. I'd like for you to take a look at what I'm about to display and see if you can tell me what these things are," Iranus said.

The holo changed to a view of the Khamearrian army as if they were looking at it from above. *This must be from one of those machines the Hythariam had in the sky*, Verona mused. Roselyn glanced at him, and he mouthed the word 'satellite' with a half smile. The image zoomed in closer to a circle of black-clad warriors that Verona assumed were Elitesmen. They were circled around some type of large glowing object.

Sarah studied the image for a moment. "It looks like the large focusing crystal that was housed in one of the citadel towers of the Elite."

"A focusing crystal?" Iranus asked.

"Yes, it's used to recharge the other crystals like the ones used for traveling. In the tower they amplify the rays of the sun to power it, and it in turn charges the others. They must be using it to help move the army around," Sarah said.

"Can you offer any insight into how they might accomplish this?" Iranus asked.

Sarah frowned in thought for a moment before answering. "I know how the travel crystals work. The user feeds a bit of the gathered energy into it along with a clear image of where they wish to go. But that large focusing crystal by itself can't do it alone."

"If I understand you correctly, the crystal works in pairs with whoever uses them?"

"That is correct, but a travel crystal by itself can only move small groups of people," Sarah said.

"They must have found a way to use the focusing crystal to increase the ability of a normal travel crystal," Roselyn said. "It's quite smart. We studied the few travel crystals we have and we would need to crunch the numbers, but the power requirements are high. As we've learned with our own

Keystone Accelerators to open portals, even in the same dimensional space the power requirements are high to keep the doorway open so enough people can move through. That's why we're limited to two uses per each Accelerator that we use. I would think it is safe to assume that while the High King's army can move about the continent, there are limitations as to how often they can use the focusing crystals before they require recharging."

"We know it's important to them by how heavily it's guarded, but what I'm not sure of is how many of these large focusing crystals they have," Gavril said.

"Two that I know of," Sarah said.

"Then they are priority targets," Gavril said.

"They are also the most heavily guarded," Verona added.

"Worth it if we can cripple their forces for a while," Gavril replied.

"Thank you, all," Iranus said. "All of your input has given us much to consider, but we must move on to our next order of business. We've been tracking an object heading to this planet from space. It was believed that the object's origin is from Hytharia. Early yesterday morning the object made it past our defenses and was able to land somewhere on Safanar."

A tidal wave of questions spewed forth from many of them about the invading horde from Hytharia.

"Give me a moment, and I will tell you what we know,"

Gavril chimed in. "As Iranus has said, the object beat our defenses, which we can attest to the military-grade technology used to create it." Gavril stopped and brought up a map of Safanar on the display. "Based upon the last known position of the ship, the direction it was heading, the craft came in through the atmosphere over the ocean northwest of Khamearra and then disappeared. We haven't been able to find it, and we have no idea where it went after. We've had people up in the flyers, sweeping different areas of where we expected it to go, but so far it's an extremely slow process."

"Do you know what it could be doing?" Verona asked.

"We're not sure exactly," Gavril answered. "This was a last-ditch effort by the Zekara to gain access to Safanar."

"They're here," Aaron's voice said from behind the crowd, and a pathway opened up for him across from where Verona stood.

Verona's eyes darted to his friend, and he felt Sarah stiffen next to him. Remnant bruises covered his skin in a patchwork of yellows and soft purples. Whispers of his name spread throughout the tent, and Verona realized that for many this was the first time they had ever seen him. The native patrons of Safanar bowed their heads in reverence to the only surviving member of the House Alenzar'seth. Aaron's gaze swept the room as he moved in closer.

"Aaron, I think I can speak for everyone here that we're

extremely happy to see you returned to us, but I'm afraid it comes as a mixed blessing since your return would signify that the Zekara have made it to Safanar as well," Iranus said.

"Who are the Zekara?" Verona asked.

"They are what the members of the Hythariam military call themselves," Aaron said. "You must be wondering what has happened to me since going through the portal and how I got free."

"You could say we've spoken about it once or twice, my friend," Verona said, and some of the others chuckled around the room. Aaron, however, barely acknowledged the jibe.

"I was taken prisoner by the Zekara shortly after going through the portal," Aaron said.

"Why didn't you use the Keystone Accelerator to open a way back to Safanar?" Roselyn asked.

"After going through the portal, the Nanites in my system shut themselves down. The atmosphere upon Hytharia was so thin that I began choking. I tried to open a portal back to Safanar, but the Zekara soldiers captured me and brought me to their mountain base. Halcylon is alive, and he's here on Safanar," Aaron said.

Sarah took a step toward him, and Aaron turned his gaze upon her but continued addressing the rest. "They held me prisoner. Put me on trial. That was how all this happened," Aaron said gesturing to the bruises upon his face and arms.

"A trial?" Verona asked.

"I could see that," Iranus said, drawing their attention.

"They held me responsible for the barrier put in place blocking the portal from Hytharia to Safanar," Aaron said. "When they found me guilty, the crowd was allowed to extract their toll."

"How did you survive?" Verona asked.

"I'm sure they wanted to kill me, but Halcylon and his soldiers wouldn't let them."

"How did you return?" Sarah asked, her voice sounding hoarse.

"They gave me enough to eat and drink to barely keep me alive. They had me staked out in the open. Then one day a portal opened, easily the size of a building, and the Zekara started filing through it, taking whatever they could. The planet had become unstable and was in its final death throes. The last thing I saw was a dark figure before something knocked me unconscious, and when I woke up I was out in the forest a few miles away from here," Aaron said.

Verona listened to his friend speaking and almost couldn't believe what had been said.

"So we have an anonymous benefactor for your release," Gavril said with a frown. "How did they even hold you prisoner? A small number of us have seen what you can do to Elitesmen and Ryakuls alike."

Aaron's eyes grew distant for a moment, and he

shuddered, "They used the Nanites on me."

Roselyn plunged her hand inside her pocket, brought out a device, and stepped in front of Aaron. She ran the device over his chest and along his arms, then around his face.

"I can detect the Nanites in his system, but they are strange like they are dormant," Roselyn said. "I would like to do a more thorough examination."

Aaron held up his hand. "I've had enough prodding by Hythariam technology for a while, so I will respectfully deny your request."

The words were soft spoken, but it didn't take anything away from the coldness in them. Roselyn backed away, coming to Verona's side. He could tell her feelings were hurt, and he resisted the urge to reach out to her.

"You've been through a lot, my friend, but Roselyn was only trying to help," Verona said.

"I appreciate your help, my Lady, but we have more pressing things to concern ourselves with," Aaron said.

Verona didn't say anything back, but clearly the issue was dismissed.

"When I came into the tent you were speaking about the High King attacking other kingdoms?" Aaron asked.

The discussion turned to what had been previously talked about, and Verona took the opportunity to watch his friend. At times he was just as he had remembered him, and at others he appeared to be a complete stranger. Sarah was

202 | AMIDST THE RISING SHADOWS

silent through much of the conversation, but her eyes never left Aaron. She watched him closely, and more than once did Aaron make eye contact with her, but it held none of the fire it had before. Verona didn't know what to make of it. His mind was at odds with what he wanted to believe, which was that his friend had beaten the odds and had returned to them.

The session ended, and people began leaving the command tent.

"My Lady, I believe you have something that belongs to me," Aaron said, looking at Sarah. "My swords."

"I do indeed have them, but you hardly look like you could wield them. I think I'll hold onto them until you are ready," Sarah said.

"You'll find that I am a quick healer," Aaron said with a smile, standing taller.

Sarah reluctantly removed Aaron's swords from her back, "Perhaps you'd like to have a go in the training area?" she asked and handed his swords back to him.

For a moment Verona wondered whether she was going to give them back or not.

"Not right this second. I'd like to tour the camp," Aaron said, and a number of people standing around practically leaped up for the privilege of showing him around. With a nod in their direction, Aaron left them behind.

Sarah turned to Verona, giving him a pointed look and left.

Verona left the tent with Roselyn silently walking next to him. Jopher had followed them out as well.

"He seems different," Jopher said.

"How so? He was a prisoner until recently," Verona said.

Jopher frowned, putting his thoughts in order. "I don't mean his injuries. All the bowing and formalities, he didn't seem to mind it at all. It was almost like he expected it."

Verona's mind raced, going through the meeting in his mind. "Maybe his imprisonment had more an effect on him than we thought," he said, catching Roselyn's sideways glance.

"It's just not something I expected to see from him," Jopher said, and the comms device buzzed on his arm. "I have to go; my father's envoy is arriving from Zsensibar."

Verona wished him well as he turned and walked away, and then he felt Roselyn's eyes on him as the young officer left.

"I don't know what to say, my Lady."

"I know. It's strange. One moment Aaron is just as he was before, and in the next it's like we're dealing with a complete stranger," Roselyn said.

Verona felt a faint twisting in his stomach at the thought that what if, perhaps, Sarah was right. "It seems that Sarah has her doubts, as well."

The people of the camp went around them, going about their business, and Verona stopped walking when he felt

Roselyn place her hand upon his arm.

"Can you blame her?" Roselyn asked. "More than anyone else here, she wants to believe that somehow Aaron has made it back to us."

"I can't argue with that, my Lady. I don't know what I would have done if it were you trapped in a place where I couldn't reach you."

"I know," she said and leaned in to kiss him.

Roselyn left him, saying she had to return to Hathenwood and would be back in Rexel tomorrow.

***

Morning came much sooner than Verona would have liked, and he woke to the sight of Braden, who shed his normally stoic demeanor, shaking him awake with a malicious grin.

"I'm awake!"

"About time too," Braden said.

"Are we under attack?"

The sobering question sucked the mirth right out of his friend.

"No, but there are a group of soldiers we're to assess this morning," Braden said.

Verona nodded and roused himself out of bed, "You've managed to drag yourself away from Aaron?"

"He said he would meet us down there later on," Braden said.

He hadn't slept well last night. After having spent most of

the day quietly observing Aaron, and coming no closer to deciding whether it was really him or not, he went to sleep. Mostly he lay awake wondering when the world had grown so complicated. He had sworn to be at Aaron's side throughout the measure of this journey, and at times like these, Verona was left grasping where it would finally lead them.

He and Braden headed outside the city to one of the various training areas set aside for the soldiers in the FNA.

"Have you seen Sarah?" Verona asked.

Braden shook his head. Sarah had left them yesterday, and he had not seen her since.

"I did speak to her through the comms device, and she said she would meet us," Braden said.

"What's so special about this group of soldiers?"

"They were handpicked by Colind, who said they might possess the potential for tapping into the energy," Braden said.

"I haven't seen Colind in a while. The last I heard he was trying to find the old members of the Safanarion Order," Verona said.

Braden glanced the other way, saying nothing.

"When did you become the purveyor of information?"

"What?" Braden asked, a little too quickly.

"You know something. Particularly about Colind," Verona said.

"He instructed me not to say anything."

"Well, now I must know," Verona said.

Braden clamped his mouth shut and put a bit more speed in his step.

"Is this what we've been reduced to?" Verona asked, matching his pace. "Keeping secrets from each other, my old friend? Come on, what is Colind up to that he saw fit to tell the one person whom most wouldn't have thought he would confide in?"

Braden eyed him for a moment before answering. "He hunts Mactar."

"I suspected that such a thing would come to pass in time. What did you say to him when he told you all this?" Verona asked.

"What could I say to him?" Braden asked. "Should I have reminded him of his duty to the Safanarion Order? No, there are some that the world could do without, and if a colossus out of legend wants to make it his mission to take out one of our strongest enemies, then more power to him. Mactar deserves to die."

Verona was silent for a moment, knowing that Braden still mourned the loss of his brother, Eric. They all did. There were times when he expected to see Braden's twin brother at his side, and his absence was a constant reminder that any of them could die along the way.

"I can't argue with that, my friend, but one thing that I

have learned, especially in Khamearra, is that we can accomplish so much more if we work together than if we go off on our own."

"Sometimes," Braden said.

They were silent the rest of the way, coming to their designated place in the training area, marked with a white eagle. The soldiers were cloistered together listening to Sarah. Her long blonde hair was braided, and more than one soldier's eyes shone with that cautious admiration that often marked good men when they saw someone as beautiful as the High King's daughter. He had often told Aaron that he was a lucky man, and he meant it. Sarah noticed them approaching and waved them over. Braden told him he would be there in a moment. Young Sarik detached himself from the soldiers and joined them at the front. He supposed he shouldn't think of Sarik as young anymore, it was just that he had taken Sarik into his care three years ago when the lad was fifteen. Sarik was the third son of a minor house in the Waylands, and his father had been overjoyed that the nephew of their prince would take his youngest son into his service. Verona never viewed it as taking anyone into his service, but rather as adopting Sarik as the younger brother he'd never had.

"Sarik is going to demonstrate the slow fighting forms, and I want you to pay particular attention to both his form and his breath control," Sarah said.

The twenty men spread out to get a better look. They ranged in age with the youngest looking about sixteen years of age to some being twice that, but they all lined up and paid attention.

Sarik began moving his body slowly. They both had practiced what Aaron had taught them nearly every day since those days aboard the deck of the Raven. Sarik moved with effortless ease, his whole body becoming one.

"Can anyone tell me the importance of breathing?" Sarah asked.

"Because we like living, my Lady," an older soldier snickered and was quickly joined in by others.

A smile cracked Sarah's face as she joined in. "As do we all. You happened to be quite right..."

"Kay, my Lady," answered the soldier.

"Watch as Sarik moves, his body and breath become one. One cannot happen without the other. When breath is controlled you have greater endurance, which is essential to stay alive," Sarah said, making eye contact with each of them as she spoke. "Suits of armor aren't so common anymore, but those warriors who donned them had to build their endurance to wear them. A smarter, less armored warrior could easily tire out his more armored opponent if he didn't know how to control his breathing. You've all heard of the De'anjard?" Sarah asked.

The soldiers nodded, and some glanced at Braden, who

joined them.

"The De'anjard were known throughout the realm as being among the strongest of any fighting force on Safanar. Braden can you tell us why?"

"You can't fight well if you don't breathe well," Braden bellowed.

"Forgive me, my Lady, but we were told you were going to test us to see if we could tap into the energy as you do. When are we going to get to that?" Kay asked, and the question was mirrored upon every one of the soldier's faces.

"In order to open oneself to the energy around them, they must be calm and in control. Mastery of self comes through a quiet and focused mind. Practicing the slow fighting forms will help to train you to focus your mind. Only then you may open yourself up to higher forms of practice," Sarah said.

The men spread out with each trying to mimic Sarik's movement. The rest walked among them and corrected their form as they went. More than once Verona saw Braden watching Sarah as if he were weighing something.

"What's wrong, my friend?" Verona quietly asked.

"The rune-carved staff has been stolen," Braden said.

"And you believe Sarah took it?"

"I'm not sure. There weren't many who knew about the staff or where it was."

"Just all those people at the arena in Khamearra knew

about the staff," Verona chuckled.

"The guard on duty was knocked out, and he can't remember anything."

Verona glanced at Sarah who was showing one of the younger soldiers the proper form. The soldier almost looked stunned to be speaking with the princess. "Well, if Sarah did take the staff, I'm sure it was for safekeeping." *Or to keep a certain someone from taking it,* Verona thought to himself.

"And the guard?" Braden asked.

"Now that is something we should be concerned with. If whoever took the staff meant us harm then they simply would have killed the guard. Could you imagine an Elitesman leaving a witness alive?"

"I see your point, Verona. I thought things would have been better when Aaron returned, but instead it's got us all being suspicious of one another."

"Or in this case, Sarah. I agree, my friend, things have gotten more complicated. What I'm about to ask you may seem offhand, but have you noticed anything different with Aaron since his return?" asked Verona.

Braden frowned. "Nothing comes to mind. Aaron has always gone his own way."

"Fair enough," Verona said.

They spent the next hour going through the various fighting forms and then paired the men in groups for some sparring. Verona noticed a group of well-armed

Zsensibarian guards making their way through the training yard. Among them a tall, broad-shouldered man with a spiraled crown that sat atop his head. Jopher was with them. Verona liked Jopher, but had never met Zsensibar's ruler. As far as Verona knew, it was a rare event that required Zsensibar's king to venture outside his borders.

At some point Aaron arrived. He had two of the De'anjard with him and a small group of noblemen watching. Aaron waved over to him as he walked over.

"Have you come to join us, my friend?" Verona asked.

"I thought I might," Aaron said, smiling and nodding to the others in greeting. His eyes lingered on Sarah for a moment, who gave him a perfunctory nod.

"I'd like three volunteers and the rest of you to form a circle around us," Aaron said.

Two veteran soldiers stepped up, and one of the younger soldiers, Wesley, Verona believed was his name, stumbled forward. The wiry lad fell in line with the other two men.

"When the Elitesmen attack it will rarely be just you against them. There will be many coming at you all at once and without a shred of mercy. Therefore, the Elitesmen shall be granted none," Aaron said as he slowly stepped toward his three volunteers. "You," Aaron said to Wesley. "How do you think you'd do against these other two?"

Wesley glanced at the other two men, weighing his options. "I'm not sure, your Grace."

Aaron nodded. "Fair enough." He brought out a white piece of cloth about a yard in length. "Here tie this to your belt behind you."

Wesley's brows drew up. He slowly reached out for the cloth and did as Aaron had asked. Verona glanced across the circle at Sarah, whose grim-lined gaze was fixed upon the men in the center.

"The rules are to stay in the circle," Aaron said to the three men. "The job for you two is to bring me that bit of cloth tied to young Wesley's backside."

The two soldiers nodded and turned their attention to Wesley, who gulped and faced his opponents.

"Go!" Aaron said.

The two men charged, and Wesley scrambled out of the way quick as a cat. The men kept doing their utmost to grab the white cloth that trailed in Wesley's wake. After a few minutes, Aaron called for a halt.

"Are you okay?" Aaron asked Wesley, who nodded. "Two on one isn't bad, but I would have thought they would have gotten the cloth by now. I want two more volunteers. Who thinks they can bring me the cloth from young Wesley's backside?"

Two more soldiers stepped forward, and the current men in the center made as if to line up, but Aaron stopped them. "You're not dismissed yet. I want that cloth."

Verona watched as Sarah almost took a step forward, but

stopped herself. He himself wondered what Aaron hoped to prove with this exercise.

"Ready? Go!"

Wesley tried to dodge between the four men who surrounded him.

"I want that cloth. That cloth represents life and death. It will mean your death if you don't get it. Hold nothing back," Aaron called.

The men stepped up their effort, and Wesley darted through the circle. The young soldier's shirt was torn as the men grabbed for the cloth.

"Don't let them get it, Wesley; if they do it means you're dead," Aaron said.

The chase went on for a few seconds more until the men were clustered around Aaron, who still stood near the center. In a blurring movement, Wesley cried out as his feet were swept out from under him and the strip of white cloth was held loosely in Aaron's hand. Wesley scooted back away from Aaron's menacing gaze.

"Enough!" Sarah said stepping into the circle. "Five to one is too much to ask anyone, unless you'd like to dance with me, my Lord."

Aaron's head came up as he regarded Sarah for a moment, his face smooth and emotionless. "You of all people should know that there is no such thing as fair when facing an Elitesman."

Sarah helped Wesley to his feet and quietly asked after him. He still looked shaky as he went to the side and sat upon the ground.

Sarah turned her venomous gaze upon Aaron. "I know that the only thing you proved by this display is that of your own prowess, but it lacks any of its former integrity," Sarah said.

The two glared at each other for a moment, and the rest of them looked on in silence. Verona glanced around and noticed Jopher frowning, along with the impassive expression of the King of Zsensibar, who looked on silently. He had been so preoccupied with what was happening in the circle that he hadn't realized that the Zsensibarian envoy had made it to their part of the training yard.

Aaron leveled his gaze at her. "If they don't learn it here, then they are just fodder for the Elitesmen."

"The man I knew would never have taught such a lesson," Sarah said.

"Then maybe you need to accept that the man you knew is gone."

Sarah and Aaron faced off. Though they simply stood facing each other, Verona sensed that violence could break out at any moment. Part of him couldn't move, while the rest of himself urged him to say something.

Verona stepped into the circle. "Why don't we take a break? Clearly we have a difference in teaching methods here."

Verona's voice seemed to dispel the silent standoff, and each backed away.

"My Lady," Aaron called.

Sarah faced him.

"Do you know the whereabouts of my staff?" Aaron asked.

"It's precisely where you left it," Sarah answered.

"That's the thing. It's not there anymore," Aaron said.

"Then perhaps you should keep a better eye on your things," Sarah said.

There were muffled gasps from the crowd of noblemen. The two De'anjard guards started to move, but Braden held up his hand for them to stop.

"My Lord," Braden said. "I'm investigating the whereabouts of the staff. Sarah has been here all morning and couldn't have taken it."

Aaron nodded to Braden. "Thank you. I just asked if she knew where it was. I trust that you will keep me apprised of your investigation."

Verona drew in the energy from the earth, and immediately his perceptions sharpened. He heard Zsensibar's king lean in to Jopher and say, "This is the man whom you chose to follow? He's no different than the High King." Jopher began to respond, but Verona focused his attention elsewhere.

Aaron had walked back to the group of people he had with him. Verona extended his senses, trying to read into those of his friend, but he wasn't very good at this sort of thing and couldn't detect anything. He let go of his connection and noticed Sarah watching him. His mind raced. One moment Aaron was the friend he knew, and in the next he was a complete stranger. He couldn't make any sense of it.

They had decided to take a break for a few minutes, and they broke off into groups. Braden went to Sarah, and the two began quietly speaking. Off to the side, Verona noticed that Wesley stood alone. He had stopped gasping for breath and rose to his feet. Some of the other men came to check on him and then left him, heading to the watering table.

"He's different," Jopher said, coming to Verona's side.

Verona almost asked to whom Jopher was referring, but he knew better. "He was a prisoner for months. Enough time to change any of us, including Aaron."

"I know...I'm just not used to seeing him like this," Jopher said.

"But what is it exactly?"

"I'm not sure what you mean."

"Sometimes Aaron is like he has always been. Patient, especially when teaching. Hard, when the situation calls for it. When Sarah was prisoner to the Drake, he was focused, perhaps a bit rash, but definitely focused. And now...I'm not quite sure what to think," Verona admitted.

Jopher didn't say anything right away. "My father is meeting with Prince Cyrus, and I told them I would catch up."

"Go on then, Jopher, and thank you."

"For what?" Jopher asked.

"For having the courage to say out loud what most of us are only thinking about," Verona said.

A smile lit up Jopher's face at the praise. He nodded and walked away.

Verona found that his mouth was dry, and he went to get some of what passed for refreshment upon the training grounds. He had to settle for water. Heading back, he saw Wesley practicing the slow forms. His wiry body still getting used to the movement he had only just learned this morning. A hunched man watched from behind. One shoulder was lower than the other, and his gnarled hands attempted to mimic Wesley's movements. His misshapen feet lurched over the ground, and his mouth moved as if he were muttering to himself. Verona couldn't hear him, but he knew he was saying something. The man's eyes followed Wesley's movements, but when the young soldier faltered, trying to remember the movement, he continued on, and Verona noted that the crippled man knew the slow forms somehow.

Verona headed over, and a short, plainly dressed man with hair cropped close to his scalp came behind the crippled man and spoke to him. The crippled man waved off the smaller man and moved closer to Wesley. Some of the soldiers had returned and mocked the cripple.

"Mock if you will, gentlemen, but I'll wager he knows the slow forms better than any of you," Verona said.

The men immediately quieted down.

"Apologies, my Lord, he doesn't mean any harm; it's just he has a tendency to wander sometimes," the short man said.

"Not a problem, master?"

The short man grinned. "I'm called Wes, my Lord, and this is Len."

Upon hearing his name, Len's eyes darted around, and he kept repeating his own name.

"Wesley, start again. Let's see if he follows along. The rest of you follow along as well," Verona ordered.

The men immediately lined up. One thing Verona could say about the FNA is that discipline and following orders were a part of their core. Wesley stayed on point. He slowly opened his stance, bringing his arms up. As the soldiers followed in unison, Len stopped muttering to himself, and his eyes seemed to focus on the movement. The men moved through the procession of movement, and Verona was amazed that the crippled man could follow along. He wasn't physically capable of all the movements, but Verona's trained eye could tell that the fundamentals were ingrained there.

Verona joined in. His mind transplanted him to the decks of the Raven, where Aaron had given these lessons to them.

Eventually the whole crew had joined in and forged a bond between the men that lasted to this day. No matter what their station, be it soldier, captain, or prince, all were equal in the performing the slow forms.

Perfection of movement is paramount. From movement comes life.

Aaron's words echoed in his ears. Verona felt his connection to the energy around them deepen, and he spread it out away from him. He sensed Sarah's vibrant presence among them. He took in greater breath, and his movement deepened, both powerful and in control. Verona's mind cleared, and he spread his senses to the other men, seeking the spark within them. A blazing presence flashed to the side, snapping away his concentration.

Len was flailing about, waving his arms madly and lurching from side to side like a crab. Wes tried to calm him down, but Len pushed him away. Len grabbed a spear from the nearby rack of weapons and held it awkwardly.

Sarah approached slowly with her palms low and facing outward. Len's eyes widened and the spear dropped from his grasp. His eyes darted all around, and he scurried away, howling as he went.

Verona caught Sarik's eye and nodded toward the fleeing cripple with Wes trailing in his wake. "Just make sure they get out the training area without hurting themselves."

Sarik nodded and set off after them.

Sarah came over to Verona. "I wonder what set him off. Did you see him before? He was able to follow along. If I didn't know better I would say he knew the slow forms."

"In this we are agreed, my Lady," Verona said, and Sarah gave him a sideways glance. "Apologies, my Lady, my uncle believes it to be prudent that I be formal with all manner of nobility. Princesses in particular."

A small smile graced Sarah's face, and she called him a fool. She looked past him, her gaze narrowing. Verona saw Aaron across the training yard, heading away from them. At first Verona believed that it was Sarah that had set Len off, but now he wondered if it was Aaron instead.

"Sarah, you're much better at this than I am. I think a couple of these men might be able to tap into the energy, but I can't be sure."

"With months of training you may be right, for some of them," Sarah said.

"We need Aaron to use his swords. The bladesong helped open the way for Sarik and me," Verona said.

"But not all of you. It took Braden a while, and he will attest that being open to the energy comes at a price. It's not meant for the weak minded. Speaking of which, you've never said whether you've had any problems," Sarah asked.

"I guess I don't have an old soul, because the only voices or urges inside of my head are my own," Verona said.

"That's one way of putting it," Sarah said dryly.

It took Verona a moment to realize that she was joking with him. "And here I almost thought there wasn't an ounce of happiness left in the world. Thank you, my Lady, for proving me wrong."

They dismissed the men, and Verona made some mental notes of whom to include on his own team of men he was building. He set off to find Aaron, hoping that the odd behavior was some sort of misunderstanding and not some nefarious purpose.

CHAPTER 13
CATCH OUR BREATHS

General Morag Halcylon surveyed their progress. The Zekara were well on their way to setting up their base of operations. The AI had done its job well selecting this location, which was far enough away that they would know if any of the Safanarions were to come within their vicinity. The traitors living among the humans had no doubt detected the ship's presence, but the combat suite had done its job effectively, and he was quite certain they didn't know exactly where they were. The same also applied to the Zekara. They didn't know where the traitor's nest was that played home to Hythariam who saw fit to break with their own race. They had been gathering intelligence since they arrived, and getting their base of operations up and running was top on his list of priorities, along with running reconnaissance on the inhabitants of this world. He didn't get to his position by being impatient. He would study his enemy, learn the way they did things, and then he would strike. He gave a passing thought to the human they had left behind and knew that he must be dead by now. As a leader of his people, Halcylon couldn't fault the actions of the human's ancestor, but the Hythariam were superior to humans in every way. Something the humans of this world would come to know.

Ronan, his chief science adviser, approached him.

"Is the package away?" Halcylon asked.

"Confirmed; the package has been delivered and has been reporting in, but it won't last long. The process was rushed," Ronan said.

"To be expected; how long do we have?"

"A few weeks before it breaks down completely," said Ronan.

"That's fine. Our timetable won't change. Preliminary reports show various groups are already engaging in combat. That is good for us because it will keep them all occupied, giving us time to prepare."

"What about the other Hythariam here? We detect their comms signals all over the continent," Ronan said.

"The traitors, you mean," Halcylon corrected. He had been drilling into them not to think of the Hythariam here as members of their race, but as traitors.

"Yes, of course," Ronan said.

"They are working on breaking the security in place so we can see the messages. So far they've been unsuccessful," Halcylon said.

"These things take time," Ronan said.

"Indeed, they are the real threat. The primitives here have a rudimentary knowledge of how to make war."

"They're not so primitive," Ronan said.

"They have a few tricks. We're still gathering intelligence, but tricks alone won't save them from the Zekara," Halcylon said.

"The SPT flyers are ready," Ronan said.

"Very good. I want to keep a close eye on our package, and we're still adapting the drones to this world. Plus, I'm reluctant to use them too much. Right now I expect the traitors are scrambling, trying to find out where we are," Halcylon said.

"We're still looking for them as well, but they've had eighty cycles to entrench themselves. The task of finding them may prove more difficult than previously expected," Ronan said.

Halcylon eyed his adviser. "Take a moment and look around, Ronan. We're here and are no longer on a dying planet. Time is again on our side. No longer are we up against the clock. We did it. We're here. Breathe the fresh air. Drink the clean water. This is a living planet and now our home."

Ronan took a moment to look around the camp. The Zekara moved with purpose, but all of them kept looking up at the alien sky above them. Their new home. "You did it. It was you who got us here. Even when those others abandoned our people to take to the stars. You stayed to lead us, and because of that, all of the Zekara will lay down their lives to protect you."

Halcylon nodded to Ronan, and they returned to the task of setting up their new home for their race, and once that was done, they would visit vengeance upon those who believed they were their betters and had doomed them all to a dying world. Before long, these humans would learn to fear the Zekara, and after enough of them died, they would fall on their knees to serve them. Halcylon smiled at the plans he had set in motion so long ago that were only now coming to bear the fruit of his efforts.

CHAPTER 14
PERFECT ARMY

Mactar surveyed the forty Ryakuls that he and Darven had brought under their control. Once they controlled the first two Ryakuls, finding more proved easier than they had originally thought. Left on their own, the beasts would hunt for Dragons and in some cases would turn on each other. If they had set off to track Dragons all those weeks ago, finding Ryakuls would have been much easier. Dragons were becoming less common throughout the lands and kept mostly upon the fringes of the realms of men.

"They are the perfect army," Darven said.

"How so?" Mactar asked.

"We can give them any order, and they will carry out those orders or die trying. Once on task, the Ryakuls will never waver from it," Darven replied.

"Unless we deactivate the controller. Then the connection is broken."

"That's right, but we don't have to keep the instructions we give them in the forefront of our minds," Darven said.

"Agreed; they can follow instructions, but I'd be reluctant to just send them off to attack a city on their own. Too many variables. The Ryakuls would throw themselves at an obstacle, but they don't weigh threats very well, which is a shortcoming of them being under control."

Darven shrugged. "Still, I'll take them over an army of conscripts any day."

"Good. I think it's time we gave the High King a demonstration. Now that the Elitesmen have proven that they can move a sizable fighting force with the focusing crystal, the Khamearrian army is going to push deeper into the Waylands, "Mactar said.

"You knew that was going to work?" Darven asked.

"Who do you think gave the idea to Elite Grand Master Gerric?" Mactar smirked.

Darven nodded.

"I am going to have you take half the Ryakuls and meet the armies as they attack," Mactar said.

"I hope the commanders of those armies know to expect me then. I'd hate to have to worry about being shot at by a stray arrow or stabbed by an Elitesman's blade."

"Word has been sent, but the Elitesmen may still take a shot at you just for old times' sake."

Darven shrugged his shoulders impassively. Elitesmen

attacks didn't faze him. "What will you be doing while I'm off winning the High King's war for him?"

"I'll continue gathering the Ryakuls. We're going to need them."

"It can't be that long before Amorak sets his sights on Rexel and the heart of their armies there," Darven said.

"That's exactly right, and that is precisely where their defenses will be strongest. We will need more than fifty Ryakuls to take Rexel and break the back of this Free Nations Army," Mactar said.

He marked the locations of the planned attacks on the map that Darven carried. There was no way they could use the travel crystals and bring the Ryakuls with them. It simply wouldn't work even with only one Ryakul, and they hadn't figured out why. The Ryakuls were fast and could make the journey quickly. Darven leaped on top of a Ryakul and signaled to the twenty he would take with him. With a final wave, he took to the skies.

Mactar had taken a short trip back to Khamearra to meet with his network of informants there. He had known his idea with the focusing crystal would work, but wasn't sure Gerric could pull it off. Why do these things himself, when he could have others do it for him? The same applied here, which was why he was sending Darven to attack with the army. His sights were set on much bigger bounty than those of the smaller kingdoms that bordered the Waylands. He would be there to burn Rexel to the ground with a horde of Ryakuls at his back.

The battles, hardly more than skirmishes that the High King's army had fought, served as practice for the real war about to begin. Unlike other wars, there would not be endless marching and razing of town after town. Supply lines would become almost irrelevant, that is, of course, if the focusing crystals used to move the armies around weren't destroyed. So far, this Free Nations Army hadn't answered the threat of the High King, but they had shown up at some of the smaller kingdoms. The results were that castles were better prepared for the attacks, but with the Elitesmen serving as part of the army, the defenses they put together were easily overcome.

Word was spreading of Ryakul attacks on the remote towns, and they had started seeing these towns mount rooftop defenses, but Mactar had no interest in attacking the towns. They were merely a learning tool to be able to take more strategic targets. Sitting on top of a Ryakul while it flew was something Darven put forward as a better way to travel—astride the Ryakuls, rather than using the crystals—and he had to admit that Darven was right. Flying a Ryakul allowed them to send out a signal, summoning more to them. Mactar leaped atop the scaly neck of a Ryakul, and its leathery wings fluttered. With a final command, the remaining Ryakuls took to the sky at the same time and wheeled around heading east. Soon he would meet up with the High King.

CHAPTER 15
FIRE FOR FIRE

A dark castle loomed on the horizon, and Colind frowned. Night had descended upon them in the northern reaches of Khamearra.

"That has to be it," Garret said. His salt-and-pepper hair hung past his ears, and although he was into his fifties, he was easily as fit as much younger men.

"It's precisely where Sarah said it would be," Colind said.

He had expected to wander for a while before picking up Mactar's trail, but Garret had the good sense to advise him to ask Sarah, and that he did. She didn't know where Mactar was, of course, but she had been to his castle. The place was little more than a keep with but a single tower.

"It looks...kind of small," Garret said.

"Mactar doesn't hold high regard for pampering," Colind replied.

"Do you really think he's there?"

Colind frowned as he studied the castle. He reached out with his senses, and the castle itself was deserted. "I wish he was there, but the place is empty. I still want to take a look around."

When they had left Shandara weeks before, they had set out to find former members of the Safanarion Order. The task had gone frustratingly slow, because the ones that survived had become adept at hiding themselves. He had been forced to leave messages around that only members of the order would be able to decipher. If any of them got the message, they would know they should make their way to Rexel. He suspected some were already heading to Shandara, and he just needed to be patient.

The town that lived in the shadow of Mactar's castle was quiet, and Colind wondered if they knew whose shadow they lived under. *Probably,* Colind thought. They made it to the castle and through the locks that were in place to keep the local townsfolk out. There were no other safeguards, which Colind found peculiar and said so.

"Perhaps he doesn't expect to come back," Garret said.

Colind shrugged his shoulders and pushed on to the castle. The castle held the normal furnishings, and it wasn't until they came to Mactar's workshop that things radically changed. They opened the double doors, and Colind sent a tendril of energy out to the orbs that slowly grew brighter. The room was packed, which at first appeared haphazard.

"Is this a storage room?" Garret asked.

Colind glanced around trying to make sense of it all. There were broken swords and shields, along with half-burnt items from twisted crowns to silver bowls. Colind swallowed hard, recognizing some of the items.

"This seems familiar; I think I remember this," Garret said, gesturing to a leather-embroidered chair with its gold paint long since chipped away.

"It's from Shandara. It's one of the council seats from Dragon Hall, where the Safanarion Order used to convene," Colind said, glaring at the items in the room, realizing what this room was. "This is a trophy room. These are pieces he's collected from all his victories."

Garret slowly turned around, taking in the grand room, when he noticed a bare spot on the wall. "I wonder what he had there."

Colind looked over and scanned the wall seeing a dark outline. His lips curved into a smile as he made out what must have hung there for the past twenty-five years. "The standard of Shandara. Particularly the standard for the House Alenzar'seth. I imagine that at some point after learning of Aaron's existence he realized his victory over Shandara wasn't as complete as he had first believed."

Garret scanned the room with a furrowed brow. "Everything in this room is associated with death."

"There is a lot of pride in this room. Let's look through it quickly and see if we can figure out what he is doing and hopefully where he went," Colind said.

Knowing that everything in room had either belonged to someone or was associated with a fallen kingdom weighed heavily on them. They spoke in hushed tones as if they were in a graveyard, and Colind supposed they were. They came to an open area, and along the wall was a metal workbench with tools.

Colind lifted up one of the discarded pieces. "This is Hythariam made."

They found other things that looked out of place, like an old comms device that no longer worked.

"How could he have known about Hythariam technology?" Garret asked.

"Because Mactar is Shandarian. He served the Alenzar'seth when the Hythariam first came to Safanar."

"Shandarian? But he would be over a hundred years old," Garret said in disbelief.

"He hasn't aged in almost sixty years. I knew him. He was my mentor for a time," Colind said.

"I never knew," Garret said.

"Not many do, and that's because the people that did know are all dead and gone. Daverim Alenzar'seth helped establish the Safanarion Order, and Mactar was one of the founding members. He was always experimenting. Pushing things beyond their limits. Reymius had discovered some of the horrible things he had been doing. Many of the practices of the Elitesmen Order had their origins with Mactar's work in Shandara."

"What happened to him?" Garret asked.

"Reymius reported what he found to his father, and Daverim had him banished. Never to return to Shandara," Colind said.

"How is it that he hasn't aged?"

"What I suspect happened is he had help. When the Hythariam first came to Safanar, there were different factions, with some loyal to Halcylon despite his plans for the rest of us. He was injected with the Nanites, but without the constraints that are applied to normal Hythariam, which gives them a lifespan greater than two hundred years."

"How long would he live then?" Garret asked.

"Iranus believes a thousand years or more," Colind answered.

Garrett blew out a heavy breath.

"Exactly, but he won't get the chance. Not if I have anything to say about it," Colind said.

"I can't tell from this stuff what he was doing or where he is going," Garret admitted.

Colind picked up a goblet-sized black piece of metal. "This is from the Drake." He turned it over in his hands and placed it on his wrist. "It's some type of control panel like what the Hythariam wear. The question now is what was the Drake controlling?"

Garret frowned in thought, and then his face lit up. "The Ryakuls. The Drake commanded the Ryakuls, and I would wager that is a power worthy of Mactar's attention."

Colind's eyes widened. "Goddess, if he can control the Ryakuls then..."

"We need to warn the others," Garret said, bringing up his comms device.

Colind continued to scan the room while Garret spoke into the comms device. They never had an accurate count of the Ryakuls, but there were enough of them to cover a mountain. Even with the aid of the Hythariam they would be hard pressed to fight the High King's army if there was a host of Ryakuls aiding them.

"Colind, they want us to return."

"No," Colind answered.

"It's Aaron; he is back."

"He'll understand if we don't come back right away."

Garret stepped up to him. "Mactar won't get away, but they need us back there. We might be able to find him quicker with the help of the Hythariam. All we need to do is track the Ryakuls now."

Colind drew his head up, considering, and nodded. "First we burn this place to the ground," Colind said grimly.

They headed to the main doors, and Colind lingered in the entrance. He reached out with the energy, grasping all the lighted orbs at once, and shattered them. Flames spread eagerly, consuming the old relics in the room, and Colind looked on with grim satisfaction, hoping that the original owners of these relics could rest easier. Mactar had been the foremost pillager laying waste to Shandara, and a warmth spread through his body, knowing that he had been able to take something from Mactar at last.

The flames quickly spread, and soon the entire castle was engulfed. Garret urged them to leave, but Colind wasn't finished yet. He drew in the energy from the earth, pushing deep underground, locating the main supports that kept the castle standing. Tiny cracks spidered their way up, and the ground shook beneath their feet. The flaming castle wavered back and forth before falling in on itself. The hiss of the fire kissed the night air, and the ruins of Mactar's castle vanished from the skyline with nothing but a few remnant walls remaining. The townsfolk gathered outside their homes and watched the flames, but none moved to investigate, and there were more than a few who were relieved that the dark menace that had loomed over their quiet town was gone.

Colind engaged the travel crystal, and he and Garret disappeared. They emerged upon the outskirts of the FNA camp. The sun had risen in this part of Safanar, casting its warmth, and the morning dew slowly retreated.

"Why didn't you take us directly to the castle?" Garret

asked.

"Sometimes you can learn a great deal by taking the long way," Colind replied and immediately started walking.

Colind silently looked around, taking in his surroundings. They had been gone a few weeks, but they had kept in contact as best they could. Mostly it was Garret, because Colind wasn't particularly fond of the comms devices. They had their uses and were convenient, but he didn't want to use them. Soldiers who recognized him either bowed their head or saluted. The FNA camp had become a city outside the walls of Rexel, with merchants selling their wares in designated areas. No one in the FNA was foolish enough to allow just anyone to go into the camp proper.

A large group was heading toward the center of the camp, and Colind frowned seeing Aaron leading the group. He was surrounded by the newest members of the De'anjard along with members of the nobility from various kingdoms. Something in way Aaron carried himself bothered Colind. It shouldn't bother him. He had always known that Aaron would lead these people, and with leadership came the clamoring fools who wanted to carry favor. He just didn't expect it so soon and Aaron to appear so comfortable with it.

Aaron spotted them and walked over.

"Welcome back," Aaron said.

"I should say the same to you," Colind answered, studying him. His skin held remnant scars, and his eyes had a harder cast to them than before.

Aaron recounted how he was imprisoned and came to return to Safanar, and Colind quietly listened.

"Where is Sarah?" Garret asked. "I would hardly expect that she would leave your side since you've been back."

A blank look of uncertainty flashed across Aaron's face, and then his eyes narrowed. "I'm afraid that not everyone was overjoyed with my return."

Now that is a colossal understatement, Colind thought. He had helped nurse Sarah back to health while she recovered from the effects of the Nanites. During that time, the thought of Aaron was hardly a breath away from her thoughts.

He glanced at the others that Aaron had surrounded himself with and noted the absence of his closest friends with the exception of Braden's towering form. Imprisonment had a way of changing those subject to its malicious tendencies. Something Colind was intimately aware of, and the first thing he longed for when he was finally free was to see the faces of his closest friends. The need to be around things familiar and also knowing that most of them were dead had seized his heart. Since his failure to recognize the evil in his son, Tarimus, he had promised himself that if he began making excuses for someone or something that was out of balance in his life, that he would take a step back and refuse the excuses their due. Glancing at Aaron, he knew that things were out of balance here, and he was determined to find out what it was. There wouldn't be another repeat of Shandara, not on his watch.

He told Aaron to carry on and that he would walk with them for a while. It was hard to believe that this was the same person he had first encountered on Earth all those months ago. There had been an unwavering kindness in his eyes, and now they seemed to be constantly measuring everyone and everything. They went to the command tent, which was already filled with people for the morning briefing. Gavril stood in the center and was speaking quietly with Verona and Vaughn.

Gavril called the meeting to order, and after a few moments things settled down to a quiet murmur. Behind Gavril, holographic screens came to life. All of them showed different kingdoms as if someone were watching from above.

"Behind me are feeds from our satellites we have orbiting the planet. Most of them are fixed upon the continent," Gavril said, and after a moment the view on the screens changed. "We're monitoring these feeds for the next attack from the Khamearrians. We have command centers like this set up in Hathenwood, a temporary one in Shandara, in addition to one here in Rexel."

"Why a temporary one in Shandara?" Aaron asked.

"There is a better one in Shandara, but it was buried when the city fell. Our engineers are quite close to getting access to it. Once that happens, we'll have greater access to the bulk of our technology that was lost at Shandara," Gavril said.

There were gasps with some pointing to one of the screens. There was a flash of light, and emerging from the morning mist was the High King's army.

"Where is this? Is this happening right now?" Verona asked.

"This is in Lorric, and yes, the feed is in real time," Gavril answered.

The kingdom of Lorric was one of the bordering kingdoms between Khamearra and the Waylands.

"We need to help them," Verona said, his eyes fixed upon the screen, and then he turned to Aaron. "Some of the Resistance fled Khamearra and are taking refuge there."

Many in the room knew that the Resistance was made up of the former De'anjard.

"We will go," Braden said. "As Warden of the De'anjard it is my duty to stand with my brothers and sisters of the shield."

"I'll go as well," Colind said.

"You can go with the ready team we have on standby. I've will inform their king that help is on the way," Gavril said.

"We need to find their focusing crystal to keep them from escaping," Verona said and then he frowned. "I think we should divide our numbers into two groups."

"What do you have in mind?" Gavril asked.

"We need to help the people of Lorric with their defenses,

but that doesn't mean we all need to be behind the wall," Verona said, stepping up to the screen and pointing to the outer area of the city beyond the wall. "We should take a smaller force here that can move quickly and take out the focusing crystal."

"First we need to find it, but I agree. We'll use the team you've been putting together as well as some of my own people," Gavril said.

"Having the airships would help, but they can't get there in time," Verona said.

"And they won't fit through the portals. Remember the Keystone Accelerators only have two charges, and one of the charges will be used to get us there. We leave within the hour," Gavril said.

"Won't they need you here coordinating the troop movements?" Colind asked.

"Not today," Gavril answered. "Iranus will take this one."

"I'll go with you," Aaron said to Verona.

"Never doubted it for a second," Verona said.

A short while later, beyond the walls of Rexel, there was an open plain where the troops of the Free Nations Army gathered. Colind advised breaking them up into three groups instead of two. One group to assist in the defense. Another group placed behind the High King's army to strike from behind, and Verona's special squad in the outskirts of the city. They were going to use six of the Keystone

Accelerators, leaving four in reserve here in Rexel.

Colind stood near Verona at the head of his group of fifty men. Aaron and Braden joined them. A few moments later, Sarah came. Other than the barest of glances between her and Aaron, they didn't speak. Garret stood by his side, and next to him was Gavril.

A younger Hythariam approached Gavril.

"Sir, Iranus wants me to return to Hathenwood," Tanneth said.

"Did he give a reason?"

Tanneth shook his head. "He didn't say, and the message came through comms."

Gavril pursed his lips in thought and then nodded.

Tanneth saluted Gavril and took off at a run.

The Keystone Accelerator that would open a portal big enough for them to go through was as long as a man's arm and twice as wide. Legs extended from the base. Gavril tapped a few buttons upon his comms device, and the accelerator lit up. In moments, an opaque circle of light appeared before them that was about ten feet tall and twenty feet wide. Colind squinted his eyes, trying to peer through it, but it was just a swirling mass with a small vibration brushing against its skin.

Farther away from them other portals opened, and Gavril gave the command for them to go through. The soldiers of the FNA immediately rushed through, eager to face the

Khamearrian army. They were well armed with swords, bows, and spears. A select few carried the plasma pistols of the Hythariam on them, but there weren't enough to arm every FNA soldier with one.

As the last of the soldiers went through, the portals started winking out one by one. With most of the troops having gone through, no one saw the hunched man lumbering onto the field before the remaining open portal. He zigzagged like a crab, as if he couldn't make his legs work right. As the portal diminished in size, he stumbled through just as it closed.

CHAPTER 16
THE RETURN

Sarah came through the portal and immediately moved away, scanning for signs of life on the deserted streets. Sounds of fighting could be heard in the distance. Lorric wasn't the biggest city when compared with Shandara, but it was still sizable, covering six square miles. The buildings lining the streets didn't have more than two or three levels, and the streets themselves were wide open. She and Verona took half the men and gathered on one side of the street, while Aaron and Braden took the other half. Orders were given to scout ahead. She looked over at Aaron, and he nodded slowly and smiled. A faint stirring squeezed her chest. More than anything she wanted to believe that by some cruel twist of fate Aaron was still in there somewhere and the stranger before her would just fade away. She longed to fall headlong into the dream that it was him. To feel his powerful arms around her and the press of his lips

246 | AMIDST THE RISING SHADOWS

on hers. She found herself daring to believe, to go against what her heart was telling her, and give in.

The press of the travel crystal nudged against her leg. She had debated on bringing the rune-carved staff, because she knew that it was somehow connected to Aaron. She had taken it for safekeeping and had kept Aaron's medallion, which she still wore nestled on her chest.

"I'm with you, my Lady," Verona said.

Sarah glanced at him and nodded. Gavril had taken the Hythariam and scouted ahead. They caught up and found him frowning at his comms device.

"Is there a problem?" Sarah asked.

"We're getting some strange readings outside the city. I'm not sure what to make of it, but it's being reported by all three groups," Gavril said.

"Have they located the focusing crystals?"

"There is a cluster of troops hanging back from the main force attacking the city. We think it's there, but we'll have to wait for them to commit to their attack before we make our move," Gavril said.

Battle drums of the Khamearrian army thundered through the air. Sarah drew in the energy and leaped to the rooftop to get a better look. The others climbed up while the bulk of their force stayed upon the ground below. William of Lorric ruled this city and divided his troops with half upon the walls, while sending out the other half to harry the

Khamearrian army as it came through the sea of buildings beyond the wall. Sudden flashes of light from Elitesmen attack orbs took out the archers on the rooftops. A group of thirty FNA soldiers zoomed away from the walls upon their gliders. Golden bolts of energy returned fire, causing the line of soldiers to pause. Dark streaks of Elitesmen giving chase could be seen from the rooftops, but still the Khamearrian army pushed forward. Flashes of violet appeared on the walls as the Elitesmen used their travel crystals to wreak havoc upon the defenders.

Verona touched her arm and gestured toward the men being held in reserve. That's where the focusing crystal was believed to be held. Colind joined them on the roof and watched the reserve forces of men intently, his eyes scanning. Sarah could sense the energy gathered in him in waves.

"I have it," Colind said. "There is a line of wagons each marked with a designation. The focusing crystal is in one of those."

"How do you know?" Verona asked.

"I could sense the remnants of a large burst of energy. It's the only one in the line, and it would take a lot of energy to move an army of this size," Colind said.

Shouts came from the streets below. A contingent of Khamearrian soldiers had broken off and stumbled upon them. The FNA soldiers charged. Sarah drew her sword and joined them. She caught a glimpse of Aaron sprinting ahead with his swords drawn. There were no Elitesmen with them, but more than a few stopped fighting when they recognized her, bringing both sides to a halt.

"Your Grace," one soldier said. "We're supposed to bring you back with us if we were to find you."

Aaron stepped forward and held his sword to the man's throat.

"No!" Sarah said to him and addressed the soldier. "If you be true Khamearrian sons you will give up this fight."

"I have my orders, your Grace," the soldier replied.

"We can't let them live," Aaron said not taking his eyes from them.

"We can't let them fight or report back to their commanders, but we don't need to kill them," Sarah said and gently lifted Aaron's sword away from the soldier's throat.

"Bind them," Sarah ordered, and an FNA soldier complied.

After the men were bound and locked in a building, they moved on.

"That was a mistake," Aaron said.

"One of many I'm sure to make, but it was the right decision. Something you used to know," Sarah said.

Aaron was about to reply when a screeching cry echoed through the sky above them and was answered by a chorus of others.

"Ryakuls!" Verona hissed.

A great shadow plunged them into momentary darkness as a Ryakul passed overhead and blocked out the sun.

They charged forward and rounded the last corner that would give them a view of the main battle.

"Goddess be merciful," Verona whispered.

The sky was filled with Ryakuls swooping in and killing the Lorric and FNA defenders in droves. The Lorric soldiers were scattering, with groups retreating at an all-out run back to the city walls. The Ryakuls left the Khamearrian line of soldiers untouched.

The FNA ran forward to engage the enemy troops and give the Lorric soldiers a chance to regroup. Sarah darted ahead, dispatching soldiers as she went. Sounds of snarling Ryakuls and men screaming their death cries were all she could hear. The skies were full of them, and they pounced upon any attempt at a regroup.

Aaron stood with a few FNA soldiers around him and watched the Ryakuls, his head cocked to the side as if he had never seen them before.

"Call the Eldarin!" Verona screamed.

Aaron turned to him and looked as if he hadn't heard.

"Call the Eldarin; without them we won't survive," Verona said.

Sarah plunged her hand into her pocket and engaged the travel crystal.

Aaron's eyes narrowed. "She leaves us. She knows we're doomed. Run. Run for your lives!"

The FNA soldiers around them stood with their mouths agape, looking confused. Moments later, Sarah reappeared with the rune-carved staff in her hands and thrust it out to him.

"Call the Eldarin," she said.

Aaron withdrew his hands as if she held a coiled viper.

"If you don't we'll all die," Sarah cried.

"You're already dead," the man pretending to be Aaron sneered, and sprinted toward the walls, yelling for everyone to flee.

Amid the chaotic battle raging outside the walls of Lorric, a lone figure charged forward. He stumbled, regained his footing, and continued forward. His body was a mass of a poorly put together man, but still he lumbered forward amid the retreating soldiers.

"...IGHT!" the crippled man sputtered, his legs carrying him in a half trot. "Fiiiiight!"

The words spewed forth from his malformed mouth, but caught the attention of those around him.

Sarah watched as the crippled man known as Len lumbered forward through a wave of retreating soldiers. Some paused, uncertain of what they were seeing, while others turned to join him.

"Verona..." Sarah gasped, the medallion growing warm

against her chest and the crystal's glow showing through her armored shirt.

The Ryakuls screeched in unison and turned sharply in the air. Sarah's breath came in gasps as the Ryakuls closed in on them. She turned back to Len who was still more than a hundred yards from where they stood. He was down on all fours rocking back and forth, his head twisting in anguish. A slight shimmer came from under his tattered shirt.

"Verona..." Sarah called again, and he and Gavril came to her side. FNA soldiers beat back the Khamearrians who attacked.

Sarah turned to them, not believing what she was about to say, but her heart surged with the knowledge. "I think...*that* is Aaron."

Verona's eyes widened as he followed her line of sight to the crippled man. "It can't be—"

Sarah blocked them out and drew in the energy, lunging forward, closing in on Len as he kneeled upon the ground. Soldiers from both armies fought all around him. His eyes met hers, and he cried out, scrambling away.

"No!" Sarah shouted and withdrew the medallion from her shirt. The crystal in the center oozed out a soft glow. Len's eyes widened in fear, his face a mask of struggle.

It has to be you, my love. Sarah quickly reached out and placed the medallion over his head. Len cried out in a deep guttural scream. His misshapen limbs flailed about, jerking wildly, and Sarah stepped back. The rune-carved staff flared to life in her hands as a beam of light surged forth from the medallion. The energy from the staff knocked Sarah and the surrounding soldiers back dozens of feet. A beacon of light shot forth, blazing into the sky. Verona and Braden came to her side and helped her regain her feet.

Elitesmen appeared all around them in a flash, and the High King's soldiers pushed forward. She and Verona drew their swords, and Braden swung his Warden's Hammer. They kept their backs to Aaron as they fought to protect him. *They can't have you*, she thought.

The Ryakuls closed in, swooping down and landing around them, lunging with their saber-tusked maws. Thunder cracked amid a cloudless sky, and a flash of green and white washed over the battlefield. Ryakuls turned away scattering.

The ground rumbled beneath their feet as two massive Dragons landed on either side of the beacon of light. Their growls rolled through the air. The Eldarin attacked, scattering the remaining Ryakuls from the sky, and the Elitesmen pushed forward. Sarah engaged the Elitesmen, fighting with everything she had. Verona guarded her back. Braden smashed his golden war hammer against his shield, and the enemy closing in around them was driven back. Their bodies flung like rag dolls through the air.

One of the Eldarin crouched by Aaron and turned its full

attention on him. A sphere of light surrounded Aaron. Sarah focused on guarding Braden, while the power of the Warden's shield blew back the Elitesmen and soldiers alike.

***

A huddled mass coiled within a glowing sphere, oblivious to the battle raging around him. He had a purpose once, an identity, but it was gone. A massive shadow loomed over him, and he shrank back.

Yours is a light meant to shine, Shandarian. The Eldarin will always heed the call of those marked by Ferasdiam.

The deep voice that sounded like two granite slabs rubbing together penetrated the fog around him. In the recesses of his mind, an answering call came as a wave of warmth spread through his limbs.

Shandarian... The words twisted and whispered in his mind. *Shandara...* It was important. Synonymous with the name, images flashed in his mind of pristine white walls and a Dragon cradling a single rose.

Len...Alen... a voice whispered inside him. *Alenzar'seth!* Like a beacon stemming from his soul, the floodgates burst open. He was Aaron Jace, the last surviving member of the House Alenzar'seth. He felt the chains that bound his mind shatter, and he opened his eyes, seeing the battle being fought around him. He couldn't move and felt his body being lifted into the air. An Eldarin Dragon focused on him, and thick tendrils of energy locked around him.

The land needs a champion...

The bones in Aaron's body snapped and reformed so fast that the pain of it was gone before it became an impression in his mind. His misshapen legs and arms returned to normal, and a mass of red particles spewed out his mouth, dissipating in the air. Aaron felt his arms lift from his sides and his body rise farther into the air. The Dragon tattoo upon his chest flared, and he felt his heart begin to beat, his mind growing clearer.

Two golden bolts of energy came from the sky and slammed into him, knocking him to the ground. The Eldarin roared, spreading its massive wings, and engulfed him protectively.

***

"They're firing on him!" Verona shouted.

Gavril's eyes widened as he glanced at the display on his comms device and back up at the sky. "That's not one of ours."

"If it's not ours who the hell could it be?" Verona said.

Plasma bolts continued to rain down upon the Eldarin that held Aaron cradled in its wings.

Gavril's fingers flew across his comms device, and his eyes lit up. "Tanneth, we have a mark sector three from my position."

A golden Hythariam flyer sped into view and returned fire. Sparks flew from two smaller craft as their cloaks lifted and crashed into the ground followed by a small explosion.

"It's the Zekara," Gavril said.

The Ryakuls regrouped and circled around. There were two Eldarin, with one protecting Aaron while the other wheeled around fighting off the Ryakuls in a mass of tooth and claw.

The Eldarin upon the ground drew back, and a man stood. The ground smoked beneath his bare feet. He held the rune-carved staff in his hands, and a white glow surrounded his body.

"Aaron..." whispered Verona. "By the Goddess, Sarah was right."

***

Aaron drew in the energy around him, feeding off the staff, and took to the sky. He leaped to the nearest Ryakul, swinging the rune-carved staff, sending bolts of energy into each strike, and blowing out parts of the Ryakul's body in a grisly mess.

You are Ferasdiam marked. We heed your call, Safanarion.

The Eldarin's words echoed in his mind as he fought. He danced through the sky, streaking from Ryakul to Ryakul. One of the Eldarin took to the sky and followed him, while the other remained still upon the ground. The energy flowed through Aaron as it hadn't since he had first taken the Nanites into his system. He stood upon the back of a dying Ryakul as it plunged toward the ground. The remaining

Ryakuls fled over the backs of the retreating Khamearrian soldiers. Aaron's gaze focused on a single Ryakul with a figure upon its back. His first thought was that of the Drake, but the Drake was gone. Someone else was controlling the Ryakuls.

His mind was as clear as it had not been for so long that it felt as if it was working in overdrive. He turned to the lone Eldarin that flew above him.

We have cleansed your body of the taint.

"Thank you," Aaron said.

He heard a strange growl and saw the other Eldarin struggling to rise. Aaron raced back and winced at the scorched gashes upon its golden hide. The Dragon lord struggled to rise and turned toward him. One of its eyes was missing, and darkness swirled in the other like a storm cloud.

Aaron felt his heart fill his chest at the sight. He reached out, but the Eldarin snarled at him. The other Eldarin landed behind him and growled warily. Aaron leaped back and saw two Ryakul corpses that lay behind the Eldarin. His eyes darted to the wounds and felt the bile rise in his throat.

Please no, Aaron thought and turned to the other Ryakul. "It's the sickness. The same thing that turns the Dragons into Ryakuls."

The snarling Eldarin's hide faded to gray.

"Go!" Aaron shouted to the Eldarin behind him. "Or you'll

be infected too. Go!" he screamed.

The Eldarin behind him drew back its head and sent a blast of energy into the Eldarin while releasing a mournful howl at the same time. The sickened Eldarin fell back as the other took to the sky. The infected Eldarin regained its footing and followed. The two streaked away and disappeared in a green flash.

Aaron released the energy and felt his strength leave him. The staff kept him upright. He heard soft footsteps behind him and spun around. Sarah stood before him. Their eyes searched each other's as if they were afraid that the other would fade away.

"I didn't...I didn't know it was you," Sarah said.

His heart filled his chest, and before he knew anything, they held each other. Aaron swung her around in his arms, crying out, losing himself in the blue of her eyes and the feel of her in his arms. They didn't say anything, their eyes speaking the volumes that their mouths couldn't say as they held each other.

The soldiers of the High King's army retreated, no longer having the element of surprise. While the Ryakuls had been an advantage to them, the battle with the Eldarin had shaken their spirit. The Free Nations Army along with the Lorric forces pushed forward until the High King's army disappeared in a blinding flash of light. The soldiers remaining on the field cheered, but those who knew the

High King knew that this victory wouldn't go unanswered.

CHAPTER 17
WARNING

Rordan was with General Khoiron in the command tent when one of Khamearra's armies returned ahead of schedule. As the reports came in, the more the old general's furrowed brows deepened. He fingered the apprentice amulet he had worn since he had found it. If truth be told, Mactar had left it for him. Since he started wearing it, he had been able to feel more of the energy around him. He hardly noticed the muddled whisperings of souls past that spewed sultry promises of glory and power.

At first he refused to wear it, convincing himself that he didn't need it, but as time went on he found that there were advantages to wearing the amulet in spite of the cost. He could stop the beating hearts of those around him if he focused on it. His experiments on a few random people brought Mactar's attention, as if he had been expecting it all along. He'd been tempted to use his newfound ability on his sister, but decided it would be much more entertaining to watch her struggle against their father.

Rordan looked up and found Khoiron eyeing him. He always felt as if the old general was taking his measure, but his craggy old face gave away nothing in return. The High King had just joined them, having been away on one of the planned assaults. His father had said to him earlier that there were some things best observed with one's own eyes. Rordan knew that despite what his father had said, he had other reasons to go. One thing he had learned about his father was that he had an unquenchable thirst for blood, and it was only a matter of time before he would lead more attacks.

"Bottom line, they were prepared for our attack," Khoiron said.

"How prepared could they have been?" the High King asked.

"They had additional support from the Free Nations Army," Khoiron replied.

"Free Nations Army," the High King sneered.

"Like it or not, your Grace. They are a force to be reckoned with and represent our real enemies in this. Lorric was slated to be an easy victory, and the troops sent in for the attack should have been more than adequate for the job. In fact, with the additional support from Darven and his Ryakuls this attack should have been downright easy,"

Khoiron said.

The High King eyed the old general for a moment. "As usual, your counsel is as sound as your logic. So tell me how we were defeated and where is Darven."

"Before we delve into the particulars of the battle, there is another thing that warrants your attention," Khoiron said and gestured to the guards.

The guards left the tent, and four Elitesmen returned with a hooded prisoner. The prisoner was broad shouldered and taller than most men in the room. He wore the uniform of the FNA that was almost in tatters, but Rordan could see something painted on his chest. An Elitesman kicked the man behind the knees, driving them to the ground and removed his hood.

The High King's eyes flashed as he studied the prisoner before him. "What's this supposed to be?"

"Do you not recognize the face of your enemy, Father?" Rordan asked. "This is Aaron, the Heir of Shandara."

The High King glanced around the room. "No, it's not."

Rordan glanced at Khoiron. "It is him, Father. I recognize his face."

"As do I, Son, but this is not him. I would know it," the High King said and stepped up to the prisoner, grabbing his face. "The likeness is remarkable. I can see why you would be fooled."

"An impostor," Rordan said.

"He had these on him when we captured him," an Elitesman said and handed the High King two swords.

"Now these I recognize. They are not fake. They are known as the Falcons and have been in the Alenzar'seth family for generations," the High King said and drew one of the blades from its sheath. There was a crystal inlaid into the pommel, and the craftsmanship of the blades with the notches was beyond compare. "There are legends about these swords. In the hands of the right master, the bladesong unleashed could sway the hearts of men." The High King returned the blade to its sheath. "Why don't you tell us who you are?"

The impostor met the High King's gaze. "I am Aaron Jace."

The High King roared, grabbing the impostor by the throat and lifting him off the ground with one arm. "If you really were Aaron Jace, I wouldn't be able to do this to you," the High King said and slammed the impostor back onto the ground.

Rordan watched as his father stepped away. He could sense the energy gathered around his father with such intensity that he had only felt it once before by another man. His father was right, the man before them could never be the true Heir of Shandara.

The High King raised his hand, and the impostor was lifted by forces unseen. The tips of his feet dragged along the floor, but despite the blow that would have killed an ordinary man the impostor appeared to have been untouched. There was a shift in the man's eyes as his narrowed gaze found that of the High King.

"You believe you are powerful. Your people's days are numbered, human. You're already dead, and you don't even know it."

The High King drew his sword, and in the blink of an eye, a deep red slice opened up the impostor from navel to shoulder. The impostor laughed, and Rordan's eyes widened as the skin stitched itself back up again. The High King spun, and the impostor's head left his shoulders, dropping to the ground. The High King thrust out his other hand, sending a blazing orb, and the body of the impostor was reduced to ash in seconds.

"Now we can't question him," Rordan said.

"He wasn't going to tell us anything. He was a spy, judging by the fact that he had these," the High King said gesturing toward the Falcons, "he had some measure of success over our enemies."

Darven entered the tent, and the Elitesmen all but hissed at the man. Darven ignored them and glanced at the bloodstained ground with remnant ashes that swirled around his feet. He saluted the High King, who nodded back and asked him for his report.

"The Ryakuls have been proven effective in the battle, your Grace. We had Lorric on the run. They were scattered, even with the help of the Free Nations Army. Mactar continues to gather more as we speak," Darven said.

General Khoiron frowned. "My reports say you lost control of some of them."

"Yes, that is true," Darven said.

"I hope you can explain why."

"The FNA were able to summon two of the biggest Dragons I've ever seen. It was all I could do to retain control of the ones in my immediate vicinity," Darven said.

"Dragons? Like the ones that came to the arena, the Eldarin?" Rordan asked.

"The very same. As soon as they appeared, the Ryakuls seemed to give in to some primal instinct. We've observed similar behavior while hunting Ryakuls, but it wasn't until today that I learned that the connection between Ryakul and Dragons is much deeper," Darven said and then he described what he saw with the Eldarin before he had been chased off.

"You saw the change actually occur?" the High King asked.

"The beginning stages of it, yes," Darven replied.

"This would explain why we've seen fewer Dragons over the years," the High King said.

"Your Grace," Khoiron said, "we shouldn't overlook the fact that Lorric was prepared for our attack and the Free Nations Army was able to aid them awfully quick. There are only two explanations for this. Either they were already camped in Lorric since we scouted out the kingdom previously, which seems unlikely, or they too have a way to move armies instantaneously. This changes things."

"You are correct, things have changed. We've proven our point by attacking the smaller kingdoms, but now we need to be more aggressive. We need to take the heart of the Free Nations Army at their source. We break that army, and the rest of the kingdoms will fall into line," the High King said.

"A bold plan. We outnumber them, but if we take the fight to them then our greater numbers will be cancelled out because they are well fortified," Khoiron said.

The High King's lips lifted into a wolfish smile. "I find misdirection to be an effective tool in battle. We have the advantage of numbers, Elitesmen, and Ryakuls."

"I know what I'm about to say you've already considered, but I'll say it anyway," Khoiron said. "To commit ourselves to this will require the use of all of our troops and resources."

"Agreed, we have a lot of work to do," the High King said.

They spent the rest of the day coordinating how the attack was going to happen, and at some point it occurred to Rordan that this is what his father had been angling toward for some time. He studied each of the men, from the army generals to the Elite Masters. Each came with their own shroud of darkness and death upon them with the exception of general Khoiron. To him this was a game pure and simple. Though they hadn't discussed it openly, it was implied that the true Heir of Shandara was in Lorric and had turned the tide of the battle there. Rordan knew that his father relished the challenge that Aaron posed. Rordan just thought it would be convenient for him if they both killed each other off and he could be done with it. There were some in the room that didn't favor the High King's plan, but they knew better than to press the issue. One of the conveniences of absolute obedience. Loyalty and fear kept these men in line, and his father was a master at determining which would serve him best.

"I would speak with my son now. We'll reconvene tomorrow afternoon," the High King said.

The men left the tent, but his father didn't say anything.

"How long have you had this planned?" Rordan asked.

"Since the first attack on the city."

"Why not attack them then?"

"People like Mactar are full of great ideas, but without actually having our troops go through the attacks over the last few weeks, they would lack the experience needed to assure victory over our enemies. They have a few victories under their belts and have hardened a bit. Now they're ready for a real battle."

Rordan frowned. "Mactar? I thought it was Gerric who came up with using the focusing crystal to move the army from place to place?"

"Gerric has many talents, but coming up with innovative

ways to use the tools we have at our disposal is not one of them."

Rordan shook his head. "I'll never understand the alliance you have with Mactar."

"You need to understand if you're to succeed me as king one day, Son. Mactar lusts for power and freedom. He doesn't wish to rule, and he would fall short if he ever challenged me. I give him the means to carry out things he would probably do anyway, but I get the benefits of his innovation."

"Was it innovation that led Tye to an early grave?" Rordan asked.

"Your brother was ever trying to keep up with you and Primus. Should I blame you for Tye's shortcomings?"

"Of course not, but what Mactar did wasn't right," Rordan said.

His father leveled his gaze at him. "Do you honestly believe that Mactar did anything without my knowing about it first?"

Rordan searched his father's face and almost cursed himself for not seeing it sooner.

"You want to know why?" his father asked. "I had three sons, and only one of you was going to inherit this crown. I had always suspected you would outlast the others. Primus was too impulsive, and Tye was the same though with a bit more jealousy. Mactar had come to me saying that he may have found where Reymius had been hiding all these long years. That Reymius had an heir. Some of the things Mactar says I take with a grain of salt, and that was one of them."

"But you risked Tye on one of Mactar's whims," Rordan said.

"Your brother would have found another way to test himself. I didn't actually believe that Reymius survived the fall of Shandara or got his daughter, Carlowen, out of there. So yes, I allowed Tye his quest. I sent Darven with him. If he had survived, he would have been stronger for it. Good for him and good for me."

"A former Elitesman should have been able to keep him alive," Rordan said.

"Yes, he should have been able to under normal circumstances. But you ought to know by now that dealing with the Alenzar'seth is anything but ordinary. I crushed their kingdom and laid waste to their precious Shandara, but still they survive. This next battle will see their end along with the rest who align themselves with that kingdom."

Rordan was silent for a moment. "What do you think of what the impostor said?"

"I'd like to hear your thoughts on it first."

Rordan frowned, taking a second to collect his thoughts. "The way he called us *humans*, like he utterly detested what we are. Sarah believes there is another race about to invade our world. At first I didn't believe her, but with the impostor, I'm wondering if she was right."

"The Hythariam are a race apart from us. Regardless, until this race shows itself we shouldn't trouble ourselves with it. They will die just as easily as anyone else. After we deal with the Free Nations Army we'll investigate it, but don't let it distract you in the short term."

Rordan said he wouldn't, but the impostor's last words hissed in the back of his mind. *Your people's days are numbered, human.* It didn't even matter to the creature that it was about to die. The creature died believing that they were already dead. There was something in the certainty of it that bothered Rordan, but he wouldn't raise it again to his father. Not until after the attack.

CHAPTER 18
A PRICE TO PAY

Aaron breathed in the fresh scents of the forest around him. The smooth call of a lakeside bird skimmed away from them. He and Sarah were the only ones here. Being here with Sarah in his arms, he could almost forget being locked away in a hollowed out mountain, prisoner to the Zekara. The last-ditch effort for a race of beings' attempt at survival. Sarah stole him away shortly after the battle was over, telling Verona, who happened to be closest to them, that she would have him back in Rexel by morning. They had disappeared before anyone could say anything, including Aaron.

"I'll happily be your prisoner as long as you wish," Aaron said.

"They've survived this long without you. A few more hours won't make that much difference," Sarah said, snuggling into his side.

They lay there near the lapping water on a bed of their clothes. They had already been there for hours, and the sun was beginning to rise.

"I still don't know where we are," Aaron said.

"Does it really matter?" Sarah asked, propping up on her elbow. Her long blonde hair caressed her bare shoulder.

Aaron swallowed in the sight of her. "Not really."

Sarah's full lips lifted into a smile halfway between suggestion and invitation. When they had first arrived, hours before, they didn't speak. They didn't need to. They stripped off their clothes and swam in the calm waters of some unnamed lake, washing the battle from them. Hours went by, and it seemed that they had only just embraced as they lay together upon the lakeshore.

Aaron was still piecing together what had happened to him. His memories were a string of disjointed images that he kept trying to put together. Sarah hadn't asked him anything, and he knew it wasn't because she didn't want to know. They had somehow silently agreed to block out all that had happened in order to steal away this precious time to be together as lovers.

After a time he felt more like himself. The Eldarin had somehow rid his body of the Nanites, allowing them to repair the damage to his body that Halcylon had done, but it was his short time here with Sarah that began to heal his soul. He drew in the energy around them, and Sarah did the same. Their golden radiance merged together, and the connection that had gone dormant since his journey to Hytharia blossomed in his chest. Sarah's eyes widened, and Aaron smiled.

The sun had fully risen when they finally dressed themselves. Aaron had only the pants that he had washed in the lake earlier. The medallion lay on his chiseled chest, reflecting the sunlight. He held the rune-carved staff, waiting for Sarah to dress, all the while suppressing his urge to remove her clothing again.

"If you keep looking at me like that, we may never leave," Sarah said playfully.

Aaron glanced away. "That wouldn't be so bad."

"Not at all. The others, I'm sure, are eager to see you."

Aaron turned back to her and pulled her to him. "They can wait."

The comms device chimed, and after a few moments Sarah brought it up.

"You may not know where we are, but it appears that our friends do. It's time for us to return," Sarah said.

Aaron grabbed her hand before she could retrieve the travel crystal. "If it were just me, I would never leave here."

Sarah's hand brushed down past his face, coming to rest on his shoulder. "Neither would I," she said softly.

"Thank you for saving me."

"I had to keep things even," she replied and brought out

the travel crystal.

Sarah took them to the Free Nations Army camp outside the walls of Rexel. Aaron sucked in a quick breath, his eyes darting around at the massive camp that was in the midst of transforming into an extension of the city. Dark banners with the Alenzar'seth coat of arms swayed in the breeze. Men and women wearing similar green uniforms traveled in groups.

They found suitable replacements for his clothing and Hythariam-made boots that molded themselves to his feet. When he stood back up, he really appreciated how comfortable they were. The acrid smell of the Hythariam tech nearby snapped him back to the Zekara's base, where he was chained to a column. The tent walls closed in around him, and he took several deep breaths to steady himself. Outside the supply tent, Roselyn and Verona waited with Sarah, both looking relieved to see him. He pulled Roselyn into a quick embrace, and Verona laughed.

"The only reason I am here is because of the Keystone Accelerator you modified for me," Aaron said and told them of the creature that had helped him. "The portal was only opened for seconds, but Thraw pulled me through it."

"I wish I could meet this creature and thank him," Verona said.

"I'm glad it worked," Roselyn said. "I would like to examine you though, just to make sure..."

Aaron nodded. "I feel fine, but I would feel better if you did."

Roselyn's eyes widened and a smile lit up her face. She turned to the others. "How could we have ever thought that other creature could have possibly been him?"

Aaron clamped his mouth shut. Sarah had told him what had happened. Halcylon had cloned him somehow and sent it here. Some of the soldiers that passed by glanced at him strangely.

Verona leaned in. "Give it some time. After all, the other you told them to retreat and that all hope was lost."

Aaron nodded. "Have they been able to find it?"

He had been anxious to meet this creature since Sarah had first told him about it.

"There has been no sign of him since the battle," Verona said.

"I shouldn't have given them to him," Sarah said.

"Given what?" Roselyn asked.

"Aaron's swords."

"We'll get them back somehow," Aaron said.

Verona frowned in thought and looked at Roselyn. "What puzzles me is how you knew there was, in fact, an impostor?"

"It was in his blood," Roselyn said. "We had samples of Aaron's original blood when he was infected with the Ryakul poison. I compared them. They matched up almost perfectly with one exception. Age. The clone was only a month old, and his cells were deteriorating fast."

"A month old," Verona gasped. "Your people can create a full grown person in a month?"

"Apparently. We'll need to ask Gavril and my father. With the advent of the Nanites, the need for cloning anything was gone," Roselyn said and looked at Aaron, her eyes downcast. "I scanned you while you were getting dressed."

Aaron was more startled than anything else at the admission and glanced at the others.

"The impostor wouldn't let her examine him," Sarah said.

"Oh. It's all right," Aaron said.

"There is no trace of the Nanites having ever been in your system. What is quite strange is that there are no impurities at all in your system now. It's as if your body was completely remade," Roselyn said.

Aaron frowned. "Well, it's a good thing the Nanites aren't there anymore, but you look concerned about the remade part."

"As we grow older our bodies show signs of aging, but we can also tell a lot about an environment that a person has been exposed to. Toxins in the air. You come from a technically advanced society not all that different from Hytharia so you've been exposed to some of that, which shows up. Only now all that is gone. It's still you at your current age, but it's as if the slate has been wiped completely clean," Roselyn said.

Aaron pursed his lips in thought. "The Eldarin healed me, and perhaps they took care of... well, everything. I'm not sure, but I've never felt better."

"We'll keep an eye on you to see that you stay that way," Sarah said.

"You were completely unrecognizable, my friend," Verona said. "It is a strange thing that there are those who have the power to inflict such change. Now that I think back to Len's...your behavior, it was as if there were parts of you that continued to shine through."

Aaron held almost no memory of his time as Len. After coming through the portal, his memory blanked out, but he did recall Thraw telling him that he didn't look right, and it would be a mercy to kill him. He wondered where the creature was now. Sarah had told him of a man named Wes who looked after him, and Aaron made a mental note to find the man and thank him.

Braden joined them, saying that they were waiting for them at the palace. Aaron caught Braden studying him out of the corner of his eye as they made their way through the FNA camp to a smaller airship field. Braden quickly looked away. He had the rod that fanned out into a shield hanging on his belt and a war hammer of blackened steel with gold runes carved on the side.

"If you're going to be the Warden of the De'anjard, you

can't be at my side all the time anymore," Aaron said.

"We'll see about that," Braden grunted.

They came to an airfield with smaller ships that were designed to carry groups of people.

"I take it we're not walking to the palace then?" Aaron asked.

"It would take some of us longer to get there. Besides these give us a nice view of the city if we're required to go all the way to the palace anyway," Verona said.

"What are they?" Aaron asked.

"They're prototypes," Roselyn answered. "We don't have the means to build more flyers yet, but we could improve upon the design of the airships already in use. Before Prince Cyrus and the other rulers would agree to put up the resources, they required proof that it would work."

"That's my uncle. He's quit reluctant to raid the treasury unless it's absolutely necessary," Verona grinned.

Roselyn nodded. "So we built working models that could be used to help ferry people around."

The airship in front of them was only twenty-five feet in length and sported two smaller engines on the wings as well as an engine over the cell floating above the ship itself. Jopher opened the gate and invited them on board. Aaron shook hands with him and noticed the quick glance that Jopher had with the others.

They're still checking to see if it's me, Aaron thought.

Joining them onboard were two Hythariam in black uniforms. Each armed with a plasma pistol and a helmet that covered their face.

Aaron nodded to himself, both relieved that they were taking these steps yet at the same time it bothered him that they felt they needed to.

The airship lurched upward, and Jopher engaged the engines. The small airship was quite agile, and Aaron grabbed onto the railing. Sarik leaped up from the ground as the airship ascended, and Aaron helped pull him over the railing.

"Have you decided whether it's really me or not yet?" Aaron asked.

Sarah glanced at the others in surprise, but the rest of them cast their eyes downward with the exception of the two Hythariam soldiers. The soldiers glanced at each other, and their helmets folded away, becoming part of their armor. Tanneth's lips curved into a half smile.

"We couldn't afford to take any chances," Gavril said.

Sarah glared at them for a moment before laughing. "If you could see the look on your faces when he asked you if you thought it was him..."

Aaron smiled, and after a moment the rest of them joined in.

"We, being the ones who knew you best, decided to take it upon ourselves to give a final check to see whether we all agreed that you were who you said you were," Verona said. "Sarah had no knowledge."

"It was actually a good idea," Aaron said. It did feel good to be among his friends again.

The small airship got them to the palace in no time. Jopher secured the ship outside one of the taller towers nearest the main hall.

Verona darted ahead, "Better let me go in first, otherwise the welcome might not be so...welcoming."

The tension that drained out of them all on the airship seemed to creep back in. The main hall was filled with people from different places around Safanar. Jopher went to stand with his father, who narrowed his gaze when he looked at Aaron.

Colind came to his side. "When we're done here, you and I need to speak."

Aaron nodded. As they came to the front of the hall, he noticed that the throne had been removed. Hovering in its place was a large holographic map of Safanar with the major nations marked and color-coded.

Prince Cyrus stepped up to him. "Welcome back. Thanks to you and the soldiers of the FNA, we were able to keep the High King from taking the Kingdom of Lorric. Now that you're all here we can continue."

"We're planning our next move, or trying to," Colind said.

Verona and the others had told Aaron about the High

King's attacks and their ability to use the focusing crystals to teleport their armies throughout the continent.

"You're planning to attack the High King?" Aaron asked.

"That is one possibility," Colind said.

Aaron turned to Gavril. "What about the Zekara? They're here."

Gavril nodded. "We know they are here, but we don't know where they are. We were hoping that you knew."

"I only saw the portal they used to get here, but never saw where they actually went," Aaron said.

Gavril frowned. "During the battle we detected strange readings on our equipment. They turned out to be two drones that were cloaked. There were no actual Zekara in the area, but we know they're here because they took a shot at you."

Aaron's throat thickened as he recalled the mournful howl of the Eldarin. "One of the Eldarin became infected with Ryakul venom; are they beyond hope now?"

Colind shook his head. "I would never count against the Eldarin."

"They are a life form the likes of which we have never encountered before," Roselyn said. "They are able to shift between physical forms and become almost pure energy."

Aaron nodded. It was something at least. "I don't know what's already been done regarding the High King, but have you reached out to him about the Zekara threat?"

"I went to my father," Sarah said. "He doesn't believe the threat exists, and if he did, he doesn't understand the threat that they pose for all of us. Khamearra is a kingdom divided."

"That may be," Colind began, "but they are firmly under the High King's control. I don't think we have any choice but to bring this war back to the High King. I am sorry, my Lady."

Sarah nodded, and Aaron knew she understood what was at stake.

"We should give shelter and aid to anyone from Khamearra that wants it," Aaron said.

"We have been, but our resources are being stretched thin as it is, and most nations who are allied with us are facing the same issues," Prince Cyrus said.

Aaron glanced around the room and saw the same resignation. He remembered the Resistance—people who lived in fear day after day in the High King's city. "Send them to Shandara, or at least give them the option."

There was a quiet murmuring, but Aaron knew that no one could make any compelling argument. Most of them believe that Shandara was his by right, and he didn't see the harm in giving the people of Khamearra a safe haven.

"One thing at a time," Gavril said. "We have the High King to face."

"Whatever they do, you can be assured that my father will

be present at the next battle," Sarah said.

"Are we able to bring the Free Nations Army to Khamearra?" Aaron asked.

After a long moment, Gavril shook his head.

"I have an idea."

Aaron turned to see Jopher standing next to his father, who had spoken. "Firstly, my first son and heir speaks very highly of you."

Aaron looked at Jopher and gave a slow nod of appreciation. "What's your idea...uh...your Grace?"

King Melchoir Nasim drew his head up. "Jopher has informed me that you are not familiar with our customs, so I will grant that we can do away with formalities at this time and speak plainly. If we cannot take our fight to the enemy, then we need to make our enemy take the fight to a place of our choosing. Knowing the High King, he will not take the slight of defeat lightly and will yearn for a crushing victory."

"Until now, he's been hitting smaller kingdoms, but we think he'll direct his efforts at the larger ones from here on out," Gavril said.

King Nasim nodded. "With Zsensibar and Rexel being among them."

"You think he'll attack one of those places?" Aaron asked.

"Or both," the king said. "I proposed that Zsensibar quit the field and break with the alliance. Rexel will become an irresistible target for the High King."

"I can see why you like this idea," Prince Cyrus said. "It's my city being used as bait."

"Uncle, this fight would have come here eventually," Verona said.

"Regardless of what we decide, we do need to move quickly," Colind said. "There might not be an attack today, but it could come from anywhere in the next few days."

Prince Cyrus looked as if he swallowed something bitter. "The reports from Lorric are that they are using Ryakuls to attack the cities."

"Can we clear the city? Get the people who can't fight out?" Aaron asked.

The question caught some of them by surprise, and Prince Cyrus's eyebrows drew up. "Reymius would be proud of you, Aaron. He was ever one for placing the safety of his people among his highest priorities."

Despite himself, Aaron smiled at being compared to his grandfather, and for a moment his thoughts drifted to one of his last conversations with his father. "There are no perfect solutions. We can only do the best we can, but one thing we can all agree on is that the High King will strike. The question is, what are we going to do to face his armies when they do come."

"There is one thing that I don't like about this," Gavril said.

"Only one thing?" asked Verona.

"The High King is on the offensive, and besides the

Khamearrian Resistance, he hasn't been attacked at all by the FNA. We can't use the Keystone Accelerators to move an army big enough to challenge the High King, but that doesn't mean we can't hit him. There are other ways to wage war than large-scale battles," Gavril said, drawing several nods of approval among them.

"I like the idea of bringing the battle to them," Aaron said.

"What I propose is hitting their military camps, and I want them to know that the Free Nations Army is responsible. They need to know they are not safe," Gavril said.

The old Hythariam soldier spoke as one who had fought many battles, and many had come to trust his judgment, including Aaron. They continued planning and making preparations. People still stared at him when they thought he wasn't looking, and he could hardly blame them. Almost all of them had been fooled by Halcylon's clone of him, and Aaron never expected it. Not that he could have done anything about it. This whole alliance would spiral out of control if they couldn't trust one another. Prince Cyrus agreed to start moving his people to Shandara. King Nasim would order his armies to withdraw from the borders of the north and send word to the High King, offering his provisional support. Aaron wasn't sure whether the High King would believe it, but it was worth a try.

The council session was about to end when a guard came racing into the main hall. He saluted the prince and spoke softly so that only he could hear. Prince Cyrus looked up in alarm and then turned to Sarah.

"My Lady, it appears that you have visitors," the Prince said.

Sarah glanced at Aaron uncertainly. "Who, may I ask, my Lord?"

The prince hesitated for a moment. "They say they are Elitesmen. They've requested an audience with their queen."

Aaron's hands shifted to the swords that he no longer had and cursed their loss.

"They came through one of the main gates and surrendered themselves to the guards," Prince Cyrus said.

"How many of them are there?" Aaron asked.

"Twenty," the guard answered.

Braden hefted his war hammer, with more than a few of the guards following his lead.

"Stay your hands," the prince ordered. "They are unarmed and have surrendered themselves."

"Elitesmen generally don't use the front door," Aaron said.

"Look among you," Verona said. "Even if the Elitesmen's intentions were less than honorable, it would be a path to a quick end for them."

Aaron glanced at Braden, who lowered his hammer but still kept it in his hands. Gavril's fingers flashed across his comms device, killing the holo image of the continent.

"Please send them in, my Lord," Sarah said.

Prince Cyrus gestured to the guards at the entranceway to the main hall. The guard saluted to his prince, unlatched the great doors, and pulled them open. Several lines of men entered. Soldiers of the FNA flanked each of the Elitesmen, clad in their black uniforms. The Elitesmen's hands were shackled in front of them.

Aaron studied the approaching Elitesmen, and none of them held the energy. Half of their number were quite old with the rest being near his own age or younger. Some had the pristine arrogance that Aaron had come to associate with the Elitesmen, but not all of them. The last Elitesman to come in wore a dark-leather duster and had long gray hair. Isaac's gaze darted to Aaron almost immediately and then focused on Sarah.

Isaac came forward and sank to one knee with the other Elitesmen doing the same. "My Queen, we have come to pledge ourselves to you."

Sarah stepped away from Aaron's side. "You must be mistaken. Khamearra has no queen."

Isaac's eyes never left the floor. "You are Sarah Faergrace of the rightful ruling family of Khamearra. Many of our great kingdom will support your claim, my Queen."

Aaron came to Sarah's side. "Do all Elitesmen change their loyalties on a whim? Maybe not you, Isaac, but these younger men would have gladly killed any of us should we have crossed their paths."

A young dark-haired Elitesman raised his head. "You speak the truth, Heir of Shandara. Until recently we have been loyal to the Order."

"What, pray tell, has had such a calamitous effect that would lead you to change where your loyalties lie?" Verona asked.

The remaining Elitesmen looked up from the ground and their gazes shifted to Aaron, but when the dark-haired Elitesman spoke, he addressed everyone around them. "The Alenzar'seth fought our brethren in the arena, bringing to a halt a practice that we of the Elite should have ended long ago," the Elitesman said.

Aaron saw that some of the people were confused. "The Elitesmen recruit young initiates and as a rite of passage make them compete to save their families. The competition is designed to make killers out of them with none having a hope to succeed," Aaron said.

There was a murmuring of general disgust sweeping through the room, and the Elitesmen paid it no more mind than the air they breathed. They did, however, remain focused on Aaron.

"You didn't have to come here to change things in the Order of the Elite," Aaron said.

"We didn't. We came to pledge our loyalty to the rightful ruler of Khamearra," the Elitesman said. "We will die to protect her."

"Protect her!" Braden scowled. "Weeks ago you took up arms against her."

"Warden," Isaac said with a half smile for Braden, "that was not us or anyone else associated with our group." Isaac looked at Sarah. "Your Grace, those of us who honor the old code of the Elite have watched over you your whole life, and when you came of age one of our order was sent to train you in our ways."

"Please get off your knees," Sarah said. "How many factions of the Elitesmen are there?" Sarah asked.

Despite being shackled, the Elitesmen rose smoothly to their feet. Aaron kept a wary eye on them, not believing for a second that those shackles kept them from doing anything they didn't want to do.

"There is the faction that is loyal to your father," Isaac began. "They compose the majority of Elitesmen. Then there are us, who were able to survive by staying out of the way. We aided the Resistance where we could. Then there are those who either follow the majority or are too scared to do anything different. For obvious reasons we are quite careful in our own recruitment."

"Are there only twenty of you?" Sarah asked.

"No, your Grace," Isaac said. "Our numbers are in the hundreds. Most of which are serving in the High King's army. I thought a larger number to bring would be too risky, given the current tensions between the kingdoms."

Colind, who had been quiet, cleared his throat. "How can you expect us to trust you at all, Elitesman?"

Isaac glanced at the other Elitesmen and nodded. As one, the shackles binding their wrists fell to the floor, but the Elitesmen remained still. The soldiers around them drew swords and pistols alike and trained them on the group.

"As you can see, my Lord Guardian of the Safanarion Order, I think you will find us to be indispensable in the coming battle. By now you realize that the High King is preparing to strike," Isaac said.

Sarah narrowed her gaze. "You tell us nothing we don't already know. If you are truly loyal to Khamearra and would make me your queen, then you need to bring something to the table. I trusted Bek and the Resistance, but I never knew that there were so many Elitesmen who would break with the current regime."

"Understandable," Isaac said. "Most don't leave the order once inducted. We ask that you allow us to prove ourselves."

"Isaac did help us get into the Citadel tower and has been involved with the Resistance in the past," Aaron said. "Him I can extend a certain measure of trust, but the rest of you? I don't think so."

"With all due respect, we came here to pledge our loyalty and service to our queen and not to *you*," the young dark-haired Elitesmen said.

"Have a care with how you speak, Elitesman," Sarah said coldly. "You know to whom you speak, so I don't need to remind you, but know this. Aaron is my love. His voice is my voice. His will is my will. In this life we are one, now and forever. If Khamearra is to have me as their queen then they will be aligned with Shandara and the Alenzar'seth."

The silence of the hall swallowed them up, and Aaron's mouth hung open. He loved Sarah and knew she loved him. No force on Safanar or any other world would ever keep them apart, but to hear her speak those words sent shockwaves through him.

"My Lady," Colind said softly. "You speak the old oaths."

"Would you expect anything less, my Lord Guardian?" Sarah answered.

Aaron and Sarah spared each other a glance with hints of a smile.

"You would align the kingdoms of the west with those of the east?" Colind asked.

"Be more than a kingdom then," Aaron said, drawing everyone's attention. "Be a nation of men and women united. The promises and oaths sworn between kings die with them. Be a nation of people, and those laws won't die because the ruling families change."

Colind smiled thoughtfully. "It's never far from you, is it?"

"It's the best way forward. You, my grandfather, and others of the Safanarion Order began this work," Aaron said.

"Why would anyone trade one tyrant for another? The bonds of this alliance should be strong enough to survive the death of one man even if he is Ferasdiam marked."

"Not all the kingdoms would agree to this," Colind said.

"Then that is their prerogative, but given time they will come around," Sarah said.

"We still offer our services," Isaac said. "Any leader among you knows the value of having well-placed agents in the enemy. We can give you information about the focusing crystals and how they are being used. How many there are and how they are being protected."

Gavril and the other generals of the Free Nations Army perked up at this.

Sarah regarded the Elitesmen. "I'll accept your service on the following conditions, and they are not negotiable," she said, capturing all within her regal gaze. "Your powers are a privilege, and from this day forth will be used in the service of protecting others. You will have dominion over no one but yourself. The Elitesmen are not a law unto themselves and have much to atone for. Part of that atonement will be met by service in the Free Nations Army. You will enter service at the lowest possible rank, and you will only be given privileges through achievement. If you can agree to that, then you can be in my service. If not, then the door is over there, gentlemen. I won't have you in my company or in Khamearra. Is that clear?"

Isaac already nodded before looking at the others, and they spoke in unison. "By the grace of our Queen we serve."

"There is one more thing," Sarah said and then paused. "You will no longer call yourselves Elitesmen. My first act as queen will be to disband the Order of the Elite."

Some of them sucked in a breath with an angry glint in their eyes.

"What may we call ourselves then?" one of them asked.

"You have names, why don't you start with those," Sarah said. "Perhaps in time and if you prove yourselves worthy, you can apply to enter into the Safanarion Order."

Colind sucked in a breath, and Aaron felt his mouth hang open again. After a few moments' thought, he found that he agreed with her. Real change can come from a new identity, and inside he applauded her genius.

"I would honor that," Aaron said.

"But they're Elitesmen," Colind said before he could stop himself.

"Look at them. The younger ones held no part in the fall of Shandara," Aaron said.

"And what of the older ones?" Colind asked, narrowing his thunderous gaze.

"They broke with the Order and were hunted as any of the Safanarion Order were," Aaron said.

Colind drew up his chin stubbornly, considering what Aaron had said. "You took the Safanarion Oath. One day this will fall to you and the others when I am gone. I hope this isn't a mistake, but I will consider any man or woman into the Safanarion Order should they be worthy."

The council session ended. Isaac and the other former Elitesmen left with Gavril and some others, eager to glean whatever intelligence there was to be learned. Sarah stayed by his side along with Verona and Roselyn. Braden kept a wary eye on the former Elitesmen. Aaron nodded for him to go on, and Braden gave him a salute and stalked off to follow them.

Sarah glanced at him.

"Braden won't rest until he's sure about them," Aaron said.

"I thought now that you were back that things would calm down, but there is never a dull moment when you two are together," Verona said, dividing his gaze between Aaron and Sarah. "Did you ever think that Elitesmen would come asking to join us? Or more specifically, pledge their loyalty to their queen?"

"I knew there were factions, but I never thought any of them would give up being an Elitesman," Aaron said.

"Actions will prove their conviction in this case," Sarah said. "It seemed obvious that if they were going to help us then they needed to be reforged. If they follow through, they will be better for it. I just hope I haven't made us more vulnerable if they don't."

"Some things are worth the risk," Aaron said.

Colind approached them and asked to speak with Aaron. Then after a moment's consideration, he asked for Sarah to stay with them.

"What I'm about to tell you will affect you as well," Colind said to her.

They left the main hall, leaving the palace, and headed into gardens that were meticulously maintained. The fresh air felt good after being stuck inside.

"Ferasdiam marked," Colind said. "Do you know what it means?"

Aaron frowned. "I think I have a pretty good idea."

Colind's lips lifted into a small smile. "Enlighten me."

"You believe that I've been touched by the Goddess Ferasdiam. This has granted me powers beyond that of an ordinary person," Aaron said.

"You sound as if you don't believe it," Colind said quietly.

"I'm not sure what to believe. I do believe that anything I can do, can be done by someone else," Aaron answered.

"Do you think Braden can jump as high as you do? Or Verona move as fast as you do? Channel enough energy through that staff to kill a Ryakul? You've surpassed anyone who has been Ferasdiam marked before with the possible exception of the Amorak," Colind said.

"My father? He's Ferasdiam marked?" she asked looking from Colind to Aaron.

"He is," Aaron said. "When I faced him atop the Citadel

tower the Dragon tattoo felt strange."

"How so?" Sarah asked.

"It was like it was reacting to being near him," Aaron said, thinking back to his encounter with the High King. "I think he felt it too. He kept rubbing his arm."

Colind nodded. "Having two Ferasdiam marked within the same lifespan hasn't happened before."

"What I don't understand is why the Goddess would bestow her mark on one such as he? It makes me think that this is up to chance. You say my ability to move faster and be stronger than the others is a mark of me being special. What if it's just talent, like a musician's skill with an instrument?" Aaron said.

"But you've heard her message. The Eldarin honor their vows, and that is not something to take lightly," Colind said.

"The land needs a champion," Aaron quoted. "That is what she told me. What vow do the Eldarin honor?"

"Even on your Earth there must have been those among you who had talents in things that went beyond that of ordinary people. Despite you being raised on another world, your bond with Safanar is strong. I can sense your connection to it, and this is a good thing," Colind said.

Aaron glanced at Sarah, and she took his hand in hers. Safanar had become home to him. He did miss Earth sometimes, and his sister, but his place was here.

"There is a danger in being Ferasdiam marked," Colind

said.

Aaron met Colind's gaze and mentally braced himself. "What danger?"

"Reymius bid me to let you make your own way, and he was right. But if something happens to me, there would be no one left to tell you. Those who bore the mark before came during times of great change. Some were a force for good, and others became as Amorak—drunk on power," Colind said.

"It wasn't always so with him," Sarah said.

"I believe you, my Lady. Tapping into the energy opens ourselves to the knowledge of past souls. This can cause madness in some. We are defined by our actions. It is our actions that carry the weight and bares the measure of us. Too much death and destruction can wither person's soul. I remember when Amorak was much younger and not as he is today. He was seduced by the power of being Ferasdiam marked and views himself almost as a god."

Sarah withdrew her hand from Aaron's. "Worship of the Goddess is outlawed in Khamearra, but the people still do in secret."

"Exactly," Colind said. "The Ferasdiam marked have a special connection to the higher orders, but Aaron, you are quite different. You spent the measure of your life never knowing about any of this. Your dedication to people governing themselves is quite remarkable."

"Darkness can find its way into anyone's soul," Aaron said. When journeying to Safanar he had been on the path of vengeance, and it nearly sucked the life out of him to a fate worse than death.

"I knew you would understand, but there is more. The more powerful you become, the more tenuous your connection to who you are becomes," Colind said.

Aaron frowned. "Are you saying I will become like the High King?"

"It's not outside the realm of possibilities. The Eldarin are creatures of two worlds with a foothold in this realm and one beyond. They become pure energy and transcend these planes, ascending to the higher orders," Colind said.

Aaron studied Colind's face, trying to glean the meaning behind his words. "Are you saying that I can do the same?"

Colind slowly nodded. "Except that the Eldarin return to heed your call. If you were to transcend you may not return, ever."

Sarah's eyes darted to his. "I would never leave," Aaron said.

"Love keeps you here. What would you do if you lost each other?" Colind asked.

An icy weight shifted in Aaron's stomach. "Anyone who has ever loved fears the loss of a loved one. I've lost those dear to me, and while I mourn that loss each day, it doesn't define me. I won't become like the High King."

"That is good to hear," Colind said.

It wasn't beyond the realm of possibilities that Aaron could become like the High King, so he could understand Colind's concern. He didn't like killing. He killed because there was no other choice, but even those deaths weighed heavily on him at times. Colind left them, and he was once again alone with Sarah.

"Queen?" Aaron asked.

The question caught her off guard. "Of all the things that's been said, you latch onto that."

Aaron grinned. "Well it popped in there, my Queen."

Sarah punched him in the arm. "I have as much desire to be queen as you do being king. I do worry about you. You fight with honor. My father won't, and neither will Halcylon."

"We can't fight if we don't have hope. I won't become like them," Aaron said.

"Do you think that they didn't believe the same thing or something similar at one time or another?" Sarah asked.

"This is a burden shared by anyone, whether they are king or queen or just your everyday average person."

"You're right, this is a burden shared by all. Desperation has a way of sapping the souls of men, and once you make a compromise on one thing the next becomes easier, until one day you find yourself doing despicable things you never would have thought you would be doing. That is what

Colind is trying to warn you about, my love."

Aaron nodded. "I understand. That's why it's important for you to keep me in line. No, seriously, we all look out for each other. What Verona and the others did so they could be sure that I was really me and not some impostor was right on."

They came to the tower where a small airship waited to take them back to the FNA camp. Sarah stopped just before the gangplank and glanced back at him, then looked from the ship to the city beyond. She tilted her head to the side and smiled at him. Aaron smiled back and gasped as she jumped away from the tower, streaking away from him in a blur. *It's like the forest all over again,* Aaron thought and launched into the air, racing to catch up with her. They raced along the rooftops of Rexel as only they could.

CHAPTER 19
ONE LAST LESSON

Aaron met up with Verona to see the group of FNA soldiers that Colind had sent him. The training area was only half-filled, as many were helping Rexel prepare for attack. Some groups were evacuating those who couldn't fight to Shandara. Many of the local Rexellians chose to stay and defend their homes. Most of those going to Shandara were children with their mothers and older people who offered to look after the families of those staying behind. What was hard to see were the young boys barley more than teenagers, too old to go with the younger children, but not old enough to fight. Finding them jobs that kept them out of harm's way was proving to be difficult.

What had come to be known as the training area was comprised of various fields of previously unused land outside the city of Rexel. The soldiers of the FNA all went through basic field training where they were evaluated on their skills with common weapons, particularly the knife and staff. They were called upon to navigate a five-mile track that ran through the forest that held challenges of its own. After their basic training, they were divided into various groups with some being taught how to use Hythariam weapons and technology. During all of this, they were called upon to work at whatever task was required for keeping the camp operating.

Sarah had left them a few moments before, saying she would be back soon.

"We caught sight of you two from the airship. I was sorry I couldn't join you," Verona said.

"It was spur of the moment. The airship's pilot nearly jumped out of his skin when he saw Sarah leap off the gangplank," Aaron grinned.

Verona looked at him for a moment, then clamped his hand on Aaron's shoulder. "It's good to have you back, my friend. I'm glad you're able to take a look these men."

"It was a close thing for all of us. I keep thinking that the spy had unfettered access to all of you and well...things could have been a lot different," Aaron said.

Verona nodded. "Sarah never believed. Somehow she knew it wasn't you. I'm sorry to say that I thought it was some effect of her being influenced by the Drake."

"I could see why you would think that," Aaron said, suppressing a shiver at the image of Sarah attacking him.

Her blue eyes glowing yellow like the Drake's. "All of you came together in the end, and that's what's important."

"She blames herself for giving the Falcons to the clone," Verona said.

Aaron nodded and felt the loss of his swords more than he was willing to show. "What choice did she have?"

They were silent as they walked on, and Aaron glanced at the skies above Rexel. "There are a lot of airships now."

"They've been working almost around the clock on them, but there have been much more in the air lately since Lorric," Verona said.

"What do you mean?"

"Our Hythariam friends have been frantically searching for the Zekara but are unable to find them. They revealed themselves at Lorric, but have since gone quiet."

Aaron nodded.

"Will you be able to face the High King without your swords?" Verona asked.

"I won't lie to you, I would feel a lot better facing him with them than without them, but they're lost. At least for now. I still have this," Aaron said lifting the rune-carved staff.

"Oh, that reminds me," Verona said digging into his pack. "Tanneth asked me to give these to you," Verona said, handing him two small curved axes.

"Thanks," Aaron said.

"Two of them in case you miss with the first one. Isn't that what Tolvar's son said?"

"Yeah," Aaron said. "We could sure use his help."

"We can use all the help we can get," Verona grinned.

"Sarah told me that you've come a long a way in being able to tap into the energy," Aaron said.

"She did, did she? Why do I feel like there is a target painted on my back?" Verona laughed nervously.

"I recall you and Sarik getting a good laugh when I first tried to jump on the deck of the Raven," Aaron said.

Verona shook his head. "I knew that someday you would make me pay for that."

"Yup," Aaron said, coming to a halt.

"Really, right now?" Verona asked, glancing around.

"You can already do it. You just don't believe you can," Aaron replied.

"That's because I tried, and it didn't work out so well," Verona said.

"When Sarah was first trying to show me how, I was too focused on the actual act. What you need to focus on is where you're jumping to. Look at that tree branch right up there," Aaron said.

Verona grimaced. "So high up?"

Aaron leaped up to a thick limb about thirty feet from the ground and turned to face his friend. "Your turn." He watched as Verona focused and could sense the energy being drawn into his friend. Verona squatted, pushed up, rose a few feet into the air, and then landed. After a few more attempts, Aaron could see the frustration setting in and leaped back down.

"Close your eyes," Aaron said. "Trust me. Close them. Picture the limb. Build a perfect picture in your mind. Now draw in the energy and feed it into your muscles, but expand to feel it in the air around you." Aaron waited a moment before continuing. "Now I want you imagine yourself jumping to the tree limb. No need to talk." Aaron continued drawing the energy into himself. He could sense it in Verona. The potential was there. "Now imagine Roselyn is up there waiting for you."

"This is stupid," Verona said, but didn't open his eyes.

"No, it's not. The only thing keeping you from reaching that limb is you. Focus, Verona," Aaron said. "Think back to the tower. Everything is riding on you getting to that limb." Aaron felt Verona's lifebeat darken at the mention of the tower, but the energy flared within him. In a burst, Verona launched into the air, passing the tree limb, and the tree for that matter. He crash-landed beyond, and Aaron was at his side in seconds asking if he was okay.

Verona glared at him for a moment, and then his face split into a wide smile. "I just jumped."

"Yes, you did. Landings are a different skill set and will come in time," Aaron snickered and extended his hand, helping his friend up.

"You are having too much fun with this, my friend," Verona said. "But thanks."

Aaron's face grew solemn. "Better here in practice than in a battle with the Elitesmen."

Verona nodded.

"I can't tell you how many trees I crashed into trying to keep up with Sarah," Aaron said.

"Come on, they're right over there, and it looks like we have some company," Verona said.

Aaron glanced at the group of FNA soldiers and saw Sarah standing with them. Two Elitesmen—*former Elitesmen* Aaron corrected himself—were there. They had changed their clothing into the common garb of a soldier, but Aaron could sense their connections to the energy around them. They walked over, and without word, the soldiers of the FNA lined up. The two former Elitesmen joined them.

Isaac appeared, still wearing his dark-leather duster.

"I'll serve, but I'm not wearing a uniform," Isaac said.

"Have you trained anyone before?" Aaron asked.

"Traditionally the Order of the Elite required that senior members be involved with teaching. I know that the Safanarion Order had similar traditions," Isaac answered.

Aaron nodded. "I would appreciate it if you would help us train these men. Colind believes that they have potential."

Isaac's gruff exterior softened as much as his craggy face would allow. "I will do my very best, but what of the others?" asked Isaac, gesturing to the former Elitesmen.

They were close to Aaron's age, and he could tell they didn't like being demoted to a common soldier. Aaron also knew he didn't much care what they liked. "We all need to start somewhere."

Isaac stepped closer and spoke softly. "They joined your cause at great cost to themselves. They are not novices, but highly efficient killing machines."

Aaron shifted his gaze so the two former Elitesmen could hear. "That's the part we need to change. They need to be highly efficient at protecting." Aaron moved to stand directly in front of the former Elitesmen, but he addressed all the men. "Killing is easy. Anyone can kill. Whether with a weapon or with their hands, the act of taking a life is simple and permanent. With the Hythariam weapons it becomes easier still and with less training. Now don't mistake me, I'm not talking about the inner turmoil that comes from killing, even in self-defense. I mean that killing on its most fundamental level, the act of thrusting a knife into your enemy where he is most vulnerable. It is simple and yet at the same time one of the most horrible acts a person can do. Killing changes you, and the more you do it the worse it is.

"The real challenge is keeping those around you alive. Fighting for those who can't fight for themselves is worth a great deal. Teaching others to defend themselves is better still. And creating a world where we're not living by the sword every day is ideal."

"What about your enemies, do they not deserve death?" one of the former Elitesmen asked.

"What's your name?"

"Rohnek, my Lord."

"Sometimes our enemies deserve death. When it comes to survival and it's either you or them is different than using death as a means to remove obstacles in your path," Aaron said.

"But you've killed Elitesmen and many others," Rohnek said.

"They were trying to kill me—" Aaron began.

"Quite a lot of them actually," Verona quipped.

"My point is that killing should be something that is used as a last resort," Aaron continued.

The other former Elitesman raised his hand, and Aaron nodded to him.

"Zedya, my Lord. There is a war. These are soldiers," Zedya said. "There will be death."

"Yes, there will. Too much death, but eventually the war will be over. I've been to Khamearra, and I know the Elitesmen there kill for the slightest offense or to pull innocents into their experiments. We will fight this war because we have no other choice, but one day the war will be over," Aaron said.

Rohnek and Zedya both lowered their eyes. Aaron knew

there were some that relished the power of the Elitesmen Order and then there were those who had to function within its confines to survive.

"My promise to you is not to judge you on what you did to survive. You now wear the uniform of the Free Nations Army and will be judged on the actions and achievements you accomplish from this moment forth. You are part of something, and in time it will become part of you. You all have abilities and talents. You are here because there are some who believe that you have the potential to learn. Some of you already know a great deal. Help your fellow soldiers. There is no one standing here right now who doesn't need help or can't learn something new," Aaron said, walking down the line of men.

"We have a short window of time for training. Some of you will be coming with us on a mission. We'll have more on that later. Right now I'd like to see what you can do. Verona tells me that he and Sarah have already gone over the slow fighting forms. Let's see how well you learned," Aaron said.

The training session must have been rudimentary for the former Elitesmen, but they didn't complain. Their form was perfect, and they carried out whatever he asked them to do with rigid focus. Rohnek and Zedya both wore a mask over their thoughts, and at some points Aaron wondered what they were thinking.

Colind had been right to single out these men. Some had

real potential in their own unique way, but what was common among them was a strong sense of self. Something they would need if they were ever successful in tapping the energy around them. More than once he wanted to have the Falcons with him and wield them into the bladesong of awakening.

After an hour, they dismissed all but ten of the men, which included Rohnek and Zedya. They needed their help for what they were about to do. Aaron planned to keep a close eye on them and had to trust whatever vetting process Isaac had used to allow them into the Resistance.

Sarik came at a run across the yard and met them.

"Tanneth is waiting for us on the east field," Sarik said.

They met up with the Hythariam who was working among three long tables inside a tent. The young Hythariam had his fine white hair tied back and tucked into his shirt. He wore dark gloves, and next to him were a pile of octagonal containers several inches across. There were several basins that were filled with dark powders and one that contained a powder that shimmered in the light.

"Is that powder from the yellow crystals used to power the airships?" Aaron asked.

Tanneth nodded. "The black and red powders are used to ignite the charged tiny crystallized dust for a truly powerful explosion. One of these can take out this whole area."

"Is it safe for us to be standing here?" Isaac asked.

310 | AMIDST THE RISING SHADOWS

"It is if you don't sneeze," Braden said, coming from behind the crates stacked on the other side of the tent.

"Warden," Isaac greeted.

"They are safe enough to handle when I've got them inside these canisters. The outer walls are meant to break apart in a wide arc that will shred anything close by. The metal used is something we have that is highly resistant to heat, which is why they don't simply burn up during the explosion," Tanneth said.

"They are so small. How much damage can they really do?" Sarik asked.

"I planted enough of these on the structural supports of one of the Citadel towers and brought it down," Tanneth said.

"I can attest to that as I was on top of the tower when it collapsed," Aaron said. "How many do we have?"

"This is the final batch. I have three crates we can take with us," Tanneth said and picked up one of the octagonal balls. He rotated it to show a small panel. "This is the timer, which I recommend setting after these have been put in place." Tanneth started closing the canisters, and he and Braden stowed them away.

Isaac's bushy gray eyebrows raised as he looked at Aaron. "What do you plan to do with these?"

"We're going to set these around the High King's camp in Khamearra," Aaron replied.

"My Queen, there are those who would be loyal to you there," Isaac said.

Aaron's eyes darted to Sarah, who seemed to go cold in an instant; he knew this wasn't easy for her.

"There are more loyal to my father, and these same soldiers have already been attacking other kingdoms. We cannot halt our actions on the chance that they may support my claim to Khamearra's throne," Sarah said.

Isaac considered this for a moment and nodded.

Tanneth cleared his throat, getting their attention. "We'll be placing the explosives throughout the camp," Tanneth said and brought up an aerial map of the camps outside of the city of Khamearra.

The FNA soldiers had long gotten used to Hythariam technology, but it was interesting to see the reaction from the former Elitesmen who all looked stunned at the display. Aaron watched the flash of recognition as they identified the landmarks unique to Khamearra, including the High King's palace and Citadel of the Elite.

"How is this possible?" Rohnek asked.

Tanneth took a minute to explain how they had machines in the sky that recorded the images. He then entered a few commands into the holographic interface, moving the massive aerial photograph across the viewing area. "These targets in red are our high-priority targets. The ones deemed to have the most impact are also the riskiest of places for us to plant these bombs. These other locations highlighted in yellow and green have a lower priority, but we feel it will get the message across."

Rohnek frowned at the display. "Those marked in red are the command tents for the Khamearrian army, and those others are where lesser officers gather. You're not hitting the common soldier areas at all."

"That's right," Aaron said. "We're attacking their leadership."

"The plan is for us to enter the camp at these locations over here," Tanneth said gesturing on one side of the map. "We make our way through. Plant the bombs and regroup over here," he finished, pointing to another part of the map.

"They're not going to just let you walk through the camp. What's your plan for that?" Isaac asked.

"In those crates over there are Khamearrian army uniforms. We'll wear them and should be able to make our way through the camp with little difficulty," Tanneth said.

Rohnek and Zedya exchanged glances, and Aaron nodded for them to speak.

"They don't let common soldiers up near the areas you have marked without going through checkpoints," Rohnek said.

Tanneth shared a glance with Aaron and nodded. Tanneth had already known about the checkpoints, but was testing the former Elitesmen's loyalties.

"It's a good thing we have two former Elitesmen who have the authority to get us through," Aaron said.

Rohnek glanced at Aaron, considering with the slow realization that he had just been tested and passed.

"We'll break off into teams," Aaron said. Perhaps they were sincere in wanting to serve Sarah. "Rohnek and Zedya, one of you will be with either Sarah or myself. Isaac, you will go with Sarah." Aaron continued giving the team assignments that they had agreed upon earlier. The part that he didn't like was not having Sarah at his side. It wasn't the former Elitesmen that bothered him...well not too much anyway, it was there was the potential for something to go wrong. Since his last trip into Khamearra had resulted in four of them getting captured, he didn't want to take any chances. They were stronger now and better prepared for the Elitesmen, but still anyone could be overwhelmed.

"When do we leave?" Isaac asked.

"As soon as we can get changed," Aaron answered.

Tanneth approached him while the others were changing into the Khamearrian uniforms. "I had this made for you," he said, handing him a sword. "It's well made and should serve you well until you get the Falcons back."

"Thank you," Aaron said. The sword had a slight curve and single edge. The handle was long enough for both his hands to fit. The style of blade was close to what Sarah carried. He pulled it out of its sheath and tested the balance.

Tanneth was right—it was a remarkably well-made sword. Aaron thanked him again, and Sarah looked away from him.

Aaron came to her side. "It's not your fault."

"Yes, it is. I should have kept them. They've been in your family for generations, and now they're gone."

"We'll get them back. I truly believe that."

"But we don't know where he went," Sarah said, letting out a frustrated sigh.

Aaron gently caressed her shoulder. "I've been giving this a lot of thought. Either he went back to Halcylon, or he's been captured by your father's army. There wasn't a trace of him left in Lorric, or we would have found him. If he's with you father, then there is a good chance I will get the Falcons back again. The same goes for Halcylon."

"How do you know that either of them won't just melt them down?" Sarah asked.

"Oh, you can't," Tanneth said, who had been listening. "The Falcons aren't made of ordinary steel. It's some type of foreign metallic alloy that we've never come across. I looked into it when you first fought the Drake. No ordinary sword would be able to cut through our armor. Not that the Falcons with the holes cut into the blades could be ordinary, but still quite interesting."

"I never thought about it before. My grandfather left them to me, but I don't know much about their origins. Would you be able to recreate them?" Aaron asked.

Tanneth's gaze drew downward as he shook his head. "I tried at Hathenwood, and while the blades appear to be like your swords, they weren't quite right. When I tried to add the holes into the each blade, they lost too much of their integrity to do you much good in a real fight."

Aaron nodded, hiding his disappointment, but wasn't completely surprised. "I appreciate you trying."

He still had the rune-carved staff, which was leaning against the side wall of the tent. Aaron went to retrieve it, and as his hands grasped the staff, he felt a deep pull from the pit of his stomach.

"Are you okay?" Sarah asked.

Aaron shook his head to clear it. "Yeah, I just had a strange feeling."

"What about?"

"I'm worried about the Eldarin. One of them became infected with the Ryakul poison. I don't plan on calling on them anytime soon, but then again I didn't plan on calling on them that last two times either," Aaron took a moment, thinking about what he wanted to say. "They healed me, Sarah. Took the Nanites from my system and reversed what Halcylon had done to my body. The Dragons and the Eldarin are going to be pulled into this again, and I'm afraid that we'll see an end to them all because of it."

"They chose to honor you, my love. You are Ferasdiam marked and her champion. If they come to your aid, they do

316 | AMIDST THE RISING SHADOWS

so by their own intent," Sarah said.

"Ferasdiam marked," Aaron said. "I'm the possibility of what anyone can achieve."

Sarah shook her head. "What will it take before you accept that the things you do is what puts you beyond ordinary men? It's your heart that makes you great. Not the power that you're capable of. You affect all those around you. They look to you and give better of themselves. They follow you, not because you're Ferasdiam marked or the last scion of the Alenzar'seth line. They follow you because you light the way for us to have something more than we've ever had before. The Eldarin had it right, my love. *Yours is a light meant to shine.* And if they sacrifice themselves so that we might survive these times of trial then we should honor their sacrifice by remaining true and become something greater than we are today."

Aaron lost himself in her eyes. "You heard them?"

Sarah nodded.

Hearing her speak the Eldarin's words ignited their voice deep within. There must be a way that he could help them.

Verona came quietly to his side. "It's time to go."

Tanneth had them gather on one side of the tent. He brought out two metallic cylinders about a foot in length and handed one to Aaron. Aaron glanced at the Keystone Accelerator and gave it to Sarah, who looked at him questioningly.

"I'm not leaving without you. So you hold onto it," Aaron said.

Tanneth opened a portal, and Sarah led her group through.

"Braden and Sarik will be with her," Verona said.

Aaron nodded, "Let's go hit them for a change."

The soldiers of the FNA grinned hungrily, and Rohnek gave Aaron a firm nod. Tanneth opened another portal and handed the spent Keystone Accelerator to the soldier remaining behind. Aaron stepped through the portal with the others following closely on his heels.

CHAPTER 20
TRAP

Khamearra had become a place where its citizens were required to contribute to the High King's war. There were still pockets of those who left messages urging the return of the Faergrace line, and Rordan wondered how his perfect sister felt about that. He hadn't seen or heard from her since she openly defied their father, who had attributed her display as being under the influence of the Alenzar'seth. Rordan knew better; no one told Sarah what to do. He knew his father didn't really believe it either, and was using Sarah's open defiance as a means to get what he wanted. He had been watching his father closely, and for him it was a matter of pride and possession. His father yearned for the heads of his enemies, especially the Heir of Shandara; too many times the man had slipped through their fingers. He suspected that his father welcomed the challenge, as no one since the fall of Shandara had dared oppose Amorak. Not since Reymius Alenzar'seth, and the fact that his grandson had returned to Safanar did appear to have awoken something in his father.

Rordan finished strapping on his light armor, the same that the Elitesmen would be wearing, choosing to rely on their powers rather than be weighed down by heavy armor. He engaged the travel crystal and emerged on the fields outside the city. Khamearra's army was mobilizing, preparing to execute his father's plan and end the insurrection in the Waylands and in Shandara before they could fester any further. Rordan nodded to the guards and stepped into the command tent.

"Have you tied up the loose ends?" the High King asked.

"There weren't that many to begin with," Elite Grand Master Gerric answered. "The ones we could find have been dealt with. The bulk of the Order have been preparing for the attack."

"That's something at least," the High King said and lifted up two sheathed swords and put them on the table.

"Are those the Alenzar'seth's swords?" Gerric asked, unable to tear his eyes from them.

"Yes, they are. One of my favorite trophies," Amorak said.

"Your Grace, these blades are legendary," Elite Grand Master Gerric said.

The High King glanced at him. "I'll make them a gift to you after the campaign."

"You honor me, your Grace."

"Rordan, I see you're ready," the High King said. "You will be with the Elitesmen."

Rordan nodded. "What of Zsensibar?"

"I've sent word that their offer was accepted," the High King said.

Rordan frowned. "That's it? You accept their offer?"

"Absolutely. I don't trust King Nasim in the slightest, and I will deal with our friends to the south after we crush the Waylands and their Free Nations Army. Zsensibar is quite fond of its slave practices so let's see how the entire kingdom copes with being slaves," the High King said.

"Father," Rordan said, "after we conquer the Waylands, won't our troops be too preoccupied with holding Rexel to be able to fight a war in Zsensibar?"

His father turned to face him, his cold gaze could crack the heart of a stone. "I don't plan to occupy the Waylands, Son. I plan to burn it to the ground. When we're finished there, no other kingdom will dare oppose us."

Rordan nodded and was about to say something else when his father knocked him to the ground. In a flash of light, they emerged some distance away from the command tent. Plumes of orange blossomed throughout the camp, and soldiers closest to them collapsed, clutching bleeding wounds that appeared to come out of nowhere.

Rordan sprang to his feet, his sword drawn, and drew the

energy into himself. Elite Grand Master Gerric was nowhere to be found.

"Stay with me," his father said.

Soldiers raced around, trying to keep the fires from spreading. There was nothing but scorched earth near the tent they had been in. The blast actually came from several tents over.

"Could it have been one of the crystals?" Rordan asked.

Soldiers recognizing their king and heir gathered around them, grim faced and weapons drawn.

"This was no mishandled crystal," the High King spat.

The armies had already been gathering to prepare their attack, and the forces remaining with the tents were scheduled to follow soon after.

"Sweep the area. I want them found!" the High King bellowed.

Rordan watched as his father closed his eyes for a moment and he felt the waves of energy coming from him in staggering proportions. Elite Grand Master Gerric stumbled over to them. He had a trickle of blood running down his neck from a shallow wound behind his ear. Khoiron came up the hill, leading a company of soldiers with some breaking off to methodically search the area in teams.

The High King opened his eyes and called for a report from the general.

"This was a coward's attack. Explosions have been set off

throughout the upper and lower camps. I don't have a confirmed number, but marking where the smoke is rising, they looked to have targeted us pretty well." Khoiron said.

"Which means we have spies among us," the High King said.

Rordan noticed an Elitesmen walking along the next row of tents leading a group of soldiers.

"Elitesman," Rordan called as he came to the other line of tents.

The Elitesman stopped and turned around, but the group of soldiers kept going.

"Your Grace," he said and bowed his head.

"Do you know if the other camps have been attacked?" Rordan asked.

"Apologies, your Grace, but I don't know," the Elitesman said, glancing up at the group of soldiers.

Rordan nodded for him to carry on and returned to his father.

"The attack goes as planned—"

"Shouldn't we assess the damage before moving on with the attack?" Rordan asked, looking to Khoiron for support.

"I would advise patience, your Grace," Khoiron said.

"This cowardly act is an attempt to put us off balance, and it will not work. We leave now," the High King said.

Rordan took one last glance at the city behind him and left to join the Elitesmen.

***

"We're overdue as it is. Who was that?" Verona asked.

"That was Prince Rordan," Rohnek answered. "He didn't suspect anything, but I thought we had more time on the timer."

Verona shrugged his shoulders. "Let's catch up to the others. Their armies are assembling, which means they are about to attack."

Aaron looked up as Verona and Rohnek caught up to them. Making their way through the camp had been easier than they originally expected, but they could not have made their way to the command tents without the former Elitesmen. Elitesmen authority was unquestioned in Khamearra. He kept glancing at the massing army, knowing there were other camps just like this fed the growing fear that they simply didn't have enough soldiers. Verona relayed their brief meeting with Rordan, and Aaron's gaze fixed upon where they had come from, knowing that the High King wouldn't be far from his only living son.

"This isn't the time," Sarah said. "He's too strong here. When you face him it must be with an army at your back."

Aaron frowned. "If we could take out the focusing crystals we could gain more time. Time enough to prepare--"

"They are too well guarded, my love."

"Not for me they're not," Aaron said, clenching his teeth. Then he whispered, "So many people are going to die,

Sarah. If I could prevent that I would."

Sarah reached out, taking his hand in her own. "I know you would, and more importantly everyone else serving in the Free Nations Army knows it too. It's why they will fight."

Aaron nodded, saying nothing, but in his mind he was still judging the distance to where he suspected the High King was, but when he looked up they were gone.

"It's time," Tanneth said quietly. He engaged the Keystone Accelerator and opened a portal back to Rexel.

They filed through the portal. Rohnek paused in front for a moment, tilting his head. He spun around, drawing his sword, and raced past Verona. At first it appeared as if he was swinging his sword at the empty air, but then Aaron heard the kiss of steel on steel.

"Keep going," Aaron shouted and dashed ahead to catch up.

"You betray us, brother," an Elitesman said, releasing his shroud that had kept them from seeing them.

"You betray yourselves," Rohnek said, lashing out with his sword maneuvering around the two Elitesmen.

"The penalty for treason against the Order is death, and you will die alone," the Elitesman said.

Aaron brought his staff down, and the Elitesman crumpled to the ground. Rohnek took advantage of the distraction to sweep the other Elitesman off his feet, but paused with his sword at his throat.

The Elitesman on the ground cursed. "Mercy is for the weak, brother, and you will find none here." The Elitesmen tried to roll away, but Rohnek's blade bit into his neck.

"They won't change," Rohnek said, cleaning the blood off his blade.

"Some of them won't," Aaron agreed. "But some will."

The camp around them plunged into silence, and Aaron felt the faint stirring of energy crawl along his skin. There was a massive bubble of energy growing near the center of the High King's army. The flaring brilliance stretched out, engulfing everything in its path. Tanneth shouted for them to hurry, that the portal wouldn't stay open. The rest of them went through the portal until only Tanneth and Aaron remained.

This is it, Aaron thought to himself. They stepped through the portal and emerged upon the quiet fields of the FNA camps outside of Rexel. Aaron scanned the horizon, expecting the High King's army to appear at any moment. The sky was full of airships hovering along the borders of the city and FNA camps alike. The others glanced around at the sky for a moment, and then Verona tore off his Khamearrian soldier's uniform.

"Don't want to be mistaken for the enemy now, do we?" Verona grinned as he put his regular clothes back on from his pack.

They all quickly changed their clothing, and the comms devices began chiming at once. Tanneth answered.

"The High King's army is attacking," Iranus said.

"We're in Rexel, and the army isn't here," Aaron replied.

"Not there. They are in Shandara."

Aaron felt his gut clench as if he had been kicked. They had sent the women and children along with those who couldn't fight to Shandara, believing that the High King would focus on Rexel.

"Roselyn is in Shandara," Verona gasped.

"We're going," Aaron said.

"We can't use the Accelerator until it charges," Tanneth said.

"We can use the crystals," Sarah said and tossed one to Aaron.

Aaron caught it. "Tanneth, you and Sarik head back. We need you in the flyers." He almost said in case the Zekara chose this moment to show themselves, but they had enough to deal with without worrying about the whether Halcylon would attack or not.

Tanneth withdrew two rods from his pack and handed one to Sarik. Two foot pads opened up at the ends, and they stepped on. Within a moment they rose into the air and were racing to the field where the flyers were kept.

Those who remained closed in around Aaron and Sarah, each putting a hand upon the shoulder of the person in front of them until they were all linked. The FNA would be sending soldiers to Shandara at any moment. With a nod to Sarah, they engaged the travel crystals, and the group disappeared.

They emerged in Shandara in the Dragon Hall. The sun was shining, casting its warm glow upon the city. Aaron hadn't been to Shandara since he had brought down the barrier between Safanar to Hytharia. Then the city had been a place of twilight, where the deathly shadows held the land by the throat. It had been months since he had been here, and without the Drake and the Ryakul around, the land was slowly starting to heal.

They raced through the city amid the soldiers heading toward Shandara's walls. Aaron drew in the energy, launched himself into the air, and landed atop of a taller building. He was followed by Sarah and Verona. The former Elitesmen crested the top with ease. Braden came last, pulling himself over the edge. Aaron was relieved to see the gaping holes in Shandara's pristine walls had been repaired.

"They've been fortifying the city since you've been gone," Sarah said.

"That's good. At least now we know we have a chance," Aaron said.

Battle drums could be heard in the distance. Aaron glanced at the others and launched into the air, speeding toward the walls. The others followed as best they could, and only

Sarah was able to keep up with him. Aaron reached back, sensing the energy in the others and urged more speed from them. Verona immediately started to break away from the others, quickly followed by Braden. Rohnek and Zedya remained closed off to him. They crested the walls, seeing groups of FNA soldiers spread out. Some of the FNA carried Hythariam weapons and were spaced out among those armed with bows. Nearest them was a group of Hythariam clustered around a large mounted gun. Aaron scanned along the walls and saw others spaced out along the massive walls of Shandara.

"We found them and other weapons hidden throughout the city," Verona said.

"And they work?" Aaron asked.

"We're about to find out, my friend."

Sarah turned toward them. "Iranus was trying to clear a path to the command center, but it has been buried in an area of the city still under rubble. He said they needed you in particular to open it for them."

Aaron nodded and stepped closer to the edge to get a better look at the Khamearrian Army spread out. They were just out of bow range, but Aaron was certain they weren't out of range of the Hythariam weapons. The Khamearrian line stretched far, and Aaron couldn't begin to guess at how many soldiers were out there. There was little movement, and the soldiers appeared smallish from their vantage point.

Aaron narrowed his gaze, scanning down below. "I don't see any Elitesmen."

Sarah frowned, her eyes darting back and forth, searching. A bright light flickered behind them from the streets below. A portal opened, and more soldiers of the Free Nations Army poured through. Aaron noticed similar portals being opened throughout the city below. Squad captains spread the word to hold their fire until the High King's army advanced.

A seed of doubt took root in Aaron's gut. Everything about this felt wrong. He scanned the sky, searching for any sign of Ryakuls, but there was none.

"This is a trap," Aaron said.

"What do you mean?" Sarah asked.

"How else do you explain the lack of Elitesmen presence and no Ryakuls? Prior to Lorric, all of the High King's attacks included the Elitesmen, which were instrumental in taking the smaller kingdoms. Yet here the Khamearrian Army stands, and they do nothing. It's like they're waiting for something."

Aaron brought his comms device. "Gavril, I think this is a trap. The High King wants us to divide our forces. Stop sending soldiers to Shandara."

"How can you be sure?" Gavril asked.

"The army here is just waiting, and there appears to be no Elitesmen in sight. What would the High King hope to gain by attacking Shandara? Even if he had to guess he would know that the bulk of the FNA is in Rexel..." Aaron's eyes widened. "They're coming for you at Rexel."

The comms device went silent. Aaron called Gavril's name, but no reply came. Aaron let out a frustrated breath, his mind racing. Verona tried using his comms device.

"Captain," Aaron called. The FNA captain came over to them. "I want you to start shooting at the High King's army."

The captain frowned. "We have orders to hold fire unless they start attacking."

"This is a diversionary force sent here to draw us out of Rexel. Right now they are out of bow range, but my guess is that they don't realize that you can still get to them," Aaron said.

The captain's eyes widened. "But with our forces divided... I will give the order," he said and left.

"What do we do?" Verona asked.

Aaron glanced at the city behind them and then back to beyond the walls. The FNA armed with Hythariam weapons fired on the High King's army. Screams echoed from down below, and the soldiers scattered, trying in vain to take cover from the golden bolts.

What could they do? They needed to defend the city, but the High King would bring the bulk of his forces to Rexel. He glanced at Braden, whose cold eyes dared him to ask him to stay behind.

Sarah placed her hand on his arm. "You can't be everywhere, and we are needed elsewhere. Trust that the soldiers here can hold the city. We must go."

Aaron swore and grabbed a clump of his hair on top of his head, despising himself for not being able to stand with the FNA to defend Shandara, but Sarah was right. If the High King committed himself to destroying Rexel and the heart of the Free Nations Army, then that is where he was needed most.

Aaron turned to Braden.

"My place is at your side," Braden said.

"A Warden of the De'anjard defends the helpless."

Braden glared at him, but continued the oath. "Through cunning and strength."

"Stands the watch," Aaron continued.

"Protect that which matters most."

"Honor those of the shield," Aaron said.

"Stand as one...sacrifice for the many," Braden finished.

"The Warden's Oath is meant to guide the De'anjard. Be a shield to these people here. Sarah is right. I can't be everywhere at once. I need you to hold this city. Shandara is more than the Alenzar'seth," Aaron said, holding out his hand.

Braden looked at Aaron's hand before taking it in his own. "I swear to you that I will not let this city fall."

Aaron thanked him, and Rohnek and Zedya stepped up.

"We would like to stay and help," Rohnek said.

"Why?" Aaron asked.

"We renounced the Elitesmen Order to join the Free Nations Army. You said that we should focus on protection. The people behind these city walls, some of which are from Khamearra, need protection," Rohnek said.

Zedya gazed at him intently. "People truly follow you. At first I thought it was through fear, but that is the way of the High King. What you are is different. You make us want to give more. Here in this place, at this time, let us use our skills in a cause worth something more. Let us stand with the Warden of the De'anjard and defend these walls."

Aaron looked at them for a moment and then to Braden, who nodded.

"All right," Aaron said, "good luck."

He brought out the travel crystal, and Sarah did the same. The others closed in, and they left the walls of Shandara behind.

CHAPTER 21
WAR

The alarms blared through the city of Rexel, reaching into the palace. The FNA soldiers raced to their pre-battle-plan assignments. Colind glanced at Cyrus, who already wore his armored plate covering his torso. Full-plate armor had become less practical over the years, and with so many changes sweeping across Safanar, Colind knew the days of hardened metal armor were numbered.

"I knew this day would come," Cyrus said. "As soon as Aaron showed up at the palace, I knew that this battle with the High King would happen."

"Aaron may be the catalyst for this, but you and I both know that this battle would have happened eventually. The High King wouldn't have settled for treaties," Colind answered.

Prince Cyrus watched the feeds come in on the Hythariam's holo displays. Amorak's army had arrived outside Rexel's walls on the west. Rexel's walls were nowhere near the size of Shandara's, but with the Elitesmen the size of the walls didn't matter.

Cyrus called for his guards then turned to Colind. "You didn't think I'd wait out the battle in here did you, old friend?"

Colind shook his head and followed Cyrus out to the waiting transport that hovered just outside. Garret met them at the small airship, which heaved upward after they were onboard. The skies over Rexel were littered with airships patrolling. Some were still in hiding and waited for the orders to provide support where they were needed. The soldiers with them were armed with swords and Hythariam pistols, putting to use the number of weapons found in Shandara. The shields of Shandara were in short supply, but at least they had more than just the two that been found by Aaron's companions.

"I know you'd rather be hunting Mactar," Cyrus said.

"My place is here doing what I can to help defend the city, and I have no doubts that he will present himself here today," Colind said.

The prince eyed him for a moment. "You should stop blaming yourself for Tarimus's choices."

Colind pressed his lips together. "I can't absolve myself of my son's failings. Who else can his failings fall to if not his father? I keep thinking that perhaps if I had done things differently..."

"Tarimus was always power hungry; even as a child the potential was there. And he paid the price for it. The past...whatever else it is, my friend, is gone. We still need you."

"I have given everything I have for the Safanarion Order, and I understand what you're saying, but I blame *him*. Goddess how I blame that man," Colind said, balling his hands into fists, feeling the blood rush to his chest. He yearned for Mactar's blood and as much as his wrath focused on him, deep inside he still blamed himself for Tarimus. His son of all people should not have been pulled into Mactar's web. *I should have protected him better. Why couldn't Tarimus have been stronger? Why didn't he come to me?* Colind drew the energy into himself on instinct and glared to the west where the High King's army waited.

Why couldn't I have listened better?

Mactar would pay. He could do that much at least. There would be no rest for him until one of them was dead.

Cyrus ordered the pilot to take them higher into the air to get a better vantage point of the battle below. Bright flashes belched from the muzzles of the Hythariam weapons, pouring their destruction into Khamearra's line. There was fighting on the walls as Elitesmen utilized the travel crystals to their advantage. The tactic worked well against the other kingdoms, but the Free Nations Army had been preparing for this type of assault and had designed the posts on the wall to also function as defensible positions. This slowed the Elitesmen down but didn't stop them completely. They needed Aaron. Full-sized airships roared by with their engines at full blast, dropping a lethal mixture of crystallized dust that exploded on impact. Attack orbs from the Elitesmen upon the ground raced up, tearing into the airships as they went by.

The High King's army swallowed up the land beyond Rexel's western walls in a great shadow. Siege towers made their slow progress toward the walls. Cyrus ordered the pilot to take them to what the Hythariam referred to as the operations base, where they could coordinate the battle.

"Be safe, my friend," Colind said after they touched down.

"Where are you going?" Prince Cyrus asked.

"To where I'm needed. The wall," Colind replied.

Garret stayed at his side as they ran with the soldiers heading toward the front line. Garret pulled him to the side as a portal opened on the street before them and out came Verona leading a group of FNA soldiers. Aaron and Sarah soon followed, and the portal closed behind them. Sounds of the battle rocked the walls in the distance, drawing their attention, and Colind noticed Aaron glance at the skies.

"Not yet. They haven't brought the Ryakuls in yet," Colind said.

Aaron nodded. "It's only a matter of time."

Isaac, the former Elitesman came to join them, wearing his dark-leather duster over his FNA uniform. He led eighteen other Elitesmen that had pledged their loyalty to Sarah.

"My Queen," Isaac said, bringing his fist over his heart.

"The Elitesmen are attacking the walls," Colind said.

Sarah nodded and looked at Isaac. "Have your men go and help hold the walls."

Isaac motioned the men ahead, and all but four left them. "We will stay to help you with whatever it is you are planning."

Aaron glanced at Colind. "Has Zsensibar's army returned yet?"

Colind shook his head as a new barrage of alarms raced through the city.

"Aaron," Iranus said over the comms device. "The High King attacks with another army on the eastern side of the city, beyond the FNA camp. They're unprotected there. The army appeared out of nowhere."

All attacks had been assumed to come from the western side, and the High King had obliged their assumptions.

"We need King Nasim to bring his men up behind them. We'll head over there now," Aaron said and closed the comms device.

"Shandara?" Colind asked.

"A smaller army attacks there, but it seems as if the bulk of Khamearra's forces are here. They mean to overwhelm us.

Braden stayed behind to help defend Shandara from attack," Aaron said.

"Good. That's really good. He will do well I think," Colind said.

Aaron nodded and frowned. "The High King learns fast. He brought a portion of his army to Shandara first, knowing that we would send some of our number to defend the city. And now here he has divided his forces again."

"He seeks to put us off balance," Colind said.

"I believe it's working," Verona said.

Aaron glanced at Sarah, knowing that she intended to stay at his side.

"I'm with you," Sarah said.

Aaron drew in the energy, and the runes on his staff glowed. He extended tendrils of energy to the others around him, strengthening their own connections. The others around him gasped, including the former Elitesmen.

"Ferasdiam marked," Isaac whispered and with his thumb and forefinger made a small circle upon his brow, marking the sign of the Goddess.

"Today we fight as one," Aaron said.

He came to Colind, saw the blazing orange of his lifebeat, and sensed a deep hollowness. Aaron's eyes widened, but before he could say anything to Colind, a plume of smoke rose in the distance. A faint shimmer rippled through the ground at his feet. Aaron launched himself into the air, and the others followed, moving at speeds blurring them from vision. They raced onward, and miles slipped by as they closed in on the FNA camp. Shafts of light burned from different points along the Khamearrian line, wreaking havoc in the camp. Anyone caught in the beam was cut down almost instantly.

"Oh Goddess, they're using the energy from the focusing crystals," Sarah gasped.

The focusing crystals were housed in small armored domes mounted on wheels. A team of Khamearrian soldiers maneuvered the domes before firing. The FNA were focusing their own fire in waves of crystal-tipped arrows upon the Khamearrian line. For each group of men that fell, more took their place.

Aaron streaked ahead of the others, pulling a torrent of energy through the rune-carved staff. He moved so quickly that he was atop an armored dome before the soldiers could react. Aaron slammed down the staff, releasing the pent-up energy. The crystal inside cracked, and Aaron leaped off just before an explosion demolished the dome into a malformed husk. The soldiers around him attacked, and his staff whirled through the air, beating them back. Each blow sent men back, and the Elitesmen converged on his location, oozing through the ranks of fleeing soldiers.

Aaron dodged the Elitesmen attack orbs and for a fleeting moment wished he had his swords to block their attacks. He closed in on them and brought the fight in closer. Sarah and the others joined in, and more Elitesmen fell until their attackers stepped back looking uncertain at those who came to Aaron's side.

"You betray the Order," one Elitesman said.

"We serve our Queen, the rightful ruler of Khamearra," Isaac answered.

The Elitesman's cold eyes narrowed. A wave of shadows rose in the sky overhead amid the screeching roars of the Ryakuls.

"Then you've chosen death," hissed the Elitesman.

Isaac's sword flashed, and the Elitesman was dead before he realized that Isaac had moved. The FNA regrouped and pushed forward, throwing themselves at the High King's army.

Aaron's gaze drew to the Ryakuls, and a red cloud blossomed around his vision. The Ryakuls were shadows of their former selves. Dragons fallen from grace with death as their only release. He hadn't seen this many Ryakuls in one place since the Drake commanded them, but the Drake was gone. The sky was full, and the Ryakuls spread out, slicing into the FNA with some breaking off to head toward the city.

"Mactar," Colind hissed.

"He's controlling the Ryakuls? If we take him out then they will scatter," Aaron said.

"Excellent, then maybe they will attack the High King's army as well," Verona said.

Aaron nodded and saw another focusing crystal down the line. "I have an idea."

They closed the distance in seconds, but instead of destroying the contraption, Aaron took out the men around it, and the others followed his lead. Aaron studied the different levers, and after a bit of experimentation, figured out the ones to maneuver the dome. He aimed the focusing crystal into the sky and fired at the approaching line of Ryakuls. The energy blast tore through them easily. The Khamearrians pushed forward, eager to take back their asset, but the others fought around him, giving him time to shoot. FNA soldiers caught up to them and began establishing a perimeter. Aaron motioned for one of the soldiers to take over.

The Free Nations Army clustered together in pockets, trying to avoid the attacking Ryakuls that threw themselves relentlessly at their lines. The crystal-tipped arrows helped, but at the rate they were using them they would exhaust their supply in no time. The burning roar of airship engines at full blast plunged over the battlefield, firing their payloads into the Ryakuls. The dark beasts swarmed a single ship, tearing it apart, and Aaron saw men fall to their deaths in the distance. Gritting his teeth, Aaron launched into the air, heading directly into the swarm of Ryakuls. The breath caught in his throat as a dark-speckled presence kept pace with him.

"I hunt Mactar," Colind's voice said from the swirling mass, which charged off in another direction. The Ryakuls took no notice of it.

Aaron landed upon the deck of an airship, unleashing the energy from the staff into the Ryakuls that attacked it. The sailors regrouped and reloaded the platforms that held the giant crossbows and fired. For all the Ryakuls' power, their weakest point was the head.

Aaron leaped from the airship, and a dark swath cut deeply into the lines of the Free Nations Army. Bodies of men were tossed in every direction, and their cries were pebbled amid the snarling Ryakuls overhead.

The High King, Aaron thought. He saw the dark figure slice through lines of FNA soldiers, becoming a tornado of death. The soldiers pulled back, fighting with the weapons that seemed all but ineffectual against the High King. A spark of energy lanced across the Dragon tattoo upon Aaron's chest. He landed upon the ground and launched back into the air, heading straight for the High King.

A Hythariam lay on his back, firing his plasma pistol using his Nanite-augmented senses, but he kept missing. A dark blade hissed through the air, but for once it missed its mark, and the Hythariam gained his feet.

The runes flared on Aaron's staff, and the High King's

sword hacked against it, sending sparks into the air. As the High King moved, a trail of darkened shadows followed in his wake. Aaron sensed the tendrils of energy coming from the High King, but instead of strengthening the connection to the energy of those around them, the High King fed from it.

The High King broke off his attack, and the shadows around him faded into the earth. The wailing moans of men dying littered the battlefield around them.

"I've been waiting for you, Shandarian," the High King sneered. "What, no talk of impending doom to strike across the land? No offer of alliances?"

Elitesmen materialized around them and stood waiting. Strapped to the High King's back were the Falcons.

Aaron glanced at the dead FNA soldiers that were sprawled upon the ground and then back at the High King. "You have something that belongs to me," he said.

The High King brought up his sword, a curved blackened blade. "Well, then by all means, take them back. Let's see how well Reymius taught you."

The High King charged, and Aaron sidestepped out of the way on pure instinct alone. The attacks came from all directions, and Aaron moved the staff, blocking the High King. With each blow a small shower of sparks was sent raining to the ground. Silver streaks blurred around the two combatants. A thunderous blow knocked Aaron back, and his body skidded to a halt. A silver-clad Elitesman reached out hungrily for him. Another Elitesman planted his foot, locking the staff to the ground, while another grabbed Aaron by his hair, dragging him up and away. The medallion became as ice against his chest. He let go of the staff and scrambled to bring his feet under him. Aaron clutched the hand that held him and twisted, kicking out with his foot, infusing the crushing blow with energy. The Elitesman cried out and was knocked back. More Elitesmen closed in on him, but Sarah appeared by his side, quickly followed by the others.

"I thought I'd help even things up," Sarah said and engaged the closing Elitesmen.

Aaron sprang to his feet, his eyes locking on the rune-carved staff less than twenty feet from him. The High King kicked the staff away and smirked at him invitingly. An Elitesman charged in front of him, cutting off his view of the High King.

Aaron snatched the curved axe from his belt and hurled it with an energy-enhanced throw. The axe streaked through the air and burst through the Elitesman's chest. Aaron bolted across the fallen Elitesman, avoiding the High King's sword and locking his grip upon the High King's gauntleted wrist. The High King roared, bearing down upon him with all his strength, but Aaron didn't yield. They locked together, two opposing forces matching strength against strength. The

High King spun, and Aaron felt himself lift into the air, but he didn't let go. His feet touched the ground again, and Sarah was there swinging her sword down. The High King shifted at the last moment but caught the tip of her blade on his arm. Aaron kicked the side of his knee, sending the High King off balance. Aaron quickly maneuvered around him, grabbed the hilts to his swords, and tore them from their sheaths on the High King's back.

The Falcons were once again his.

***

Colind flew through the sky, opting to use darker arts to travel through the battlefield. To the untrained eye, he was a dark mist swirling through the air. He had limited time for which to travel this way, lest he not be able to regain his physical form.

The battle raged beneath him. At least they had been better prepared, unlike the firestorm that engulfed Shandara during the fall. He sped along, and while the Ryakuls were focused upon the FNA, he still couldn't locate who was controlling them. Mactar had to be around here somewhere and within view of the battle. Colind sank to the ground and pulled his essence together. He reached out with his senses, following the flow of energy. The battlefield was a wash of clashing forces, but what he sought was much older, and in spite of Mactar being a master manipulator, there were some things that he couldn't hide. Colind bolted for a small hill upon the rise.

Mactar was so focused on the battle before him that he didn't sense Colind's approach until he was almost upon him.

Mactar spun around, his eyes widening. "You never were adept at the dark arts."

Colind pushed his hand out, sending a bolt of energy searing into Mactar, who raised a shield and deflected the bolt.

"You should have wasted away in that prison I left you in," Mactar spat.

"I almost did, but you underestimated *him*. All of you have."

"The Heir of Shandara has proven to be a formidable opponent. Your last hope to rebuild the Safanarion Order," Mactar said.

The two men circled each other.

"If that is his will. Aaron walks his own path. Do the promises of the Zekara still sustain you? Reymius always suspected, but I wasn't sure until the Ryakuls began fighting for the armies of the High King. Then I knew you had somehow harvested the power of the Drake. After all, how else would you know how to repair their technology? That is why you ran from that mountain. Aaron had already defeated the Drake, but you had gotten what you came for and probably would have been gone if it weren't for

Tarimus dogging your every move."

Mactar's eyes narrowed, and his face drew down in a sneer. "Reymius," Mactar hissed, "was a fool to spurn the Zekara, like Daverim before him. They are the true power behind the Hythariam and not the pitiful band that remained holed up in Hathenwood after Shandara burned."

Colind clenched his teeth at the mention of Shandara, and then his lips lifted in a satisfied smile. "Speaking of burning. I returned the favor and found a castle overlooking a small town in northern Khamearra. Sarah was kind enough to share that information with me. Your trophy room was particularly interesting. There isn't much left of it, by the way."

Mactar's face twisted into an evil sneer as he lashed out with an attack orb, and at the same time Colind launched his own attack. Colind was knocked back, and the putrid smell of burnt flesh invaded his nose. Mactar's left arm was a charred wreck where the orb struck.

"What have you done!" Mactar cried out, clutching the remains of his wrist.

Echoes of the Ryakuls' mad shrieks could be heard across the skies of Rexel. Colind turned toward the whispers of the bladesong he heard in the distance. To the east, the sky became washed out in a dazzling display of sunlight reflecting off the majestic hides of Safanar's remaining Dragons.

Mactar's mouth fell open at the sight. Colind pulled a dagger from his belt and plunged it into Mactar's back. The essence of Mactar began to dissolve, and Colind brought his hands up, pulling on the energy around them to keep him from escaping. The dark swarm of Mactar turned and enveloped him in a swirling mass.

"You can't stop me," Mactar's voice hissed.

Colind kept his focus, and the energy flowed freely even as parts of him tore away, but still he held Mactar in check.

"You'll kill us both!" Mactar screamed.

"*I know*," Colind whispered.

***

Sarah spun around, sensing the attack coming from behind. Rordan grinned, dodging her sword thrust and grabbing her arm. Using the travel crystal, he took her to another part of the battlefield.

Sarah lashed out with her blade, knocking the crystal from his grasp and continued to hack away at her half-brother. Rordan broke off his attack and dashed away. He made a show of glancing off to the side, and it was then that Sarah realized she was surrounded. Elitesmen melted into view from the smoky battlefield, circling around them. She steadied her breathing and held her sword at the ready.

"Afraid to face me, Rordan?" she asked, allowing the energy from the earth to seep into her.

Rordan raised his head, tilting it to the side, studying her through the eyes of a stranger. It was gone in a blink, and he shook his head.

Sarah chanced a look at the Elitesmen surrounding her. "I know some of you don't hold with the Order. Some of you have already made your loyalties known. Are there are any among you that will stand with me now?"

Sarah slowly circled around, but she was met with the hardened gazes of men who had long ago lost any semblance of a moral code. *So be it,* Sarah thought and clenched her teeth.

"You're alone, Sister," Rordan hissed, his pale face and sunken blackish eyes regarded her coldly.

Sarah saw the tendrils of energy flowing into Rordan. He seemed to be drawing upon the Elitesmen around him. Feeding off of them. Rordan raised his sword, and darkness swirled from the tip of his blade.

Sarah stepped back, her eyes darting to the bulge nestled upon Rordan's chest. "You fool," she said, her eyes widening in understanding. "Take off the apprentice amulet before it's too late."

Rordan's face lifted into evil sneer, and when he spoke his voice sounded inhumanly deep. "But I've become so much more. The amulet allows me to tap into undreamed of powers."

Sarah cried out, wincing as something burned her from beneath her skin. She focused the energy around her, calling on her training with Verona, and formed a shield. The burning stopped immediately.

Rordan leaped forward, swinging his sword. Sarah sidestepped, knocking his blade to the side. She had fought Rordan before, but this time it was different. He was descending into madness in his lust for power. The apprentice amulet that the Elitesmen used to unlock the powers and knowledge from souls past had opened a door to something else. Braden had sensed it when they were in Khamearra, but she hadn't.

Sarah maintained her shield and fought her brother. Why the Elitesmen didn't attack she didn't know. She couldn't spare any thoughts for them as all her focus was on the fight before her. Rordan moved as quickly as she did, and in their deadly dance their blades met in a harsh clang.

Rordan broke off his attack and shook his head as if to clear it. Sarah circled around and stretched out with her senses. Along the fringes she heard the bladesong, and her connection to Aaron blossomed like a flower in the dawn. Releasing the shield, she leaped up into the air and closed the distance to Aaron. Rordan's screams echoed in her wake. Dark shadows pursued her. Sarah went as fast as she could, skimming across the Ryakul-filled sky. She heard the snap of saber-tusked teeth as she went by and occasionally the cry of a pursuing Elitesmen. Getting her bearings, she headed toward where Aaron fought. Determined to be at his side, she pushed all other thoughts from her mind as she sped across the battlefield.

***

The swirling mass of darkness tried to consume Colind, but he stubbornly held on, allowing years of rage to give him vast reserves of strength. This was a reckoning, and he didn't care if he died, just so long as he took Mactar with him. That was all that mattered. He owed all the ghosts of Shandara that much for his failure. He had fulfilled his vow to his old friend, Reymius. Aaron had grown into the champion that Safanar needed. The bladesong reached out to him, and he felt the touch of Reymius's heir, Ferasdiam marked and the last scion of the House Alenzar'seth, he would go beyond any of his forefathers. A weariness spread within him, consuming his remaining strength. The swirling mass receded once again, forming into the man that had haunted Colind's dreams since the fall of Shandara.

Mactar fell to his knees, covered in his own blood. He raised his weary head, his face twisted in pain and surprise. Colind still held him even as his own lifebeat diminished, his essence leaving his body just as the blood soaked the ground beneath it.

A flash of light lit the area around the two dying men.

"Darven," Mactar whispered.

The former Elitesman that had become Mactar's apprentice regarded him and the battlefield around them.

"It seems you have nothing left to teach, my Lord," Darven said coldly, his gaze wandering to Colind before dismissing them both. "The Ryakuls cannot be controlled anymore. Your plan has failed. You are no longer of any use to me," Darven said.

Mactar struggled to rise, and in a swift motion, Darven caught him, holding a knife to his throat.

"You need me," Mactar said, his voice barely above a whisper.

"No. I don't. And I'm going to do to you what you would have done to me eventually," Darven said. His knife bit into Mactar's throat, quickening an already fast approaching death.

Darven engaged the travel crystal and was gone.

Colind had nothing left to give. His vision faded, and he felt his essence, being pulled farther away, drawing him far to the east into the gardens of a palace known as the White Rose. Armies fought along the pristine white walls of his beloved Shandara. The golden shield of a Warden of the De'anjard flashed, driving the High King's army back. The Hythariam fought at his side, and Colind felt himself drawn farther into a grove of trees. Home to a lone white tree where he had been summoned once before by the ghost of his friend, Reymius. The tree sparkled like a beacon of stars washing him in the warm glow of the Goddess, who at last welcomed home her wayward servant.

***

The lines of the armies blurred, and Sarah sped across the battlefield that had become a place of madness. Elitesmen fought Elitesmen. Ryakuls swarmed anything that moved. Airships littered the ground in burning wrecks. There were still some in the air that continued to fight however they could, but the FNA fleet of airships had been cut in half. The airship captains were careful to avoid the Dragons, who threw themselves at the Ryakuls with reckless abandon.

Sarah continued on, heading toward the heart of this battle being fought between the man she loved and the man who had been her father. Aaron had been careful to avoid the topic that one of them would die in this battle. He would have found another way if it were possible, but Sarah knew that her father was a monster. None of them would be safe from her father the High King until he was stopped. The Resistance in Khamearra had tried to rebel and resurrected the old call of the Faergraces, her mother's line. Even now she heard the rallying cry, and her heart wept at the death upon the battlefield below. If they didn't stop her father here, they would all die, for her father would offer no quarter, and (truth be told) the alliance that had become the Free Nations Army would never surrender. Aaron would never yield to her father. It wasn't a prideful plea for power that pitted Aaron against him. It was his indomitable will to survive and protect those around him. To step up when fate called upon him. The Goddess had marked her champion well, and the Eldarin honored it. She knew deep in her heart that Aaron wouldn't call on the Eldarin again, believing that they had given enough, but she wondered if they would be drawn to this battle anyway. Too many of the Dragons had died along with a horde of Ryakuls for them not to appear. She needed to be at Aaron's side. To fight beside him for their future. This war would plunge Safanar into a time of darkness that they might never escape from if it didn't end here. She raced onward, drawing steadily toward the source of the bladesong that could be heard by all.

***

Aaron wielded the Falcons, unleashing the bladesong in a battle medley that adapted his style to thwart the attacks of the High King. This battle had taken him out of time. They blurred in and out of the vision of the men around them, but all could hear the wild cracks like thunder splitting the sky open when their blades met. Aaron gave himself over fully to the dance and opened himself to the wisdom of souls past. Ancestral voices sang in unison, lending their skill to his blades beyond what anyone could achieve in one lifetime, but it wasn't enough. In the back of his mind, Colind's warning of too much death corrupting the heart of the Ferasdiam marked kept coming to his mind. Dead Elitesmen and soldiers littered the ground at his feet, but it wasn't until soldiers from the FNA began to attack him did he suspect that the High King was exerting his influence over them.

"I am a god among men," the High King bellowed and leaped into the air. He landed with such force that a small crater dotted the battlefield. "I hold the lives of men at my fingertips." The High King gestured with his free hand, forcing a handful of soldiers from their hiding places. The tips of their feet dragged across the ground. A Hythariam soldier shot at the High King with his plasma pistol, but the shield he had in place deflected them.

"You're no god," Aaron said through clenched teeth, slamming his swords down.

The High King whirled out of the way, and the soldiers dropped to the ground. Aaron swept out with his leg, but the High King leaped away. Aaron bounded after him. Each attack was deflected. They would land, and the dance would begin again. The High King and Aaron were lost within a cocoon of blessed steel and the energy of a raging storm.

"We have no right to control the lives of men," Aaron said.

"We have every right," the High King answered, lashing out with his sword. He dashed forward and seemingly appeared at Aaron's side.

Aaron scrambled out of the way, but the High King kept coming.

"You've felt it, haven't you? The thirst. That feeling of holding people's lives in your hands. They are so easy to manipulate and control," the High King said and smirked.

Aaron risked a glance to the side. Verona stood with a crystal-tipped arrow drawn, his face was a mask of struggle and apprehension. His body shook, straining against the force of the High King.

"Let him go," Aaron said.

Verona's fingers shook as he struggled to hold the bow string taunt. "I can't hold it!"

The arrow flew from his bow, and Aaron dove out of the way. The arrow exploded as it hit a cluster of soldiers upon the field. Aaron moved toward the High King, but Verona called out to him. He had another crystal-tipped arrow drawn. The shadow of a Dragon flew overhead, and Verona cried out as the crystal-tipped arrow was let loose. The arrow struck the Dragon, and the explosion took out part of its wing. The Dragon let out a mournful wail as it tumbled to the ground and the Ryakuls pounced.

Aaron raced to the High King. The crystals set in the Falcons began to glow. Aaron unleashed a barrage of attacks. The High King deflected the blows, but Aaron kept coming, driving him back inch by inch. The High King feinted to the side and backhanded Aaron, sending him sprawling to the ground.

"No, you don't," Sarah cried, startling the High King.

The High King stepped back, blocking Sarah's attacks until she stopped in mid-swing of her blade.

"You see, Shandarian. There are none beyond my power," the High King said.

Verona cried out, aiming a crystal-tipped arrow at Sarah.

"You're so high and mighty, Heir of Shandara. The only way to save them is to control them. If you don't, they both will die," the High King said.

Aaron reached out with the energy to his friend and the woman he loved. The power was there. He could manipulate the lines of energy and had done so to save Sarah when she was infected with the Nanites, but this was different.

"Do it, Aaron!" Verona cried.

Aaron couldn't. If he did, he would become like the High King. The soldiers around them from both armies stopped fighting and circled around them. They had blank expressions, and the High King grinned. The soldiers came closer and held whatever weapons they carried to the throat of the people nearest to them.

The bladesong churned within Aaron, and he felt the energy around him that connected every living thing. He couldn't move, paralyzed at the scene before him. He couldn't protect them all. The knowledge of souls past couldn't help him here. None of them had been Ferasdiam marked. He silenced them, clearing his mind of their influence.

"This is not your purpose," Aaron said.

"My *purpose*," the High King spat. "An accident of birth gave me these powers, the same as you."

"Maybe, but it doesn't take any great insight to know that forcing people into subservience is a weak man's ploy. You would burn this whole world if it didn't function as you saw fit."

"Weak, am I? I hold the armies on this field within my grasp. Your own friends turn against you," the High King said.

Aaron smiled. "You haven't turned anyone against me. They are your actions through them. You have no followers, but those who are too afraid to do otherwise."

"Fear *is* power!"

Aaron pulled the energy inward and poured all his focus on the High King, whose eyes widened in shock. "I don't need to control anyone on this field. I just need to keep you from doing it."

The crystals in Aaron's sword flared to life. He shot forward, circling the High King and slicing through the web of energy extending from him. The lines of energy melted away as Aaron pushed forward and prevented new lines from forming. The High King howled in rage, slamming his dark blade down. Aaron came to a stop and crisscrossed his blades, blocking the High King's attack. Aaron pushed up, knocking the High King backward and spun, slashing through his armor with glowing blades.

The High King looked down at the shallow wounds that bled from his torso and then up at Aaron in disbelief. Then his face twisted in rage, and he threw himself at Aaron, roaring as he came. Aaron stood his ground, relying upon the strength that came from a calm, focused mind, and met the High King's attack. Each time Aaron knocked the High King's blade aside, he would swing again wildly and with little skill, but still he charged forward. Aaron stepped back just enough to allow the blade to hiss by, but quickly felt his feet be kicked out from under him. Aaron toppled to the ground and scrambled to his feet, but could already feel the downward swing of the High King's blade bearing down upon him.

The death blow never came. Sarah stood over him, catching the blow with her own sword. The High King regarded his daughter with baleful eyes. In the blink of an eye, he knocked her sword aside and held her up by the throat.

"No, don't!" Aaron shouted.

The High King's gaze switched between Sarah and Aaron. Sarah grabbed the dagger from her belt and plunged it into the High King's shoulder. She dropped to the ground, and Aaron rushed forward, plunging his swords through the High King's chest. The High King's eyes widened in shock and his gaze slipped to Sarah before falling to the ground.

The soldiers around them all seemed to move at once, shaking their heads to clear them.

Aaron reached out to Sarah and pulled her away. She resisted for a moment and then buried her face in his shoulder.

"I couldn't let him take you," she whispered.

Aaron just held her amid the stunned silence of those around them from both armies.

A dark vapor rose from the High King's body and lifted away along the breeze. A large swath of wind blew, carrying a deep resonance of the Dragons around them. The Ryakuls had scattered and quit the battlefield with no one there to control them. The Dragons banded together, with some groups flying off to the east while others pursued the Ryakuls.

News of the High King's death spread among both armies, with the late king's generals raising white flags despite the protest from certain groups within the Elite Order. There was so much infighting among the Khamearrian soldiers and Elitesmen alike that had the FNA chosen to do so, they could have decimated the once-superior force.

CHAPTER 22
AFTERMATH

In the days that followed, Sarah was proclaimed the High Queen of Khamearra with fealty being sworn by the surviving generals of the army. Rordan, along with a faction of the Elite Order, were nowhere to be found. Other factions of the Elite Order had fought their brethren during the battle, confirming what the former Elitesman Isaac had suspected. Without the High King and certain Elite Masters, the already crumbling Order would fade away. Sarah's first order as High Queen was to formally disband the Elite Order and revoke all their authority. They were to be absorbed into the Free Nations Army and were to be watched carefully. The former members of the Elitesmen were offered a choice: to serve in the FNA or stand trial for their crimes and abuses of power. A number of them fled and were being hunted, but the bulk of them had chosen to take the High Queen up on her offer.

In Shandara, Braden reported minimal losses and that the Hythariam were instrumental at defeating what had come to be known as the High King's diversionary army. The term was used loosely, because they had learned that while the army was sent there to divide the FNA forces at Rexel, they had orders to take the city if they could.

Prince Cyrus of Rexel was all too happy to see the Khamearrian army return to their homelands using the portals created by the Hythariam. A sizable force did stay to integrate with the Free Nations Army, but there were already plans to move them, as the strain on the natural resources in the area around Rexel was proving too costly. Many eyes drew toward Aaron as the option of moving the bulk of the Free Nations Army to Shandara was discussed.

There were still many people missing, with Colind being most notable among them. Some believed the Lord Guardian of the Safanarion Order would turn up, but Aaron felt a deep-seated fear in the base of his stomach that Colind had not survived. Mactar was also absent, and Aaron firmly believed it wasn't happenstance that the two were missing.

At Iranus's urging, Aaron returned to Shandara with Sarah and Verona. There had been no Zekara activity since Aaron returned to Safanar, and while the threat of High King Amorak was gone, those high up in the FNA knew it was but a temporary lull in a larger storm. Aaron had no doubts that Halcylon was preparing for his attack at this very

KEN LOZITO | 363

moment, which was one reason Aaron was in Shandara. The other reason being a pressing need to get away from the battlefield. Amorak had turned the gift of being Ferasdiam marked into something monstrous, and he was left wondering if he was walking the same path. Amorak had referred to it as being an accident of birth, but too much of what Aaron had seen led him to question things of that magnitude being up to chance. Was his being here an accident of birth, or was it destiny that brought him to Safanar?

The combined Shandarian and Hythariam defenses of the city could only be unlocked by a member of the Alenzar'seth line of which Aaron was the last. Aaron's great-grandfather, Daverim, had insisted that if they were to give shelter to the Hythariam, than what they accomplished together would be freely shared with the people of Safanar. When it came to Shandara's safety, its defense and control would fall to a member of the Alenzar'seth. For better or worse, it was agreed and was a primary reason why Iranus was so keen to get Aaron back to Shandara.

"There it is," Verona said.

They had used one of the smaller airships to bring them to the command center. The Hythariam had cleared a road to the place, but there were still remnants of the rubbled remains of buildings in this part of the city. The growing population had set themselves to the task of rebuilding. The progress they made was like night and day since Aaron had first seen Shandara all those months ago. It had been a long time since he had first left Earth, and yet so many things had changed. His life on Earth seemed like a dream.

"What is it?" Sarah asked gently.

Aaron looked at her for a moment, knowing that she was hurting inside and there was nothing he could do but give her time. Taking her father's life had saved them, and he knew she didn't regret it in the least, but still the pain was there along the edges of her eyes.

"I was thinking of my sister, Tara. I left her so she would be safe."

"I'm sure she is fine," Sarah said.

Aaron nodded. "I know, but it would be nice if the two of you could meet someday."

"Perhaps," Sarah said.

Aaron had no wish to return to Earth on any permanent basis. His home was at Sarah's side here on Safanar, but Tara was his only link to a life he had before. In the wake of so much death and destruction, it seemed like such a random thought, but the more he thought about it, the more he wondered if it would ever happen.

The small airship landed, and they followed a path that led them underground. Orbs lit the way, and the pathway opened up to two large metallic doors.

"Gavril, we're here," Roselyn spoke into her comms device.

Next to the door was a silver panel, and Roselyn urged Aaron to place his hand upon it. The smooth surface warmed to his touch, but nothing else happened. He drew in the energy and probed with a tendril behind the plate, and a smaller panel opened above, revealing a circular depression. Aaron withdrew the medallion and pressed it to the surface, and after a moment, both panels withdrew into the wall. There was a great shudder beneath the floor, and bits of rock and dust sifted down from the ceiling. The doors slowly opened, and interior lights flickered on, revealing a large cavernous room that extended well away from them. Holographic screens flickered to life, and Aaron could hear the gasps behind them largely from the Hythariam. A map of Shandara came up on the main display with different sections reporting in sync.

They entered, with people exploring in different directions. Aaron eventually came to a set of doors across the way.

"One of those will take you up to the grounds near the palace," Roselyn said after checking one of the screens.

Aaron came to the doors, and they opened automatically, revealing a small chamber beyond. *An elevator?* He stepped on, and Sarah followed. His comms device chimed, and the panel lit up before them. Aaron selected the button that would take them to the surface. After a few moments, the doors opened to an overgrown path. After climbing through, he and Sarah emerged into a grove.

"I know where we are," Aaron said. "Come on, this way."

He and Sarah ran through the grove, coming to a clearing where a lone white tree stood bathing in the sunlight. Shimmering at the bottom of the tree was a translucent cloaked figure that beckoned them forward.

"Colind!" Aaron gasped.

Sarah threaded her fingers in his as they approached the tree where the shade of the last Lord Guardian of the Safanarion Order waited for them.

CHAPTER 23
EPILOGUE

"Sir, have you seen the latest feeds?" the Zekarian soldier asked.

General Halcylon nodded, watching the summary feeds from the drones they had monitoring the continent. "They may be more powerful than we thought. There are definitely some things we can use."

"There is still the issue with powering our equipment," Ronan said. "The power sources we brought from Hytharia will be depleted in a few months."

"They have sources here we can use," Halcylon said. "Besides, since we haven't been able to find the safe haven where the traitors have taken refuge, we've detected another alternative."

"Where?" Ronan asked.

"Just moments ago a place showed up here on the eastern side of the continent. There is a source there that could power whatever we wanted for the next hundred years."

Ronan glanced at the map, and his eyes widened. "Shandara?"

Halcylon's lips curved into a smirk. "That's what the humans call it. When we take over this place it will all be renamed in a fashion more befitting the Zekara. But I have another task for you."

"What is it?"

"I need you to solve the problem with the longevity of the Akasul," Halcylon said.

"I thought we only needed the one to put the locals off balance while we did more reconnaissance?"

Halcylon nodded. "That was the plan, but now I think we have further uses for them, and we'll need many of them."

Halcylon returned his gaze to the feed showing the battle that had unfolded in the center of the continent. The humans were more powerful than he thought, but were weak in every way he already suspected. The wheels spun in his mind as he proceeded with the next phase of his plan. His enemies already knew of their presence here even if they didn't know their exact location. It was a tactical risk to have the drones fire on the Alenzar'seth, and he shrugged off their failure to destroy him. After all, there was nothing one human could do to prevent what he had been planning.

Safanar would be brought under the dominion of the Zekara.

ABOUT THE AUTHOR

I've been reading Epic Fantasy and Science fiction nonstop since the age of eleven. Before long, I started writing my own stories and kept adding to them throughout the years. As a father, I began telling my kids about the stories that became part of the Safanarion Order series. It was their enthusiasm and constant "Tell us more Dad," that lead me back to the keyboard. My main focus is to write books that I would like to read and I hope you enjoy them as well.

If you would like to get an email when I release a book please visit my website at KENLOZITO.COM

Say Hello!

If you have questions or comments about any of my works I would love to hear from you, even if its only to drop by to say hello at KenLozito.com

One Last Thing.

Word-of-mouth is crucial for any author to succeed. If you enjoyed the book, please consider leaving a review at Amazon, even if it's only a line or two; it would make all the difference and would be greatly appreciated.

Discover other books by Ken Lozito

* * *

Safanarion Order Series:

ACKNOWLEDGEMENTS

First my thanks to you dear reader and to anyone who has reached out to me about the series. Your words of encouragement mean a lot to me and I am eternally grateful.

Next up is my family, you've all been the cornerstone to my foundation. To my children, who with silent demanding, dared me to be better than I thought could be.

My editor, Jason, thank you for all the feedback and words of encouragement.

Then there are my "beta readers," Tim, Milosz, and Phillip who helped put the final touches on the book and provide an excellent sanity check for the story as a whole. Thank you so much for you time and support.

31994956R00236

Made in the USA
Middletown, DE
18 May 2016